Her Leaves Remain

Her Leaves Remain

Remain

A NOVEL

Ashley Owens

This is a work of fiction. Names, characters, places, and incidents either are the product of the author's imagination or are used factiously. Any resemblance to actual persons, events, or locations is entirely coincidental.

ISBN: 9781654354398
Imprint: Independently published

For the ones who believed in me from day one.
(You know who you are…and so do I. Love you!)

Prologue

Thunder claps just outside the dorm room window, shaking the building to its core. The rain streams down the window swiftly, with one drop racing another to reach the windowsill.

Rain pelts my face. Drenches me from head to toe. It sloshes inside my shoes as I squish through the muddy grass toward home. I replay his venomous sneer hovering above me, and the vomit rises again.

"Don't forget your zit cream."

Tilly snickers and throws my acne medicine straight at me, pulling me back to the task of packing up my dorm room. I catch the tube of medicine just before it hits my face and lay it in the open suitcase on my freshly stripped bed.

You're not back there, Lyv. I repeat the mantra over and over in my mind. _You're not back there. You're not back there. You're not back...yet._

When I invited Tilly over to help me pack for home I think I knew deep down she'd be of no use. She's been my best friend since diaper days. I should've known her restless mind couldn't handle something as mundane as packing up an entire dorm room to go home for the summer.

"I don't understand why you didn't just ask your mom to come down and help. You know she would've jumped all over it."

She has a point as she rolls her long, black hair around one finger.

But while my mother is the most organized person I've ever known, the kind of woman who makes lists of what lists she needs to make, she's also the most overbearing person I've ever known. On my first day of high school she used her PTO mom status to wander the halls, sneaking by my classrooms to make sure I found my way around my schedule in my new school.

And yes, a present parent is better than an absent one, but even still, she sees what she wants to see in me and everything else falls to the wayside.

So no, I didn't call my mom to come help.

"C'mon Tilly, it's really not that much to pack. Don't be so dramatic."

Asking Tilly not to be dramatic is basically like telling the tides to stand still.

"You're joking, right?" She pauses while I keep folding clothes. "You literally have an entire dresser full of clothes left, Lyv."

She rolls her onyx eyes but picks up a shirt to pretend-fold anyway.

"Trust me, if I had the option to stay here over the summer and not have to pack everything up, I would," I mumble at my suitcase.

"C'mon, Lyv. How bad can going home really be?" Tilly picks up the mate to a stranded sock and rolls them together. "You went home once this year for Christmas, and even that was only for a week before you came running back to campus. Summer will fly by and be over before you know it."

In Tilly's mind, going home for the summer is a black and white concept. Home is mock tails with pretty pink umbrellas floating on top. Home is a pool in her massive back yard with the hot tub you can hop into when the day filters to night.

To Tilly, home is safe.

Tilly doesn't know that, years ago, the town we were supposed to feel at home in betrayed me in the worst way; let in a monster so vile I can hardly look at the place without being back in that moment when it all went so wrong so fast.

So, to answer her question, going home could be dreadfully bad.

Going back to the town I tried leaving behind for an entire summer is more than my worst nightmare. For me, "home" stopped being "home" a long time ago and once I was out I never looked back.

Until now.

Tilly (short for Matilda) followed me to college, though. Not that I'm complaining. Everyone likes a little familiarity, right? We've just finished our freshman year at the University of Colorado Denver and I'm 110% sure I wouldn't have survived it without Tilly.

"You're stressing again," Tilly takes the shirt I just folded out of my suitcase and throws it at my face, trying to make light of the thoughts she undoubtedly reads on my face. But under her humor she's worried. I see it in the crease of her forehead and the way her dark eyes go squinty when she stares at me. "Breathe for a minute."

It's been years since my last panic attack; right after *it* all happened, to be exact. Then, about two weeks ago one hit suddenly. I blamed it on finals prep, but have a nagging feeling going home was the trigger. Tilly's been witness to most of them, so she knows all the ways to coax me out of the dark.

I do as she says and focus my mind on my hands folding shirts, sleeve with sleeve with shirttail. I focus on the yellow hue of it, remembering the time my mom bragged about it bringing out the green of my hazel eyes. We sit on my bed—correction, *Tilly* sits on my bed—packing up the last few contents of my tiny, five-drawer dresser chest she so drastically overstated.

She pops a bubble with her gum for the tenth time and my patience wears thin.

"Could you knock it off, please? Your bubble popping is distracting me and I have to be out of here early in the morning. I need to stop by The Cinema to pick up my work schedule."

By some unknown force (i.e. my mother) my old job had a vacancy I was able to fill for the summer. I have a love/hate relationship with The Cinema. While it's great because I get to sneak and watch some of the new movies without paying, there's a smell to a movie theatre that clothes seem to kind of trap deep in the fabric to the point it's there forever. I can already feel the sticky counters I'll have to scrub down after a group of rowdy teenagers rub their grubby hands across them.

"You need a job," my mom had said. "You have a car now, remember?"

Of course I remembered. How could I forget when she reminded me every chance she could?

"And I'm not being dramatic," I stop Tilly before she can counteract me. "We can't all have a glamorous city pool lifeguard job, can we? Not to mention working at a movie theater has absolutely nothing to do with what I really want to do with my life."

I grab a pair of already folded jeans and refold them for good measure, shooting a pointed look in Tilly's direction. She rolls her eyes but drops the subject. Only because she knows I won this battle. No arguing the fact that her summer lifeguarding job is a cakewalk compared to mine. Granted, I don't think I'd take her job if I had the chance, if I'm being honest. Tilly has more of a figure for that sort of job anyway. She's tan and slender and tall—the kind of girl who can buy whatever she wants without having to try anything on.

I'm not overweight by any means, but my mom blessed me with curves that fill out those lifeguard suits a bit too much for my personal tastes.

Despite working at The Cinema this summer, photography is my passion and the route I've decided to take for the foreseeable future and it kind of sucks doing anything other than that for the summer.

"All I'm saying," Tilly picks up a pair of underwear and tosses them into the suitcase unfolded, "is maybe this summer will be good for you. You can always take pictures on the side, or do a little freelancing. Maybe start planning out your program entry project for next year. It could help distract you, you know?"

She glances at my face for a reaction but I give her nothing. She's phishing, I know, and brings up my program entry project like it will get me to talk about Connor. But I don't want to talk about him. An ex is an ex for a reason.

Because she's Tilly, she goes on.

"Have you talked to him?"

12

"Why would I? We broke up. There's nothing to say."

I keep folding, repeating the steps.

Grab, fold, and pack. Repeat.

I try not to picture his sweet grin smiling at me. I ignore the image of his almost gray eyes and floppy, blonde hair trying to sneak its way back into my mind. I've been putting those memories and details out for the past couple of days, but of course Tilly brings them flooding back.

If I see the pity on her face I'll defend myself against her ridicule.

And I'm just really tired of constantly having to defend myself.

"Are you sure about this?" She stops folding. That didn't last long. "Connor was such a great guy. I don't want to see you pass up another good one. Here, lets make a pros and cons list for him to help you sort through it all."

And there it is. The ridicule.

She grabs a pen and notepad still left unpacked on my desk and pushes it toward me.

Apparently breaking up with someone who just happens to be a good guy is against some moral code I've not read yet.

"Tilly, a pros and cons list is not a fix all. Some things aren't so black and white," I push the pen and notepad back into her chest. "I'm just so done with talking about it."

She huffs.

"That's the thing though. You've not even talked about it at all. With anyone! Not even me," she sits up on the edge of the bed and crosses her long arms. "I mean, one minute you seem to be happy go-lucky with the guy, then the next you drop him like a bad habit. I just don't get it."

"I don't need you to get it. I need you to respect my choices and support me, Tilly. It just wasn't working."

I move away from my bed and from Tilly, away from the conversation at hand. Truth is, Connor is an amazing guy. He's kind, thoughtful, supportive, funny—all the things a girl could want. He's also in one of those punk, alt bands, which only helps his case. But when push comes to shove, there's more to a healthy, functioning relationship than just those aspects.

Connor wanted a part of me I promised to keep to myself a long time ago and keeping him around seemed unfair to everyone. Then there's the uncanny resemblance between Connor and *him* that my mind was for whatever reason drawn to when we first met. Same blonde hair. Same blue eyes.

Different personalities though. Completely different personalities.

Regardless, on the last night of finals week I met up with him and told him things had changed for me. I didn't feel the same way anymore. He took it like I imagined, never calling me names or showing any type of resentment. He accepted it, kissed my forehead, and walked away.

Tilly's a different story. She refuses to let it lie.

I work on moving everything on my desk into my backpack even as she shoots daggers at the back of my head. Unfortunately, my small height has never been beneficial when I'm reaching for high places, so Tilly has to help me grab my backpack from the top shelf above my desk. Still, I keep my back to her and mutter a small "thank you".

"So you're just going to   ignore me then?"

15

I can tell Tilly's frustrated without even turning around. It's all in her voice and the way it goes flat and emotionless when usually it runs up and down like a rollercoaster.

"Yes, as long as you keep talking about Connor."

"Suit yourself, but when you finally pop from holding all this in I *will* be there to say I told you so."

"I'd be worried if you didn't," I turn to sneer at her and get another shirt thrown my way.

"Speaking of worried, how's your mom? Is she awaiting Princess Lyv's return with streamers and balloons and the whole deal? Wittle Wyv is finally leaving the teen years behind."

There's the other dreadful place my mind didn't want to go: my birthday. Typically I love my birthday, and this year I'm turning 20 while Tilly has been there for months now. But I'm not really in the celebrating mood. Not that this small detail will stop my mother from celebrating when I get home tomorrow.

Tilly's moved from sitting on my bed to lying on her back, feet kicked up on the wall like she's trying some restorative yoga pose while she assesses her cuticles.

"I really hope not. It'd be great to come home to a nice, quiet welcome. I'd even settle with just a simple hug from my parents and a snarky remark from Max. I'd even be OK with a gift or two and a small cake. Then I want a hot bubble bath before I sleep for 24 hours straight. Nothing too grand."

Tilly giggles.

"Yeah, right. Like that'll happen. Your little brother is a terror and your mother is a maniac. There's no way they'll let you brush your birthday under the rug."

She has a point. Max is two years younger than me but age is merely a number as far as he's concerned. He's basically 17 going on 7. He wasn't always that way, though. But these last few years have left him more on the immature side despite his getting older.

"I'm sure you're right. It's worth a shot though."

I shrug and she shakes her head in doubt.

"What about you? Aren't you excited to go home?"

Tilly is filthy rich. She'd die before admitting it, but it's the truth. I can't imagine it's too much of a drag going back home for the summer when you're going home to luxurious shopping trips whenever you want them and a top-of-the-line hot tub right outside your back door.

"Eh, I'm as excited as you can be I guess. I don't know. My mom and sister have been so busy planning Mona's wedding that I'm sure they won't even notice I'm home."

Tilly's sister, Mona (who's more like her twin even though she's four years older than us), has been engaged for about three years now and apparently she's finally tying the knot this summer. They're going the traditional route with the bride's family paying for the wedding, so it's going to be huge. I'm talking celebrity-wedding level.

"What, you're not excited to be the maid of honor?"

I laugh but Tilly sits up right so suddenly she has to regain her composure from the head rush she gives herself.

"Oh, but didn't I tell you? I'm not the maid of honor. No, that's going to be her douche-bag fiancée's sister Lissaaaa."

I assume "Lissaaa" talks with a seriously nasally voice.

"That's awful! I guess I just automatically thought you would get that title, since you're the sister and all."

"You and me both, girl."

She lies back down in her previous position but I can tell she's no longer in the mood to talk. It looks like I'm not alone in this Debbie Downer boat after all.

We finish packing and Tilly makes her way back to her own dorm (we couldn't room together thanks to Tilly's late enrollment) and I'm left alone to ponder my thoughts.

I would never admit this to Tilly, but I know she's right about Connor. Eventually these pent up emotions will bust. Kind of like the popcorn kernels at the theater when they break into big, puffy clouds. I shudder to think of the "when" or "where" or "how" it'll happen.

For now, though, I'll settle for my bottled up emotions and hope for the best. That night my dreams go to a weird place of Connor serving popcorn in nothing but an ugly purple bowtie, signature grin in place, and sleep escapes me.

Chapter One-Lyv

My alarm was set for 8 a.m. this morning, but I wake up at 9:30 a.m. instead.

Happy birthday to me.

I'm a punctual person and I come by it honestly. If my mom isn't thirty minutes early for an event, she thinks the day is ruined.

"If we're on time, we're late," she always says.

My dad and Max, on the other hand, were cursed with sloth speed and have to be woken up a whole hour earlier than me just to have enough time to get going. It's like my mom gave me all her organization traits and Max got all of dad's.

This morning, though, I'm more on Dad and Max's time. Luckily my roommate is already home for the summer and I run around the room like a mad woman with no interruption.

There are a few birthday wishes on my phone, some from family, one from Tilly, and a bunch on social media from people I haven't talked to in years. But they'll have to wait and I slip my phone into my purse so it's ready to go when it's time to leave.

Today is a no makeup day and I throw on a ball cap to cover my unruly bedhead. Curly hair tends to have a mind of it's own this time of year, especially in the morning. The brown tendrils stick out from beneath the hat, but there's no time to stop and fix it. After tossing on my favorite ratty crop top t-shirt, my worn-in, high waist shorts, and flip-flops I wheel my suitcases toward the door with my backpack strapped on my shoulders.

Sweat rolls down my spine as I rush toward the elevator.

If mom could see me now, I think to myself.

One long exhale releases the tension in my shoulders from rushing around as I push the lobby button and start the descend.

Once I'm to the front counter I convince myself the entire world is against me. There sits Heidi, my-tolerable-but-just-barely RA. She's dutifully answering the phone and dutifully annoying me as she puts me on hold with her finger up in the air.

Deep down I'm sure Heidi is a decent person—way, way down. Skip one freshman event during move-in week, however, and you're on her bad list for the rest of your life.

"Ahh, Lovely Lyv. Birthday girl!"

I think she started that nickname to mock me, but I like to pretend she really thinks I'm lovely.

"The one and only," I curtsey with a smile that I'm sure looks more like a grimace.

"Are you all set to go?"

Her smile seems genuine enough, but it doesn't quite reach her eyes.

"I think so."

"You think so, or you know so?"

She giggles at her own lame, patronizing joke and my last shred of patience rips.

"Yes," my teeth grit.

"Lovely! So your belongings are all moved out?"

I nod.

"And the bed is lowered to its original position?"

Another nod.

"And your fridge is unplugged and fully thawed?"

"Yes, Heidi. Everything is good to go. You can go check if you want," I slap the key down on the counter in front of her and instantly regret my suggestion. Knowing Heidi she just may take me up on that.

"Oh, Lyv, I trust you! If you say it's fine, it's fine. You just need to sign here to say it's all clear, here to say you've handed in your key, and here to say we've had this little chat."

She slides a pen and clipboard my way and points to three highlighted lines I'm supposed to sign.

"Have fun on break! I wish I could go home but they've got so many summer programs going on and, you know, RA duty calls."

She flips her fiery red hair and props her manicured hands under her chin.

"That's great, Heidi. Enjoy."

With a slight nod and another grimace/smile I walk toward the exit. Just before I get to the doors Heidi calls after me.

"Oh, and I'm so sorry to hear about you and Connor!"

Word travels fast, huh?

I pretend like I don't hear her and walk on. It stings, though, despite it all. I'm usually good at pushing Heidi's snippy comments off to the wayside but this one sticks.

I'm trying to figure out how Heidi of all people found out about Connor and me when I spot a silhouetted figure standing at my car. The figure waves dramatically and a few passerby's eye us curiously.

"TYLER!"

The only person who calls me that ridiculous name is Tilly's boyfriend, Mason. He's 21 and just a year older than us. Mason goes to our rival college about 20 minutes away, so I see a lot of him.

He looms over me now with his blue eyes shining in the morning light. I'm slightly annoyed at having to glance up into the sun just to see him.

When we were about fifteen Mason thought a horror movie marathon sounded like a good idea, even though it was dead of summer. So, there we were (we meaning Mason, his groupies, Tilly, our old friend Emily, and myself) watching scary movie after scary movie. We had an old sheet hung up on the back balcony with a projector Mason's mom rented from the public library. For the drive-in effect, she'd said.

It was a perfect night, really, apart from the fact that *The Strangers* was on that list and Mason was obnoxiously obsessed with

24

Liv Tyler at the time. Lucky me, I was the only other "Liv" he'd heard of, even though I repeatedly told him it was different because they weren't spelled the same. From that point on he thought Tyler suited me better than my actual name.

I think it makes him feel special to be the only person on the entire planet to call me that.

"Hey Mason," my voice sounds tired, even to my own ears. It's further proven when Mason raises his perfectly arched eyebrows. I swear I think Tilly plucks them but she insists they're naturally that sculpted.

"Staying up late with my girl, Tyler?" He wiggles those raised brows suggestively and gives a goofy grin. I resist the urge to reach up and smack him now that I'm close enough.

"Good one. No, I woke up late and it's just not been my morning. I had to deal with Heidi before getting my coffee kick and no one should ever have to handle Heidi Clearwater without some kind of caffeine high," all of this comes out in one breath.

I move past him to my car with one bag strapped across my shoulder and two more dragging behind me on the ground. Mentally I thank myself for moving the car closer the night before. Mason doesn't offer to help in any way, though I'm not surprised. He's plenty strong enough to grab everything I have at once, but his strong is more of the "Look at my super huge muscles!" rather than "I'm actually strong and not just trying to look cool."

"Man, that Heidi. She's a mental case but she's got a killer ra-

"

He cuts himself off, probably remembering he's talking to his girlfriend's best friend. That's the thing about Mason: he means well *most* of the time, but he's about as dumb as a box of rocks. What comes to his mind comes out of his mouth, and sometimes that's fine. In Mason's case, however, it's typically not.

But for reasons beyond my comprehension, Tilly is madly in love with him. So I keep my opinions to myself.

We don't say anything for a few beats as I toss my bags into the back hatch. Mason finally clears his throat to break the silence once everything is in and I move toward the driver side.

"Well, I guess I'll go try to wake Tilly up. You know how hard it is to get that girl moving in the mornings. See you back home, Tyler."

I merely mumble a resemblance of a goodbye and wave before getting in the car. He doesn't wish me happy birthday, though I don't really expect him to.

The thought of seeing Mason back home makes me cringe. The thought of ever hearing that stupid nickname ever again in my entire life makes me want to scream. The thought of being at the theater all summer makes me panic.

Or sitting through a whole summer's worth of conversation with my parents asking about school and boys and my unclear future and dealing with my bratty testosterone-driven brother for three months...it's all too much.

But it could be worse, I tell myself.

I could be here all summer, at school. Connor is here all summer playing shows with his amateur band. At least I won't have to chance running into him at home, I guess. I could be stuck here having to risk seeing him in the breakup aftermath.

So yeah, I guess it could be worse.

Out of habit I check my phone for a text or a call from him. It is my birthday after all. Surely he's sent me a message, but there's nothing.

A clean break.

That's what I'd wanted and apparently he plans to keep his end of the bargain.

With each passing mile I get from CU Denver, home sounds a little less like a death sentence.

<u>*Chapter Two-Lyv*</u>

I spend the entirety of my two-hour drive home mentally preparing myself for the moment I walk into The Cinema. It'll be the first time I've done so in a little over a year and, to my surprise, I'm a little excited about it the closer I get. I guess it won't be *that* awful.

Hopefully.

I'm less than surprised when Reggie is the face I see when I walk into the theater.

Reggie is your stereotypical movie theater employee. He's lanky and dorky, with glasses wrapped together in the middle with tape (I kid you not). His shaggy hair would be problematic if he were anywhere near the popcorn, but since he's manager he stays in the office unless things get too busy. He's a movie junkie to the core and cherishes The Cinema more than life.

I'm pretty sure he believes his job is secret service level of importance.

I once watched him corner a girl in the lobby and explain the significance of cinematic media and how it "breeds an imagination no book or album ever could".

Poor girl was just trying to get to the ticket booth but Reggie had to make his case in the name of The Cinema.

"Knock, knock," I make the motion at Reggie's office but can't actually knock since the office is sans door. I can't say why, exactly, but my guess would be something involving Reggie and his desire to cut out barriers between the moviegoer and the staff.

"Lyv, how great to see you again! Please, come in."

Reggie waves me in with the goofiest grin you could imagine. He has a couple of snaggleteeth on his bottom row of teeth but that never seems to stop him from smiling.

"It's great to see you too. I just want to thank you for having me back. I really do appreciate it."

I lucked into this job as a high school freshman. I'd been at the lake with some friends all day and hadn't used the restroom all afternoon. The Cinema was the only thing open between the lake and my house by the time we left the lake that night, so we stopped in. And there it was, the "Help Wanted" sign on their door. I took an application when I left and Reggie's been taking care of me every summer since.

"Oh, it was no problem. As soon as your mom called it was a no brainer. You've always been a delight within the great walls of The Cinema. Now, I do want to bring something to your attention."

He pulls out a piece of paper from under a stack of folders on his impossibly messy desk. The clutter makes me itch and I crave the moment I get to come in and organize that mess.

"OK, what's the problem?"

"No problem, really, it's just that we couldn't give you as many hours as before."

Before college I technically worked as part-time, but my hours were borderline full-time hours. He turns the paper around so I can read the schedule. I see my hours aren't just decreased a little; they've been drastically cut.

"I know, I know. They're significantly smaller. We've got a plethora of new employees and we had to decrease hours in order to keep everyone under the cap. I hope you're not too upset."

I almost laugh but control myself.

Upset? Ha!

I thought I would walk out of here with a Monday-Saturday workweek, six hours a day like

31

before. But here I am with my name listed next to four days, none of which are the weekend, and only five hours under each shift.

That's so much time to myself this summer. Time to read and lie by the pool and photograph the sleepy town I never planned on coming back to for long.

"Hey, no hard feelings, Reggie. I know you have to do what works to keep everyone at peace."

Sucker.

"Ah, I'm so glad to hear that! And that is exactly why we like having you around. You just understand. Of course, you can always pick up a shift if someone takes off a day."

I smile broadly. Creepy as he may be, the guy knows how to hand out a compliment.

"Alright then. I'll be seeing you back in here in a few days, correct?"

"Monday morning. I'll be here."

And with my schedule in hand it's time to go home. I'm sure my mom won't be too thrilled about my minimal workweek but it's really out of her hands, or so I plan on telling her.

My house is only a few blocks away from The Cinema so it only takes a few minutes to get there. My neighborhood is something straight out of a '50s sitcom. Streets line with mirror-image homes and evenly cut, green lawns border rounded cul-de-sacs.

Perfect USA Suburbia where nothing goes wrong and everyone lives happily.

Tilly lives just a few houses down, which came in handy growing up when we needed a girl's night or a riding buddy to the mall.

I almost choke on the water I just took a sip of when I pull into the drive. There stands my mom waving her long, slender arms around like a maniac under the front porch awning, streamers and balloons taped above her tall figure. Suddenly I have the urge to punch Tilly. She always has to be right, doesn't she?

"Wow mom, you really shouldn't have."

I plaster my best fake smile and go in for a hug once I'm out of my car. She made it to me before I even had my door open so the hug comes as soon as I'm on my feet. Her graying hair clouds my vision as I take a step back for a breath.

"The birthday girl is home! I'm so happy to see you! How are you? How was your drive home? Did you get your work schedule? Oh, here let me help you with your bags."

She's already moving around me to grab my bags out of the hatch. That's something else about my mom. She tends to ask so many questions all at once that you don't really have time to answer any of them in particular.

It's odd my dad isn't out here to help already but I don't linger on the thought for more than a couple of seconds.

As we walk up the sidewalk to the front door I notice there's no movement in the living room. The front window is wide open and the blinds are up with a clear shot to the empty house.

Something's not right.

My dad should be in his recliner by now flipping through sports channels. Max should be on the couch completely invested in his phone. Our new German Sheppard pup, Daisy, should be running around with her favorite rope chew toy.

But we step through the door and there's no one. No dad. No annoying brother. No rowdy pup. It's a ghost town in the McDowell house.

"Where is everyone?"

I'm suspicious now, even more so when I turn to my mom who's bright hazel eyes are about to pop out of her head with excitement. She's biting her lip to weaken her smile, but it's on the brink of busting out across her already summer-tanned face.

"Ummm, I think your dad's out back by the pool. Here, lets drop your bags off by the stairs and we'll go see what he's up to. I'm sure he'll want to see the birthday girl."

Now I know something's up.

My mom isn't the kind of mom to just "drop your bags" anywhere unless it's in its designated spot in the closet once you've emptied the bag.

I follow her anyway.

It's fine, I think. *Everything's normal.*

We put an in ground pool in my seventh grade year and it was the talk of the neighborhood the whole summer. We had so many pool parties that summer that we had to turn them into BYOF (Bring Your Own Food) parties because my friends almost ate us out of house and home.

It'd be nice if I stepped through those double doors onto the back deck to find my dad by the grill. He'd give me a peck on my cheek, wish me happy birthday, and I'd dive into the pool and swim around in peace until dinner.

But, of course that's not how it plays out.

The moment I step through the sliding glass doors the air around me erupts.

Poppers pop and air horns blow. Confetti flies toward me. It takes me about ten seconds to realize I've just had my first successful surprise birthday party. We tried this once before for my thirteenth birthday but Max intentionally blew the cover.

"So, how'd we do?"

My dad steps forward out of the crowd of various friends and family. I smile despite my growing grudge against anyone and everyone involved in this setup.

"Hi dad, you did good."

It's easier to forgive my dad than my mom.

I know that's awful to say, but my mom and me are too much alike so we're always budding heads. My dad is my polar opposite.

Despite his occupation as a middle school principal he is too carefree to ever really cause much strife in my life.

"Your mom did all the brunt work," he boasts, despite the drops of sweat resting at the edge of his salt and pepper hairline.

He kisses me on the top of my head like I'm five again.

It's a comfort I've missed in my time away.

"Now, now. You did your part. You put up all the decorations."

My mom wraps me up in another one of her famous Ginny McDowell bear hugs and I sink into her completely.

"So we really did good, then?"

"It's perfect, mom."

I smile genuinely and hug her thin frame tightly.

Max is nowhere to be seen, of course, so I skip that reunion. It would've been a train wreck anyway.

Before I greet the crowd I run back to my bags by the stairs and grab my camera.

I can't believe how many people showed up for this.

For me.

There's mom's sister Ann and her husband. Their kids are at the edge of the pool with their feet in the water. There are two of them, twins, and they're Max's age. I wave but keep moving. Next is Uncie Brad ("uncie" because I couldn't say uncle when I was little) and whatever flavor of the month he has this time around. I smile and do my best not to make the greeting awkward before moving on. My dad has one older sister but she lives in New York with her family and I'm sure she didn't have time to drop everything for her niece's surprise party in Colorado.

Finally I see Granny and Pop Pop McDowell standing with my mom's parents. I hug the McDowell grandparents first because I know it'll be short, sweet, and to the point. The Buckley grandparents, however, make the hugs last. Granddad Buckley squeezes the life out of me before passing me on to Nana Buckley. She doesn't hug but kisses my entire face, smudging her terrible orange lipstick on my cheek.

I break free from the attack of the grandparents and make a quick escape for some air to breathe and a napkin to wipe my face. My grandparents spoil me like every grandparent should but sometimes they push spoiling right into smothering.

38

They mean well, though. To them I'm still just little Lyv, innocent and untainted as ever.

Once I step away from the crowd I snap a few photos. Some people expect it, like mom and dad, and strike a pose while others laugh on unknowingly, giving me the perfect candid.

I have been thinking about my program entry project, after Tilly's suggestion. It's sort of like an audition, only through picture taking instead of singing or dancing. This project determines if I have what it takes to get into the program at all.

I'm still not completely sure what I want to do for the project but I know I want something to do with people. There's something special about catching human emotion in such a lasting forum like photos. The layers and facets to a person are endless, so I know it'll be a solid place to start.

Next I move my lens toward the group I call my friends. I spot Tilly hanging back with Mason and one of his friends from college. I think his name is Sean, maybe? Or Seth?

Finally, a birthday wish comes true: Tilly is within arms reach.

I get a light punch in but   she just laughs.

"How could you not tell me?"

I shout whisper on the off chance my parents could hear me complain.

"What, and miss the look on your face right now? No way. That's comical."

She's still laughing and eventually I chime in. It is funny, I guess, now that the initial shock has passed.

"Happy birthday, Tyler."

I point finger at Mason next.

"And you! I talked to you this morning and you didn't say anything."

"I said 'see you at home'. Like, word for word, that's what I said."

"I didn't think you meant literally."

I shake my head and search for Max. We aren't too close anymore, not like we used to be, but I figured he'd at least be here to celebrate my birthday.

"Hey, Mase, isn't that Asher?" Tilly points to the door and we all follow her line of vision. "Why is he with Emily?"

Emily is one of our old friends from high school. She went to a local college but we still hang out when we're all in town.

Asher is also an old friend, but more so one of Mason's friends than mine, so I'm a little surprised to see him here. I've been around him enough to be familiar since he also goes to the same school as Mason, but I wouldn't expect to see him here. Most of Mason's friends, and Mason, still have a sixteen-year-old mindset.

But Asher is different than the rest.

He leveled up on the maturity scale. Not to mention his style compared to Mason's is like comparing diamonds to pebbles. It's something anyone with eyes could see about him, the fact that he always seems to be one step ahead of his friends—in more ways than one. Even when Tilly and I would join Mason and his friends at frat parties, Asher stood out in the crowds.

Asher's got that urban street wear perfected, with his dark jeans and random tattoos, while Mason goes for the hard frat look; colored shorts and graphic tank tops for days.

I'm not even sure how two people so different can be such good friends.

Tonight he looks like he stepped straight out of a Tumblr aesthetic page. A white long-sleeve button up hangs loosely over the graphic t-shirt tucked into his black jeans, which stand out against his white scuffed vans.

He's chic in a way only Asher Brooks could be.

Then there's Emily in her maroon t-dress and over-dressed wedges.

"Who knows," Mason comments on the pair. "Maybe he's banging her."

"Really, Mase? Are you twelve? As if Asher's the type to just bang someone anyway." Tilly rolls her eyes, putting air quotes around "bang". He just shrugs and waves them over.

Emily is busy greeting my parents but quickly follows after Asher who's heading our way.

"Lyv, happy birthday! It's been too long."

She gives an air kiss to each cheek. Apparently she's become French since I last saw her. I ignore the way Tilly's face scrunches up in confusion and awkwardly follow Emily's lead.

"It really has. Thanks so much for coming."

"Of course! I only wish I could've been here sooner."

42

At this she gives Asher a reprimanding look and I imagine Mason's earlier assumption is correct.

"Don't look at me. That's all on Emily."

Asher gives a sheepish smile and actually blushes a bit, but I simply wave him off. Now that he's closer I notice a simple gold chain hanging around his neck. He's an attractive guy, I admit, and my eyes are drawn to every little thing about him: his chocolate eyes underlined by dark circles, like he's not slept in weeks. Or his crooked smile filled with teeth whiter and straighter than any I've ever seen.

Then there's the mystery of the little tattoos lining his arms, not to mention ones I may not even be able to see.

On Asher it all fits.

"It's fine. It's not like you could've saved me from the bucket of kisses Nana Buckley dumped all over my face if you were on time, so it doesn't matter to me either way."

He laughs like it's the funniest thing he's heard to date and I admire the sound. It's a full laugh that you can practically follow all the way down to the base of his throat.

Dimples form around his   wide smile.

Emily clears her throat.

"So, what's to eat? I'm starving."

She's easily the skinniest one out of the group but somehow always eats the most.

"I think my dad has burgers on the grill if you want to check that out."

I point her in his direction and she heads off in search of food. The boys follow, which leaves Tilly and me.

Her dark eyes bore a hole in the side of my head and I'm surprised to see her squinting accusingly my way. Tilly's got eyes and hair dark as night with skin a perfectly caramel color, so every look or gesture she makes looks intense.

"What's with you?"

I grow more and more uncomfortable with every second and try to hide myself behind the barrier of my crossed arms.

"What's with *you*?"

Me? She's the one staring like I have three heads.

"I'm not sure what you mean."

"I mean you were just eyeing Asher like a piece of meat. Again I ask what was that about?"

44

Now she's talking crazy.

"Are you insane? I wasn't eyeing him like a piece of meat. I wasn't eyeing him at all. He was talking. I was listening. The end."

"Mhmm."

She drops it but still glances at me out of the corner of her eye.

I wasn't eyeing Asher.

I can't possibly explain to her just how wrong she is; how I'm not at a point where I can eye any guy right now.

Not here with all the history I battle being back in this place I was forced to grow up in.

I'm not even sure why I'm mulling it over. I wasn't eyeing Asher.

The party carries on around us with food and presents. Cake follows and for this Max actually shows up.

At least, it kind of looks like Max.

This guy in front of me is not the sixteen-year-old boy I left a year ago. Sure, turning seventeen is a monumental step and everyone's so health-conscious and gym crazy in today's world, but

Max has really filled out. I'm talking muscles and height and broad shoulders—all of it.

He still has that same, cropped hair cut and it's the same brown that matches my own. He still has that goofy grin stretched across his face, causing his hazel eyes (also matching my own) to squint from the smile.

But he's taller, much taller, and his shoulders seem broader than I last remember. My dad's a tall, broad man, so we all expected Max to follow behind him. I just never expected him to grow so fast in such a short amount of time.

"Whoa, Max. Don't they test you all for steroids in football anymore?"

I try to ruffle his hair like I used to but can't reach the top of his head.

"Your brother has really been working on his toning this summer. He's trying to get a football scholarship to Colorado State. Isn't that right, kid?"

My dad steps up to us and punches Max's shoulder, chest puffed out proudly. Max returns the smile but it never reaches his eyes. I know that look of averseness. I know it because I've had it a million times before.

When what you want for yourself and what others want for you don't line up it creates chaos in your mind you can't always tame.

Both my dad and mom are oblivious to Max's obvious gloominess on the subject, so I change it.

"Hey mom, I was thinking. What if we split this party up? You know, give us youngsters a chance to catch up?"

I know she'll go for it.

Anything to make the birthday girl happy.

"Of course, dear. Today's your day! Just let me get a picture of you and your brother first."

She removes the camera strap from my wrist and pushes Max toward me.

"C'mon Mom, is this necessary?" Max whines but swings an arm around my shoulder anyway.

"It most certainly is."

She counts down from three and just as she gets to one Max rubs the top of my head, pushing my hat so it sits crookedly. I retaliate with a pinch in his side but there's really not much fat to get a grip on anymore.

Mom settles with the picture we give her, probably knowing she won't get anything better than that.

"Alright, we'll just get out of your hair now."

And then it's just us 20-somethings and Max. We light the bug-repellent torches and fire up the pit in the middle of the circled patio chairs. It cracks and sizzles, sounding an awful lot like my adolescent days. The sun slowly fades.

It finally feels like summer.

"So, Lyvie, are you mad you're not the biggest sibling anymore?"

I kick Max hard in the shin. First, because he just called me fat. Second because he knows I hate when he calls me Lyvie. Third, I just really want to kick him.

"Shit, Lyv. Why'd you have to kick so hard?"

He moves toward me menacingly and I admit I'm a little nervous. Now that he's all around bigger I know I don't stand a chance against him.

"What do you think, Tilly? Should I toss her?"

He grabs my upper arms and I freeze.

Not this again.

Tossing me into the pool is a birthday tradition I hoped he'd forgotten since he only decided to show up five minutes ago.

"Don't Max. I'm warning you."

I try to wiggle away but it's no use.

He's bigger and stronger than me now.

I panic as his grip tightens. The panic runs deeper than he could ever imagine but I try to keep a cap on it.

"I think you should," Tilly chimes in and I shoot her my hardest glare.

"Shut up, Tilly."

Max pulls me closer and my heart races. Scenes from a time long ago flash in my mind in black and white sequence, but the world around me spins faster.

"Yeah, I think I should too."

And with that he throws me over his shoulder like a rag doll and walks me toward the pool. I kick my feet and claw at his back but my efforts are useless. He's got enough manners to toss my hat to the side and move my camera out of the way, at least.

"Max, I swear I will get you back for this. I swear I will. Put me down!"

I hide the dread behind my empty threats.

He just laughs and my "friends" cheer him on. I hear the faint sound of the happy birthday song starting up behind me but I'm screaming at Max too loud to really hear the taunting melody. He goes to throw me in and I try to wrap around him so he comes down with me, but my grip isn't tight enough.

I sail through the air alone.

The water smacks against my thigh. I'm sure I'll have a red mark when I get out. Chlorine burns my nose, but I stay under longer than necessary. Better to stay under and collect myself than to come up reeling from the trip down memory lane in my head. I cough for a few seconds when I come up but once I gain my voice, and composure, I go right at my annoying half-wit brother and toss a handful of water at his face. The water barely manages to reach the tail of his shirt but at least I got that much of him.

I pull myself up the edge of the pool and start for Max, but a draft on my stomach prompts me to glance down at my outfit choice for the day.

Not ideal for a dip in the pool.

The crop top, now soaked to the very last thread, not only has holes in it but also sticks to my skin like it's part of me. The side is raised just below my bra, making way for chill bumps when the light summer breeze hits my bare skin. My shorts, once held tight in place by my healthy-sized thighs, have ridden up enough to count as denim underwear.

My cheeks heat and I position my arms to cover as much of my skin as possible.

Luckily Tilly runs to my rescue, handing over a dry towel to cover me up.

"You're next," I point a shriveled finger at her but she just laughs. We both know she could take me.

"Let's just get you upstairs to change."

Emily gets up to follow us into the house and I shoot a middle finger in Max's way. He pretends to catch it and puts it in his pocket.

I didn't notice Asher standing so close to the door before but now I see him and I burn with embarrassment. My stomach flips with it.

Even my parents laugh as we walk past them, me dripping wet and the girls following quickly behind me.

"Another birthday tradition," my mom shakes her head like a reprimanding parent but smiles anyway.

We barely get to my room before Tilly slams the door shut and smiles in excitement.

"OK, but am I the only one who felt the testosterone radiating off Asher? Was he feeling our girl or what?"

At first I think she means Emily but then Emily chimes in too.

"Right? I thought he was going to try to jump her then and there when she came up out of that pool with her clothes all clingy and dripping."

They laugh at my expense.

"Oh whatever! Besides, didn't he come with you, Emily?"

She dismisses me with a wave of her hand and shakes her head.

"Only because he lives down the street and my car broke down. No honey. Asher is completely on the market. Also, your brother got hot. Like really hot."

"Gross Em, it's Max we're talking about. Right Tilly?"

I look to Tilly for support. Max is practically her little brother too, so I know she'll agree.

"Sorry, Lyv. I'm with Emily on this one. Max has sprouted into a bona fide man. He's got muscles in places I didn't know a 17-year-old could have muscles."

They laugh.

I throw a pillow at each of them and gag.

Even with the humor circulating the air around us I'm still reeling from the pool fiasco.

"Okay, but for real," Emily stops laughing long enough to redirect the conversation. "Let's get back to the real topic here. Asher and his steamy gaze."

She winks and I roll my eyes, still wrapped up in myself.

"Shew, I had to fan myself, I was getting so hot just watching him throw that smolder your way."

Tilly fans herself with her hand and falls to my bed as if she's fainted. We all crack up then at her dramatics and I throw the wet towel at her.

I can't deny, though.

The man's got a smolder.

Fifteen minutes later I put on my best smile and we're giggling with the rest of the party outside. By this time the sun disappears completely and there's a draft in the air.

"There they are!" Max claps his hands excitedly and I hold back another kick to his shins. "Have a seat, ladies. We were just about to start up a game of Never Have I Ever."

We take a seat, but not before one snapshot of the group circled around the fire.

So, the game goes like this. Everyone starts out with their fingers up. We go around the circle and name something we've never done. If you've done whatever is said, you put a finger down. If you haven't done it you keep your fingers up.

The objective of the game is to be the last one standing with the most amount of fingers up, but it always feels more like a competition for who's the most mischievous.

When I say I'm the worst at this game, I mean the literal worst. I'm no goody-two-shoes by any means but compared to my friends I'm basically a nun. Which means I'm always left with the most fingers left.

So, I win the game but lose points for unruliness.

"Do we have to?"

I know I sound like a baby, but it's my birthday. If I don't want to play the game we're not playing the game.

Except we are because everyone hoops and hollers at me, calling me a party pooper. I can't be a party pooper at my own party.

"Alright, birthday girl goes first," Emily nods her head my way and we all put our hands up to start the game.

"And no dorky ones."

This comes from Max.

I scold him but he knows me too well.

"Okay. Got it. Never have I ever thrown up on an elderly couple in an Ihop."

This one goes out to Tilly. True story, too. She said she was only going to drink one or two beers that night but her and Mason were fighting at the time so she drank plenty more than planned. I was sober but stupid and thought food sounded good. That poor couple didn't even know what hit them until it was too late.

"Hey, that's no fair!"

Tilly dropped a finger   but we still laughed.

"You can't direct it at me like that. You know I'm the only one who can drop on that."

Asher clears his throat and we all look to see he too has one less finger held up.

"Asher, man, you too?" Mason slaps him on the shoulder proudly. "What happened?"

He scratches absently at his jaw before answering, drawing my attention to the thin arrow inked into his forearm.

"In my defense, it wasn't because I was trashed. I was just a kid and the eggs weren't completely cooked. I took a bite and a gooey piece fell out. I tried to get to the bathroom but didn't make it before upchucking allover this poor old man and woman waiting in the lobby to be seated."

We laugh until we cry and Asher blushes in the most adorable way. He smiles that dimpled smile of his.

The last time I saw a smile that beautiful I found myself in a situation I never want to be in again, so I look away.

"Alright, alright. Let's move on. Emily, you're up."

Max brings us back down and suddenly I'm nervous. He's too eager about getting to his turn. I just know it's something that'll embarrass me.

"Mine's perfect," she pushes her long, blonde hair behind her ears and smiles wickedly. "Never have I ever been caught hooking up in Molton's parking lot."

Another hit to Tilly, and to Mason.

Molton's is a grocery store in town where Tilly and Mason liked to fool around senior year. That is until Mr. Molten, the storeowner, caught them after hours and ran them off.

"Now I know you guys are singling me out!"

Tilly drops another finger and this time she doesn't laugh with the rest of us.

"Oh chill out, Tilly. I needed something to drop another person and Mason fit the bill. You were just collateral."

Emily tries to lean over Asher and pat Tilly's arm but Tilly's leans away from her expertly and avoids the contact.

"Asher's turn."

Tilly mumbles the words and I know she's plotting something good in her head. Whether that'll be for Emily, or me it's hard to say.

"Let me think," Asher scratches the back of his neck as he thinks. His eyes squint and he bites his lower lip.

"Got it," he snaps his fingers and grins. "Never have I ever had a parent walk in on me watching porn."

Mason drops another finger and shrugs like "whadya gonna do?" and I feel queasy.

"Wait, Max is your finger down?"

Emily leans forward and stares at Max's remaining nine fingers with a mischievous gleam in her eyes. I'm not sure I like that gleam. I'm definitely sure I don't like where this game has gone.

Some things you just can't unhear about your little brother.

"Atta boy, Max."

Mason fist bumps him and I cringe. Physically cringe. Last thing I need is Mason influencing my little brother in any way, shape, or form.

"Tell us what happened."

Emily is extremely intrigued with this and I'm not thrilled about it. Max blushes, actually blushes, and glances at me awkwardly.

"Let's not and say we did," Tilly jumps in to save the day once again.

I mouth a thank-you her way and she nods loyally.

We go around the circle. Tilly gets one on Max, Emily, and me with a line about never being kicked out of a movie for being too loud. Mason gets one on Asher about never coming into his house "piss drunk" and passing out in front of his mom. Seth or Shane or whatever gets one on Mason so that Mason is now losing.

When we get to Max I know I'm in trouble.

As kids I could always tell when Max was up to something. He'd always get jittery and kind of hop from foot to foot, chewing on the inside of his jaw with his hazel eyes so similar to my own squinted in concentration.

The signs are all there. His right foot bounces on the concrete and his jaw probably has a sore spot on the inside from chewing so hard. His eyes squint and I chew on my own lip with nerves.

My heart thumps in my chest and I brace for what he's come up with.

"Never have I ever ruined a favorite outfit one summer in the rain and cried about it for days   after."

59

The line seems harmless to the rest of the group, just another targeted attack, but tears prick my eyes.

The outfit pans out clearly in my mind. It was my favorite skater dress in a perfect champagne color. The dress wasn't the only thing tainted that night, but to Max it was just a dramatic mental breakdown over a ruined dress.

I can't fault him for not realizing what he's saying.

But still my chest burns.

I drop a finger and glance at no one but Tilly who stares at me with that same wrinkled forehead as yesterday. Everyone else laughs obliviously. I'm completely and utterly done with this game but I can't lose it here in front of everyone.

I have to finish the game. I have to brave it. I have to—

"Alright, I'm calling it quits. I've got to work in the morning and I can't save kids if I'm tired."

Tilly for the win.

"What? No! We've only been one round."

Max throws his hands up in complaint. His age shows in his mini temper tantrum.

"Right, so it's a good stopping point. We can finish it some other time. Just not tonight."

Sometimes the tables turn and Tilly ends up being my knight in shining armor, like now.

"She's right," this from Asher as he looks down at the watch wrapped around his wrist. "It's been a long day. I'm exhausted."

He catches my eye and something about that look tells me he saw the tension everyone else missed.

Something tells me he's the kind of guy who catches a lot of moments other people miss.

We all break away from the fire pit and put out the bug torches lining the patio. Max puts the lid on the fire pit but doesn't comment on my newfound quietness. Instead he bids everyone goodnight and goes into the house.

Emily hugs me and Mason waves goodbye with Sean/Shane and wishes me a final happy birthday. Tilly's hug lasts longer than Emily's. She pulls back and inspects my face thoroughly.

"You OK?"

It's a loaded question.

To be honest, I'm not sure. I thought I would be but every time I let my mind go its own way it goes to dark places in my past I don't have the energy to keep up with. It's like my whole chest is filled to the brim with an iced chill and I'm about to cave.

I nod.

She smiles encouragingly and chases after the rest of the group.

It's then I notice Asher is still there. He's so quiet I didn't even notice he'd hung back until everyone was gone.

"I hope this wasn't, like, the worst birthday party you've ever been to," I laugh awkwardly but the feeling's not really there. This doesn't get past Asher.

He smiles very much like the way Tilly had moments before. Pity oozes from the smile's edges.

"It was great. Better than any Mason's ever drug me to, I can promise you that."

That can't be true. I've been to some of the parties Mason and Asher have been to. Those can get crazy wild. This one was anything but crazy wild.

"Well, I'm glad you came anyway."

62

"Me too."

He smiles again only this time it's not out of pity. This time it's got thunder rolling with it. This time it brings some heat to my chest where it had felt like ice just moments before.

"Happy birthday Lyv."

He puts his hands in his pockets and smirks to the ground as he walks past me.

Slowly but surely, and probably temporarily, those dark memories evaporate into the summer sky above.

⊙⊙⊙⊙⊙

I'm not sure if I've mentioned I'm not much of a morning person.

Am I punctual? Yes. Am I organized? Absolutely.

But do I wake with a smile and birds chirping around my head every morning? Not even a little bit.

For whatever reason, my body wakes itself up at 9 this morning and the night before rushes back. My covers feel great at the thought of my birthday endeavors, like they're hiding me from the reality of the outside world.

Ten more minutes.

If my body could just give me ten more minutes to lay here and soak in this Saturday slumber, I'd be satisfied.

But there'll be no slumber for me. Not if my body has a say.

It's not such a terrible morning when I untangle from my covers and stumble into the hall to find Max's room just down the hall is empty.

"Max?"

I yell out, but no answer.

"Mom? Dad?"

Still nothing.

I welcome the silence.

I carry on with my regular morning routine as if I'm back in high school and haven't been away from home for a year. My teeth are brushed and my face is washed, but still no sign of family moving about downstairs.

Once I get to the kitchen I find a note on the fridge.

Lyv,

Gone to Max's summer football bowl. Be back this evening.

Love Mom, Dad, and Max

Though Max crossed out his name in some early morning humor.

I'd be lying if I say I'm not relieved.

Time to you is always important.

My nature gets the best of me and I make a to-do list of how I'll spend my relaxing day. First, I'll get the mail and take Daisy for a walk. Then I'll eat some breakfast. Maybe I'll take a dip in the pool while I have it to myself. Or drive around looking for some project shots.

It's a new day.

A new morning.

My birthday is done and last night forgotten.

When I get back to my room to find some clothes for the day my groan echoes throughout my room at the piles of suitcases I need to unpack. I'm not the kind of person who lets suitcases sit full for weeks after a trip but the thought of unpacking right now sounds like torture.

So, that won't be making my to-do list.

Maybe I'll take it a step further and not even plan a day for it.

It only seems appropriate I wear my pastel pink "I'm not a morning person" shirt tucked into my acid wash high waist shorts. I don't want to break my "No Unpacking" rule so my flip-flops from yesterday finish the outfit off.

It's not an outfit made to check the mail and walk a dog but it's the first thing I find without taking everything out of my bags.

Daisy comes running from Max's room the moment she hears me jingle the collar of her leash near the front door. She jumps up and down as if there's a trampoline beneath her, wagging her tail in swift movements. I swear puppies have more energy than a toddler with a sugar high.

"Who wants to go outside? Does my Daisy girl want to go for a walk?"

She laps my face up as I bend down to pat her small head.

If all humans were as warm and lovable as Daisy I'm sure we'd reach world peace with no troubles.

Once she's all leashed up I step out into the bright day and breathe in that fresh Colorado air.

It's going to be a good day.

Daisy is entirely too excited for this walk to sit still for the mail, so that'll have to wait until the way back.

I've never walked a dog before but I imagined puppies would be a little more manageable. Daisy, however, is all of 20 pounds and she's dragging me around like a full-grown dog.

But it's fine.

We're fine.

Except Daisy is really picking up speed. She's gone from stopping at every tree to mark her spot to a full trot down the sidewalk. There's a curve up ahead and I hope it slows her down but it's not looking too likely.

"Slow down, girl."

That doesn't work.

She hears my voice and her energy spikes, if that's even possible.

And then she's running.

I chase after her around the corner. As luck would have it, there's a fence in the yard where the sidewalk curves, which creates a blind spot for anyone making the turn.

And that's how I come to a full crash with an unsuspecting runner going the opposite way.

We hit hard, hard enough for me to fall straight on my back. That concrete sidewalk is an unrelenting thing and I'm sure I'll bruise by morning. Daisy, of course, hasn't a scratch and sits obediently as if she didn't cause this mess. Somehow the guy got wrapped up in Daisy's leash and fell knees first to the ground. The poor runner took the brunt of the fall.

Blood runs down his leg and I look toward his face to apologize.

Caramel eyes stare back at me.

The poor runner is Asher.

Asher is bleeding in front of me.

Asher is bleeding *because* of me.

So much for my good morning.

"Oh no. No, no, no. I am so sorry."

I apologize over and over again but Asher laughs.

He actually *laughs* while the blood runs on.

"Are you OK?"

"Yeah, no, I'm fine. It's just a scratch."

He untangles himself from Daisy and valiantly holds his hand out to help me up. When I grab his hand he flinches but just slightly.

"Is your hand hurt?"

"No, it's fine."

He wipes his hand on his white shirt and streaks blood down it.

"Your shirt's ruined. Here, let me see."

Instinct kicks in from years of patching up Max and I reach for his right hand. Hesitantly he gives in and lets me see. When I turn it over so a small dice tattoo on his hand faces down and palm faces me I see bloody skid marks across the meaty part. I mentally question how I never noticed all the little ink markings that seem to decorate so much of his body.

Dusty pieces of loose concrete litter the blood.

All in all, it's not too bad.

"You should let me clean that up."

"I wouldn't want to bother you."

"You're joking, right? My pup just knocked us both over and wrecked your hand. Not to mention your knee. It's the least I could do."

Daisy yelps on cue and Asher kneels down to pet her. She jumps in his arms and licks his face.

Lousy pup.

"What's its name?"

"Her name's Daisy."

"Well, no hard feelings, but only because you're so cute."

He scratches Daisy's chin but looks at me through long, dark lashes when he says it.

My heart lurches out of my chest and I keep my eyes on Daisy.

"Let's go then. I'm just around the corner here."

Like he wasn't just there less than 24 hours ago.

The way back home is much like the beginning of the walk when Daisy wonders on aimlessly. I pretend like it's me walking Daisy and not Daisy walking me.

"So, you run often?"

Mental note: work on people skills.

"I do, yeah. It helps me blow off steam."

My mind races with what he'd need to blow off steam about. Races with wonders about this stranger I've known practically all my life.

"You and I have two very different ideas of blowing off steam."

He laughs and it fills the space around us, even in the open air outside.

"And what does Lyv McDowell do to blow off steam?"

I'm no good at this but I think he's flirting. He smiles with those dimples and looks at me with those hooded eyes and I think he just might be.

My eyes drift back to Daisy.

"Usually I venture out alone and do a little bit of photography. You know, capture peaceful scenery to remind myself it's not all bad out there."

He's still looking at me but I keep time with my feet hitting the concrete.

I watch one foot fall in front of the other and ignore the heat his gaze leaves.

71

"That's different. I like that."

One quick peak at his lopsided grin sends me straight back to Daisy who is now casually walking with her tongue stuck out of the side of her mouth.

"Here we are."

I don't think I've ever been so excited to see home.

I let us both in and unlatch Daisy. She runs straight up the stairs, most likely to Max's room. The little brat has Daisy brainwashed I think. That's the only explanation for why she prefers his room and company to mine.

"Right, so I think the first aid kit is in my parents' bathroom."

Asher follows behind me.

It feels strange having him here. Last night was different. Last night we were outside and with other people. But now he's here and inside and it's just us. It feels different.

Scarier.

There's a silence between us; a tension I can't quite put my finger on. It's not a bad tension, necessarily, just a noticeable one.

"This house is amazing, by the way."

"Thank you," and because I can't help myself I take the focus off me. "You should see Tilly's. It's ridiculously massive."

"Yeah, I've been there a couple times with Mason. I could get lost in that house if I'm not careful."

We get to the bathroom and Asher goes straight for the bathtub.

"Now this is what you call a bathtub."

He takes a look over the edge and admires the tiled sides.

"That bathtub is my dad's pride and joy. He remodeled it a few years ago. It used to be a regular white tub but he put all the tile up around it and installed a new spout and everything."

That bathtub was dad's one and only project that winter. He drove us all crazy with his renovation ideas and the poor guy didn't even finish any except the tub.

The first aid kit isn't exactly where I thought it was but after some digging I finally find it.

Asher sits on the edge of the tub and watches as I go through the contents of the kit. My first instinct is to run and hide under his heavy stare. It's so unnerving to have someone look at you so straightforward.

I've been looked at blatantly before, and in ways more repulsive than I can recount. But never in a way like this where it seems someone's looking straight through me.

Despite my urge to get away from those steady eyes of his I stay put.

"Alright, first lets look at the knee."

Without thinking I kneel down in front of him, never mind the awkward position I'm putting myself in.

"This is going to burn."

The alcohol pad sweeps across his bloody knee and he flinches enough to almost throw himself back into the tub. I reach out for him and he latches onto me with a vise grip.

"Easy there, there's only so much I can do for a cracked skull."

I smirk at the pink warming his cheeks but casually unlatch myself from his hold on me.

"Sorry, that just burns more than I expected."

"Yeah, Daisy sure did a number on you, didn't she?"

Please, God, if you're listening don't let him see my hands shaking.

"I feel sorry for that puppy. Poor thing has to take the fall for your clumsiness."

I stop with the alcohol and stare at him in mock confusion as I switch to the ointment.

"I think you have me mixed up with someone else. I'm pretty much the least clumsy person you've ever met."

Asher shakes his head and a few strands of his dark, unkempt hair falls against his forehead. It's sweaty and beautiful and I can't stop staring at it.

It's really nice hair. Not too long but not too short. Like Brendon Urie post *Death of a Bachelor*.

"Right, because falling into a pool and tripping over your dog isn't clumsy at all."

"Let me just stop you right there," I hold my ointment-covered finger up. "I didn't fall into the pool, I was thrown by my runt of a brother. Also, I didn't trip over Daisy. *You* tripped us. So if anything, you're the clumsy one."

He laughs, but this one is bigger than the rest. This one makes him throw his head back and eyes shut.

It's contagious, that laugh of his, and I find myself joining in.

"Whatever you say, Lyv."

He shakes his head at me with a smile.

"I've picked this Band-Aid just for you."

He looks at his knee as I smooth a wide, bright pink Band-Aid over the ointment-covered skin and he grins widely.

"It's perfect."

"Now for the hand."

His hand is a little messier, what with the pieces of concrete mixed in and all, so I lead him to the sink to wash it out.

"Make sure you use soap."

"Yes, mom."

He gives me a side-glance and smirks.

Great.

I sound like a mom.

Who would want someone who sounds like a mom?

Not that I want him to want me.

"I think it's all clear."

He gives me his hand for inspection and I dry it off with the hand towel hanging up. Next comes the alcohol pad.

"So how'd you get to be so good at patching people up?"

He stands so close I can feel his breath on the top of my head. I'm average height and he hovers a solid two feet above me at least. The close proximity puts me on edge and I slightly and subtly slide a little away from him.

"My brother didn't always hate me so much. We actually liked each other when we were kids. He was the rowdy one and I was the safe one. I kind of just made it my thing to be the one to fix his bumps and scrapes."

The truth of that settles a little close to home.

"And who fixed your bumps and scrapes?"

His question almost knocks me off my feet. My hands pause their work and I glance up to his wondering eyes. He's not malicious or sarcastic, but genuinely begs the question.

So I genuinely answer.

"I fixed my own."

Though it's something I'm still working on.

Asher doesn't answer right away, but when he does he reverses the conversation back to Max.

"I don't think he hates you at all, you know. It seems like he's pretty fond of you from where I'm standing."

I laugh sarcastically and continue on to the ointment.

"That must be why he likes to embarrass me at every chance he gets."

"Ah, I think that's just part of having siblings. You didn't see how bad he felt after that game last night. I think he could tell he bummed you out."

And so we're back to the embarrassing birthday.

"Yeah well, if he felt so bad about it he shouldn't have brought that stupid outfit up in the first place," I move on to the band aid and take a little more time rubbing the sticky edges down than I did with the knee.

It's a welcome distraction from the current conversation.

"About that, Max didn't give all the details," my heart pounds in my heating chest. "He doesn't *know* all the details, I mean. I didn't just break down because I ruined my dress. That was a stressful day and I ju—"

"Hey, Lyv," he shakes his head at me and frowns. "You don't have to explain yourself to me."

78

I nod, glad he stopped me before I could've said anymore. With a racing pulse I stare on at his hand until he scrunches down so our faces are even.

"I'm serious. You don't owe me or anyone else an explanation for that. You want to cry? Cry. You want to scream? Scream. You want to run people down with your ferocious dog? That's fine too. Just please let it be someone else next time."

He nudges me with a smile and eventually I crack a genuine smile.

And then I realize I'm staring into his unrelenting eyes while I'm still holding his pink bandaged hand and I'm feeling that heat Tilly and Emily teased me about it.

His eyes get this little glint at the edge and they stay locked with mine. I'm the first to break.

"Well, um, I guess you're free to go then. Get back to your run and all that."

I drop his hand and he scratches the back of his neck.

"Yeah, I've got all this pent up aggression towards this chick's German Sheppard puppy, so I should probably go run that off."

79

His smirk will be the death of me.

"So I'm downgraded to some 'chick' now. A girl can't catch a break around here, can she?"

He shoves me playfully and I stumble over the bathroom rug. Thankfully Asher catches me before I make a total fool of myself but not before he gets in a good joke.

"I'm going to have to keep you close, Lyv McDowell. You're a hazard to yourself."

I lead the way out of the bathroom, mostly so he can't see me smiling like a giddy schoolgirl.

We reach the front door and Daisy runs to Asher's feet, jumping with all her might to get his attention. He bends down to coddle her.

"You be a good girl. Don't go knocking over every runner on the street, all right? I want to be the only guy you two knock off his feet."

He raises back up and I swear my heart stops a second.

"See ya around, Lyv."

With a smile and a wave he's out the door.

What's he playing at?

Who does he think he is coming into my own house and stealing my breath like it's his to take? And who am I thinking I can keep up with a guy like that?

He's dangerously close to having me right in the palm of his bloody, scraped up hands when I've barely been home for 24 hours.

I've been there before with a different guy in a different life. Head over heels, out of control, always trying to catch my breath.

That's a place I never want to be in again.

As soon as he's out of sight Daisy races to the glass panel beside the door to see him off. She barks after him, whining like she misses him already.

I guess he has that effect on people.

I pet behind her ears but still she stares after him.

"Me too, girl," I shake my head at her. "Me too."

Chapter Three-Asher

When I was a kid my dad called me Hamilton, like Billy Hamilton, the baseball player.

See, I played baseball from kindergarten until I graduated high school, and I was good. From the very beginning I ran faster than any of the other kids. I'd steal bases without losing a breath.

He was the only one who called me Hamilton. It's been almost 6 years since he's died—6 years since I've heard his laugh or proud voice call me Hamilton.

I miss that.

And so I run.

Run to remember him. Run to put the world away for a while. Run to clear my head.

After the night I had I need a run this morning. I didn't get much sleep last night thanks to a hazel eyed, curly headed girl.

Images run through my mind as my feet hit the concrete below me. I tell myself to breathe steadily even as my heart beats wildly inside my chest.

All because of Lyv.

I've known Lyv most of my life. We run in the same crowd and she's only a year younger than me, so I was always around her during high school. I'd always just known her as a friend of a friend, nothing more.

But she sneaks up on you, that Lyv. One minute you're at high school, roaming from girl to girl just to get some kind of attention. Then the next thing you know you're at a college party standing on the other side of the room seeing this quiet, reserved mystery of a girl, seemingly for the very first time ever. I watched her that night, holding herself back from the rest of the crowd, and wondered why I hadn't noticed her before now.

I remember it all so vividly.

I'd come to the party that night with Mason just to get some relief from the stack of homework I'd been ignoring. When they walked into the frat house (I couldn't tell you who's, to be honest) Tilly marched straight for me and Mason. But Lyv didn't. Lyv drifted toward the side of the room, eyes constantly roaming around at the strangers filling up the room.

I remember those eyes searching the faces in the dark until they landed briefly on me. It lasted all of about 5 seconds, but she paused on me and my stomach lurched. Her smile was small and hesitant, gone in the blink of an eye, and then she was back to scanning the crowd. Even as Tilly snickered at my obvious draw toward Lyv, even as Mase snapped his fingers in my face to get my attention, even after their relentless taunting the rest of the night— even then, I knew something was changing.

With college, I guess, spending time with people is a bigger deal than high school. In high school, it's like you're almost forced to be around whoever is in your town and that's it. But at college, you get to pick based on people you actually enjoy.

And I realized I actually enjoyed being around Lyv.

I almost went for her once. A couple of months after that brief eye contact, we were all at another party together. I almost went up to her then and there.

But some pretty boy, punk guy beat me to it. They've been dating since, so I'd let Lyv fade to the back of my mind.

Until now. Now she's back, full throttle. The same thing pulls me in now as that night at that beer-reeking house. I feel like a moth drawn to a flame around her. It's like she tries sinking into the background wherever she goes, but tends to actually do the complete opposite.

It's the eyes, I think. They're green and brown all at the same time; attentive and moody, like she has all these secrets to life hidden behind them.

It's those eyes I see now, as I see her so clearly in my head from last night.

I see her standing next to her friends and family at her party, outshining them all.

Breathe.

I see her get out of that pool, clothes barely hiding anything while her bare skin drips wet.

Breathe.

I see her at the end of the night with her round face drawn into a frown, forehead wrinkled with some battle she fights within herself. I want to kiss that frown away. I want to smooth that wrinkle out of her pretty head.

Damn it, Asher. Breathe.

But it's no use.

The universe is against me.

Because just as I work to get her out of my head I crash to the ground mid run with a dog leash wrapped around my legs and clutched in Lyv's hand. She looks up at me and my breathing goes to shit.

She's wearing a t-shirt that says "Not a morning person." Judging by her grimace I'd say that's about right.

"Oh no. No, no, no. I am so sorry."

Blood runs down my leg and the leash still vines up my calf but Lyv looks more frazzled than I do. I can't help but laugh.

"Are you OK?"

"Yeah, no, I'm fine. It's just a scratch."

It's not just a scratch and my knee actually kind of hurts. Pride pushes the pain aside.

The puppy to blame sits on its hunches, tongue lolling. If puppies smiled I'd swear this puppy is smiling right now. Mocking us for being stupid enough to get tangled up in this mess. One of us has to unwrap the leash and it's obvious the puppy isn't going anywhere, so I stand and reach out a hand to Lyv still on the ground.

She grabs my extended hand with her tiny one and I flinch. Apparently my knee isn't the only damaged body part.

"Is your hand hurt?"

Her eyes round innocently and she bites her lip.

Breathe.

"No, it's fine."

To prove my point I wipe my hand down my sweaty, white shirt. The blood smear that follows incriminates me.

"Your shirt's ruined. Here, let me see."

Something in me holds back, just for a moment when the image of the blonde-headed guy from the party burns in my mind. But she holds my hand delicately and shakes her head in disapproval. I drag my eyes away from her focused face to assess the damage myself.

I've had worse.

"You should let me clean that up."

"I wouldn't want to bother you."

Lies.

I'd love nothing more.

"You're joking, right? My pup just knocked us both over and wrecked your hand. Not to mention your knee. It's the least I can do."

As if to prove itself the dog lets out a bark and I bend down to pet the little scoundrel.

"What's its name?"

"Her name's Daisy."

"Well, no hard feelings, but only because you're so cute."

Daisy eats the compliment up and I let her believe I'm talking about her.

Once we start back for Lyv's house it doesn't take long to see what caused the little altercation to begin with. Daisy is one mighty strong puppy and Lyv works hard to keep control.

"So, you run often?"

She breaks the silence as she gives the leash a slight tug toward her.

I don't go into all the details. Nothing like talking about your dead dad to dampen the mood.

"I do, yeah. It helps me blow off steam."

She scoffs, which is how most people react when I say I enjoy running.

"You and I have two completely different ideas of blowing off steam."

I wonder what Lyv does to unwind, what she does to block out the world. And I wonder, just for a second, what it'd be like to be the one who helps her forget it all.

"And what does Lyv McDowell do to blow off steam?"

I can't help but ask. To want to know more. She's closed off and silent most days I'm around her. Her thoughts aren't laid out for the world to see and I crave to know how she ticks.

"Usually I venture out alone and do a little bit of photography. You know, capture peaceful scenery to remind myself it's not all bad out there."

Her eyes drop to the ground and she laughs to herself, brushing the reply off like it's not that important. Whatever I thought she was going to say, it wasn't this profound. Surely she's from a different universe, one much purer than this one.

"That's different. I like that."

Her side-glance toward me lasts about five seconds. She looks away again and my chest burns.

"Here we are."

All too soon our little venture ends and I'm following her inside and down a hallway. It leads us farther into the house than I'd been last night. We pass picture frames on walls, one of which is a tiny Lyv holding an even tinier Max. It takes every ounce of me to push forward despite wanting to stop and admire it.

Eventually we wind our way back to the master bedroom.

To say it's huge is an understatement.

The whole back wall is made up of glass doors leading to an outside balcony. A wooden chandelier hangs above the center of the carpeted floor and a California King bed lines the tan wall next to the glass doors. My house is plenty enough for my mom, two sisters, and me. But this bedroom alone is the size of my living room.

"This house is amazing, by the way."

She tucks her unruly hair behind her ear and shies away from the sentiment.

"Thank you. You should see Tilly's house. It's ridiculously massive."

I've seen Tilly's house before and it is in fact ridiculously massive. Tilly's bedroom puts this master bedroom to shame.

I wonder what Lyv's bedroom looks like?

Despite being in the same friend group for years, last night was actually the first night I'd been to her house. When I'd seen Emily broken down on the side of the road she told me where she headed. So I did one of those annoying things parents always tell you not to do as a kid. I invited myself along.

Anything to get a glimpse into Lyv's life.

That same curiosity kills me now.

Is she a poster-hanging girl or bare walls? Are they painted walls or plain? I bet they're painted. Something pastel and light. Something that matches her bed.

Her bed...

Breathe.

When we make it to the bathroom I'm distracted by the giant bathtub at the back of the room.

"Now this is what you call a bathtub."

It's separated from the glass shower and tile lines the sides of it. It seems sturdy enough so I have a seat on the edge. My seat gives a perfect vantage point of Lyv

ruffling through cabinets. It's creepy, I know, but she's so focused on

finding that first aid kit.

She seems like the type to focus on everything that intently.

Finally she finds the kit and moves toward me.

"Alright, first let's look at the knee."

She drops to her knees in front of me and I stop thinking with

my brain momentarily. I hate to blame it on my anatomy, but the

position she goes down to puts my mind immediately in the gutter.

Breathe. Breathe. Breathe.

"This is going to burn."

She rubs the alcohol pad over my bloody knee and it burns

worse than I imagined it would. In my effort to get away from the

burning sensation I flinch. Thanks to Lyv's quick hands I don't

tumble back into the tub.

"Easy there, there's only so much I can do for a cracked

skull."

She teases and oh, that smirk has me reeling.

"Sorry, that just burns more than I expected."

"Yeah, that Daisy sure did a number on you."

Is she flirting?

Maybe.

I hope.

"I feel so sorry for that puppy. Poor thing has to take the fall for your clumsiness."

Flirting with Lyv is easily one of my top-10 favorite things to do. Her cheeks tint red and she's got this child-like grin she shifts into playful confusion.

"I think you have me mixed up with someone else. I'm pretty much the least clumsy person you've ever met."

I don't know her well, but I've seen enough to know she's not graceful.

"Right, because falling into a pool and tripping over your dog isn't clumsy at all."

She moves on to the ointment and gently rubs it over my knee. My mind jumbles under her touch.

"Let me just stop you right there," she puts a finger in the air to keep me in place. As if I have any intention of going anywhere. "I didn't fall into the pool, I was thrown by my runt of a brother. Also, I didn't trip over Daisy. *You* tripped over us. So if anything, you're the clumsy one."

A throaty laugh bubbles up in me. Something about her triggers me in every way. She raises her brows as if to say "I'm right, you're wrong." I know then and there, regardless of how right or wrong she is, I'll go with it.

Anything she wants, I'll go with it.

"Whatever you say, Lyv."

She smiles at the box of bandages in her hand and I'm too busy admiring her smile to notice the bright pink one she chooses until she presses it against my knee.

"It's perfect."

I smile at my pink badge of honor.

"Now for the hand."

She moves me to the sink and runs water over the dirt-filled wound.

"Make sure you use soap."

"Yes mom."

I mean it as a joke but her face falls slightly.

Once she inspects my hand and deems it clean she works on it the same way she did my knee.

"So how'd you get to be so good at patching people up?"

Maybe she's too focused on my hand to notice I move just half a step closer to her. Just enough to see her long lashes shading her downcast eyes. Enough to notice how perfect her face is without a stitch of makeup.

"My brother didn't always hate me so much. We actually liked each other when we were kids. He was the rowdy one and I was the safe one. I kind of just made it my thing to be the one to fix his bumps and scrapes."

I have this terrible habit of saying exactly what comes to mind without a single hesitation. It's one my mom says I need to work on before I go out in public around actual people.

"And who fixed your bumps and scrapes?"

Unfortunately now is not the magical moment where I break that habit. The words fall out before I have a chance to stop them.

She smiles but it's sad, never reaching her eyes or anywhere beyond her slightly upturned lips.

"I fixed my own."

95

She goes somewhere else in that moment and I wish I never asked.

"I don't think he hates you at all, you know. It seems like he's pretty fond of you from where I'm standing."

And I mean it. Sure, he joked and teased her all night last night, but it seemed like he kept his eyes on her constantly, aware of every move she made.

Still, she scoffs doubtfully.

"That must be why he likes to embarrass me at every chance he gets."

"Ah, I think that's just part of having siblings. You didn't see how bad he felt after that game last night. I think he could tell he bummed you out."

Speaking from experience, brothers are more aware of their sisters' feelings than they think. I can spot a bad day on Cali and Mia the second I see their faces. Granted, my sisters are fifteen and seventeen, so their feelings come bubbling out at the drop of a hat.

"Yeah well, if he felt so bad about it he shouldn't have brought that stupid outfit up in the first place."

Now I really wish I hadn't said anything. She rubs over the bandage on my hand enough times to probably keep it in place for weeks and she won't meet my eyes.

"About that, Max didn't give all the details," she pushes the words off her tongue with a scrunched face. "He doesn't *know* all the details, I mean. I didn't just break down because I ruined my dress. That was a stressful day and I ju-"

"Hey, Lyv," I interrupt her. Whatever she's trying to say upsets her and I don't like the pain written on her face. "You don't have to explain yourself to me."

Her nod is all but convincing, so I lean down and give her no choice but to see me, to hear my words.

"I'm serious. You don't owe me or anyone else an explanation for that. You want to cry? Cry. You want to scream? Scream. You want to run people down with your ferocious dog? That's fine too. Just please let it be someone else next time."

Finally, a real smile breaks the surface.

If I had it my way I'd spend my entire day doing whatever it takes to keep that smile in its rightful place.

"Well, um, I guess you're free to go then. Get back to your run and all that."

She drops my hand and the moment falls with it.

"Yeah, I've got all this pent up aggression towards this chick's German Sheppard puppy so I should probably go run that off."

That smile of hers will do me in.

"So I'm downgraded to some 'chick' now? A girl can't catch a break around here, can she?"

Playfully I shove her shoulder and clumsily she trips over the bathroom rug. I catch her before she falls.

"I'm going to have to keep you close, Lyv McDowell. You're a hazard to yourself."

She leads the way to the front door, which is good because with her back to me she misses the goofy grin stretched across my face. Daisy joins us almost immediately. She jumps like a maniac, so I scratch under her chin to calm her.

"You be a good girl, you hear me? Don't go knocking over every runner on the street. I want to be the only guy you ladies knock off his feet."

That last line was cheesy, even to my own ears.

But I want to make myself clear. Lyv gets to me. There's no point avoiding the truth of that. No point trying to hide it, either.

"See ya around, Lyv."

Daisy's bark follows me outside until I'm beyond the sidewalk and running again. Her bark vanishes with the summer breeze but what just happened runs on in my mind.

I've run fast before, but never this fast. I don't run home, though. Instead I run to Mason's house. He's only a couple of streets down from me; a ten-minute run I'd say.

I make it in eight.

I don't bother knocking. When you've been friends with someone for so long, things as mundane as knocking don't really matter.

"Dude, did you run here? What happened to your shirt?"

Mason pauses the game he'd been playing and rises up to make room for me on the couch but I'm too wired to sit.

Instead I bend over, hands on knees with a stitch forming in my side.

"Long story short I bumped into Lyv walking her dog and got a little scraped up."

He looks at me like I'm high.

I kind of feel like I am.

"You should probably take a breath, bro."

As if I haven't been trying to do that all morning.

"What's the deal with Lyv?"

He furrows his brows but then my motive clicks with a smirk played across his lips.

"What do you want to know about her?"

"Anything. Everything. What's she like; hobbies, quirks, boyfriend-that kind of stuff."

He scratches his chin and stares thoughtfully at the ceiling.

"To be honest she's not that exciting."

Regret bubbles up already. Why did I ever think Mason would be helpful here?

"I mean, she's cool to be around and obviously she's a smoke show, but she kind of hangs off by herself. She doesn't get into much trouble."

He skips over the biggest question.

"And does she have a boyfriend?"

His grin widens.

"As far as I know she's single. Why do you ask?"

My chest feels light and suddenly my lungs fill with air. I guess things didn't work out with that punk guy after all. For the first time since seeing her last night my head clears with the idea of Lyv, the idea of Lyv and *me*.

"Thanks, I was just curious."

"Sure you were."

He sees right through me.

"One more thing. Can you give me a ride home? My knee is killing me."

Chapter Four-Tilly

Weddings are a nightmare.

Correction: *Planning* a wedding is a nightmare. Pinterest does a great job at misleading people to believe their wedding board can be replicated down to the last detail, but Pinterest lies.

Up to this point, nothing has gone right in planning my sister's wedding. Granted, Mona herself is an earthquake. She rattles and flusters everything near her, so I'm not entirely surprised her wedding isn't any different. Of course she'll dump buckets of stress on anyone hands-on with this dreadful planning process.

Lucky for me, I'm only a bridesmaid. I plan to milk that little detail long after Mona says "I do".

I've already been practicing.

"Tilly, help your sister pick out her flowers." Sorry mom, *that's the maid of honor's job.*

"Tilly, put these center pieces on the table." Sounds like *Lisa's job to me, mom.*

"Tilly, bend and break to Mona's every demand because it's her special day, not that it's any different than how every other day goes in our house." Hard pass, mom. Thanks though.

"It's ridiculous. They're all so dramatic," I rant loudly as Lyv lies next to me on a lounge chair. She stares dazed at the pool water shimmering in front of us. "I swear I'm done with it. You won't find me stressing about this wedding anymore."

You will find me, however, poolside and relaxed with a mock cocktail in hand while the sun bakes my already darkened skin. It's my day off and I refuse to let Mona suck me into her whirlwind.

"I'm sure everyone's just feeling overly stressed right now," Lyv tries comforting me. "Once it's all over everything will go back to normal."

I scoff at her optimism.

Normal—as if my family has ever known what *that* is.

"That'll be the day," I mumble.

Sometimes I imagine how amazing it would be to just disappear. I even check out plane tickets from time to time, you know, just for kicks. My mouse will hover over the next ticket to some deserted island and I wonder what it'd be like to go where no one knows me.

Where no one would look for me.

It'd be lonely, sure, but it'd be a chosen loneliness and not a forced kind. Forced loneliness is the most treacherous of all.

Lyv is lucky in that sense.

I admit, her brother is a pain most of the time, but at least he cares. At least he notices her. He's got a funny way of showing it sometimes, but I think Max has always been Lyv's number one fan. Like that time last summer when he knocked some kid out for making a sex joke about Lyv; Max pummeled the guy.

It was impressive.

I wonder what that feels like—to have a sibling actually care enough to stand up for you instead of tear you down? I don't think I'll ever know. Mona can't take a step back from herself long enough to even notice I'm home again.

"We need a vacation from this summer vacation," I close my eyes and pretend I'm on some exotic beach on some private island. "When this stupid wedding is over, let's go on a cruise or something before school starts back. How's that sound?"

Lyv says nothing.

I open my eyes to see she's not listening at all. Her sunglasses sit perched on top of her head and her clear eyes peer out at the pool. It's like she's in a trance, following the ripples in the water under some sort of hypnosis.

"Hello," I snap my finger and her head jerks toward me. "Earth to Lyv. Did you hear me at all?"

My small laugh masks the annoyance. Here I am venting about my family problems and my best friend isn't even listening.

"Yeah, sorry. That sounds like fun."

She pretends like she knows what I said and I pretend not to know she's lying about it. It's obvious the conversation is over, so we both close our eyes again as I turn the radio back up.

The radio does little to silence the noise in my head, so I text Mason. He always knows what to say.

My favorite distraction.

Mason has this superpower where he's a ready ear when I'm desperate to be heard.

In a world full of Mona's a person like Mason is detrimental.

He texts back within 30   seconds.

M: Just the girl I was thinking about.

I smile at the screen.

T: I better be.

M: What's up, babe?

T: Want to come over? Mom and Mona are out for some wedding stuff and won't be back for a while. It's just Lyv and me here.

M: Shouldn't the sister of the bride be helping with that wedding stuff?

I sense the condemnation in his words. He's constantly telling me I'm being too sensitive about the whole thing, that I shouldn't let it ruin familial relationships and all that.

But he just doesn't get it.

T: Sure, if the sister were the maid of honor. But the sister isn't, so no...are you coming over or not?

M: Be there in ten.

I send back a quick "Love you," despite my irritation at him.

M: Love you more.

Not to brag, but I'm lucky in the boyfriend department. We've been together since I was fifteen, him sixteen, but he's still my right hand man even after all that time. At times I admit I'd like nothing more than to strangle the life out of him. He's far from perfect and slips up pretty much every day, but he gets me like no one else does.

He's been by my side through so much and that counts for something.

I just wish Lyv could see him the way I do. She doesn't hate him or anything, but I know she only really puts up with him for my sake. I think he exhausts her more than anything.

I love her for trying, though, even if I don't understand why she doesn't like him too much.

When I glance over her eyes flutter open.

"Mason's coming over. Is that okay?"

I ask even though it's already been done. Still, I don't want to mess up our girl's day, so if she's not cool with it I'll tell him plans have changed.

She sits up slightly and pulls her lip between her teeth.

"That's okay. Honestly, I was about to head home soon anyway. I promised Mom I'd help clean up the house a little bit."

Her eyes drop to the ground, a total tell for when Lyv's lying. But I let it go. For whatever reason, she doesn't like being around Mase and I'm not going to force her into it.

He pops in fifteen minutes later, with a cupcake in hand and a grin in place.

"Oh no, it's the Cheshire cat smile. What gives?"

When Mason has any sort of rumor or gossip he's like a kid in a candy store. He reminds me of that Andy Griffith episode where the men play telephone with a rumor and spread so much gossip that the town thinks Barney is dead.

Give Mason a bone and he'll chew on it for days.

Lyv stands, pulling her towel around her quickly. Used to she didn't care to walk around in her bathing suit. But as the years pass, she's become more of a recluse about it.

I don't get it. If God gifted me with her curves instead of my straight and narrow body, I'd flaunt it all day.

"I'm going to cut out," she starts picking her stuff up clumsily, trying to hold all of it at once.

"Need any help?" Mason offers but she's already shaking her head.

"No, but thank you. I'll see you guys later."

Lyv heads back into my house to change.

"What's with her?" Mason whispers and points his thumb toward where Lyv just disappeared.

I shrug.

"Your guess is as good as mine. Now out with it. Tell me the news you're so giddy about."

"I will, but it's going to cost you."

He winks and my heart flips.

"I'll be the judge of that once I hear what you've got to say."

He's at my side, already leaning toward me in my comfy lounge chair. His crystal eyes gloss over my army green bikini (his favorite) and he licks his lips.

"Not so fast," I tease him with a push in his chest. "What's the gossip?"

He sighs dramatically and plops down in the chair next to me, handing me the cupcake in the process. Just as I expected: a salted caramel mocha cupcake from Luna's Sweets.

He knows me so well.

"So, Asher just stopped by. He's totally hard for Lyv."

Old news.

"That's it? That's your big secret?"

He frowns, despite my constant warning of wrinkles.

"Mase, I could've told you that months ago."

"What? There's no way. We were still at school by then. He was with Becky What's-Her-Face half the time."

Bless this poor man and his inattentive ways.

"Becky *Hampton* was clearly a distraction. He was constantly staring at Lyv and finding ways to get close to her or talk to her. It was so obvious to everyone except for Lyv, and apparently you."

He gives a small "humph".

"I swear it's like you have a sixth sense for these things."

He rolls his eyes and swipes a finger across the icing of the cupcake I'm close to devouring.

"What all did he say?"

"Not much, honestly. But for Asher, the fact that he asked anything at all is still saying a lot."

"OK, but what did he say *exactly*. I want a word-for-word playback."

"Wait, I thought you already knew everything?"

He raised his perfect eyebrows smugly and I swat his thigh.

"C'mon, Mase, spill it."

"Alright, alright," he laughs that goofy laugh that makes my skin all warm and tingly. "Mostly he just wanted to know if she's single. He was all jittery and tuned in to everything I was saying, so he's definitely interested."

I've known Asher for as long as I've known Mason and I can say with complete confidence that I've never met another person as self aware as Asher. My guess is that's because his dad and the cancer, but bottom line is the guy doesn't waste his time, or his heart, on the trivial.

Even with Becky Hampton, he let her know from day one that he wanted a strictly platonic relationship.

"And what'd you tell him?"

"I said she's cool and single."

Lyv may have just broken up with Connor but I'm not letting her get trapped in her downtrodden summer haze she always gets in. She's the opposite of just about every other human being on the planet; where summer wakes

111

most people up, it shuts her down.

She's going to say she's not into Asher, but we'll give her a little push in that direction anyway.

"So, how'd I do? Was the information worth anything? Maybe just a kiss?"

I bite my lip and tap my chin in pretend-contemplation. Teasing Mason is one of my favorite past-times, topped only by actually giving in to him. I hook my finger into the neckline of his t-shirt and pull him closer until he hovers over me. His body heat cocoons me in a safety net I hope to never leave. His stare holds me right where I sit, not that I want to be anywhere else in the world.

It's funny how someone can hold you together and devour you all at once.

Chapter Five-Lyv

The day after my tumble with Daisy is spent entirely on the couch. The sun shines bright outside, putting a slight glare on the TV in front of me, but both times I've tried doing the outside thing it's turned pretty disastrous for me, including my terrible attempt at conversation-making with Tilly after the fall yesterday. So, most of the day I just lounge on the couch, flipping back and forth between bad reality shows.

Surprisingly, Max joins me for the latter part of the day.

Just as we settle on a rerun episode of *Big Brother* my phone rings and Tilly's name displays across the screen. Max kicks at me, prompting me to take it into another room.

"Hey Tilly, what's up?"

I move toward the stairs but not before I get a good pillow throw at Max's head.

"So, did you forget to tell me something yesterday?"

She asks it with accusation laced in her words. It feels like a trick question.

"No, I think?"

"Well, I figured since you were with Asher the whole day, you'd at least tell me a *little* about it."

And there is the source of her inquiry. To be honest, I spent the whole day trying to wrap my head around what all had happened. I didn't want to drag Tilly into it all when I couldn't figure it out for myself.

"I did not spend the *whole* day with Asher. I was with you too, remembering?"

"So you did see him then!"

This entire phone call is the exact reason why I didn't tell her about it. She'd of course blow it out of proportion and run crazy with it, like some tabloid gossip spread across a magazine cover. It's never come to her attention before, trying to put Asher and I together, but I can already hear it in her voice that the task has her full attention now.

"It was no big deal, Tilly. I saw him all the time this year at parties. This was no different."

She huffs.

"Yes it is, because this time you guys were *alone.* That's a bigger deal than some crowded party with smelly people piled into a room."

"How do you even know about it?"

"Because Mason told me."

I pause, "and how did Mason know about it?"

"Because Asher told him."

My mind starts racing a million miles a minute and my heart races faster. Did I underestimate yesterday? Was it a big enough deal for Asher to talk to his best friend about it?

"Apparently," Tilly drags on, "Asher went straight to Mason's asking questions about you after your little rendezvous."

"It wasn't a rendezvous," I shake my head even though she can't see me. "What kinds of questions?"

I hold my breathe for the response.

"Questions about you. You know, what's your story? What are your hobbies? Are you single? Those kinds of questions."

"You're serious?"

Part of me wants her to say yes. The other, more reasonable part tells me I shouldn't care   either way.

115

"As if I would joke about this. Don't act so surprised. You're a catch, Lyv. Of course he's into you. Now the question is, what are you going to do about it?"

I hesitate.

"Nothing. I'm not interested."

I can practically see her eyes roll on the other side of the line.

Chapter Six-Tilly

As relaxing as a restful Sunday is, a work-induced Monday is as equally vexing. Though, Lyv is correct in saying my job is probably the least vexing job of all summer jobs.

Still, all too soon it's 9 a.m. on Monday and it's time to punch my metaphorical card. The pool is completely empty for the first hour, because what normal human being wants to go to the Carter Springs city pool this early on a Monday morning?

"Hey Matilda, how was your first year of college?"

Either my boss forgot about all the times I've told her to call me Tilly, or she just really loves to say Matilda.

"Hi Jane, it was good. Probably could've been better, but definitely could've been worse."

"I understand that, girl. My college days were a bit on the wild side, let me tell you."

Please don't, I silently plead.

Jane finds a way to turn a five-minute story into a twenty-minute one, most of which are flashback stories to her times in college. It's like those days are all she has to live for when she's not busy managing the pool. At the end of my time on this earth I really hope my greatest days aren't condensed to just a small snippet of time like Jane.

I derail the trip down memory lane before it begins.

"So, who's on the schedule for today?"

There aren't many employees to choose from. There's me, then Natalie, and Adam, both of which I would rather not have to be stuck with.

"You're opening, clearly," she laughs and I hide a yawn behind my hand. "In an hour Natalie's coming in to take over the stand so you can show the new guy the ropes."

"Alright, some fresh meat. That's great."

"Oh, definitely. Plus, he's very easy on the eyes, if you know what I mean."

The expression speaks for itself but Jane winks anyway and twirls her bottle-blonde hair around her pink manicured finger.

It'll be a welcome change to get a new face around here. Jane is cautious about change, so that's rare. Fortunately for me, her unwillingness to change means job security for me the last three summers. Unfortunately for me, that also means I've dealt with the same coworkers for the last three summers of my life.

That gets a little old.

What's more shocking than Jane's new employee is when Asher Brooks saunters in precisely one hour later, red trunks and lifeguard tank top adorned. Strange he never mentioned he'd be working here before.

"Don't tell me you're the hunky newbie Jane's bragged about all morning."

My whistle gets caught on the sweatshirt I attempt to pull off and Asher chuckles at my expense.

"I guess I am. But in her defense, I pull this uniform off pretty well."

He slides a hand down the leg of his bright red board short trunks dramatically.

He's not wrong.

My red one-piece screams "mandatory uniform" while Asher's trunks look like any casual pair he'd wear on a family vacation to the beach. Then again, just about everything Asher wears looks better on him than it would other people.

He's got "effortless" bottled up and patented.

"Well, lucky for you, I'm your tour guide."

He bows back at my curtsey and we head toward the break room to get his whistle and sunglasses. Natalie moves to the lifeguard stand, but not before giving Asher a complete, head-to-toe stare.

I fight back my eye roll.

"Have you been a lifeguard before?"

"Yeah, back when my dad was in physical therapy they had a PT pool. They gave out free lifeguard training one year and I volunteered there just to kind of be close to him, you know?"

I nod but honestly have no clue. My dad left before I was old enough to know his face. I don't know what that kind of love feels like, let alone what it feels like to have that love ripped away from you. Tension builds around us at the talk of his dad. Mase and I weren't dating yet when Asher's dad got cancer, but I sill remember hearing about it.

Small town and all that.

I try for some humor to lighten the mood.

"Good. So you know the basics then. Don't let anyone drown on your watch."

"Yeah, I heard that's the goal. I'm 0 for 2 right now, but I'm hoping things will turn around here."

His laugh eases the pressure in my shoulders and I relax.

The "tour" takes all of thirty minutes and mostly consists of where to find safety equipment and when/how to test the pool. Two kids run past us by the pool filter, earning a screeching whistle blow from Natalie. The sound echoes after us as I lead Asher back into the break room area for paperwork.

The stack of papers typically only takes about ten minutes but I'm treating this part of the tour as an interrogation, which means he'll be reading every last word on every single page until I finish questioning him about his intentions with Lyv.

"I'm sure you know Mason already told me you're crushing on Lyv, right?"

No point beating around the bush.

He smiles through the blush creeping across his cheeks as I hand the stack of papers over to him. I can maybe count on one hand the times I've seen Asher   Brooks blush.

"I'm not surprised. Mase is a pretty terrible secret keeper."

"You've got that right."

Silence sets in for a few minutes as he reads away, occasionally signing dotted lines as he goes.

"So you really like her then?"

He hesitates, refusing to look at me. Asher's a relatively quiet guy. He doesn't speak just for the mere purpose of small talk. So I know his hesitation is his way of really searching for the right words.

"I barely know her," he mumbles, "but I think I could."

Good.

Lyv's heart is too pure to be toyed with.

"Then I just have on piece of advice for you."

He puts the paper in his hand back into the pile and directs those big, brown eyes my way. I've never known him to mess with a girl's heart just for the fun of it, but it sill needs to be said.

With his undivided attention I give him my only request.

Just one plea. No, one demand.

"Don't break her heart."

You know what breaks my heart?

Movie theater prices.

I mean, who wants to spend $20-plus on snacks when you've already spent $10 on a ticket? It's disheartening, really.

After a long first day back at work I've counted approximately fifteen people who've bought the Classic Combo.

Large popcorn, two fountain drinks, one candy.

That, plus two movie tickets, is just appalling.

People are so willing to pay a ton on something so temporary.

OK, if I'm being honest with myself I've got a little monster named Envy sitting on my shoulder, and she comes out to play every time a couple comes through my concession line. She seethes and spits when they argue over who's going to pay for the candy and where they should sit and just generally anything that draws attention to the fact that they're here together.

Connor always bought the most expensive candy offered. He'd take me to the movies, buy the Classic Combo, and pick our seats instead of saying, "I don't care, you choose."

He put in the effort it took to keep someone happy but in the end that still wasn't enough. Despite his kind heart, it all got to be too much.

Routine kicked in and I panicked.

I'm thinking of how terrifying the mundane can be when Reggie pops his head around the corner of the popcorn machine, bringing me back to the buttery counters in front of me.

"Lyv, do you mind taking over the ticket booth for just a sec? Darcy's got to take her first break."

The clock on the wall reads 7:30 p.m. and I sigh.

An hour.

I've only been here an hour.

Apparently The Cinema is another dimension where time stands still and couples do cute couple things while I stand on the sidelines layering butter for their popcorn and rub grease allover my clothes.

At least the ticket booth stands off by itself so there's no one to bother me and there are no sticky floors to fight against.

"Thanks Lyv," Darcy smiles and I step into the booth with a forced smile back.

My dream last night is the direct cause for my unusual and extremely bitter mood.

The exact details escaped me the minute I opened my eyes this morning, but I remember something like Connor picking a fight with me because he thought I cheated on him with Asher. Then there was something about a custody battle over Daisy, even though Connor's never even met Daisy and she's technically Max's pup, not mine. But that's where it all gets a little hazy.

Bottom line, the dream felt all too confusing to get over in just one day. The subconscious scenario replays over and over again in my head like a skipping movie.

Why do they call it the subconscious, anyway?

Because nine times out of ten what we come up with in our subconscious carries over entirely to our conscious, which means it's not really subconscious, right?

I'm babbling to myself in my head when a teenage girl steps in front of the window.

"Two tickets for Table 19, please."

The dainty blonde hands me a debit card, I print her tickets, and hand everything back in one gesture—just as my brother steps up beside the girl and rests his arm around her shoulder.

"Max?"

As if the name alone could put this puzzle together for me.

He drops his arm quickly, looking like a deer stuck in headlights with a wide mouth and eyes.

"Oh, uh, hey Lyv. I didn't know you were working here again."

That shows how much he pays attention to me.

"Yep, I'm here all summer."

I turn my attention to the girl now grinning sweetly and clutching his arm.

"Ohmygosh, Lyv! I didn't even recognize you behind that window. It's been so long?"

"I'm sorry, have we met?"

Max shuffles on his feet and the girl laughs like I've said some kind of joke. In reality I'm just genuinely confused at what's going on. I study her face for a moment but she's completely unfamiliar to me.

"Does Eyebrow Ellie ring a bell?"

And just like that, it clicks.

Eyebrow Ellie. An unfortunate nickname, but one she gained many years ago. Ellie's been in the same class as Max since preschool and now I see the familiarity, apart from the fact that her single eyebrow from middle school has now become two perfectly polished ones.

"Wow, Ellie. You look amazing. Explain to me why you're with Max again?"

I'm only half joking, but she laughs anyway and pats Max's blushing cheek.

"Yeah, yeah. Can we just get to the movie already?"

"Oh, calm down Max. We've still got fifteen minutes," Ellie chimes and pulls him back when he tries to escape.

"Yeah, Max," I add, just for good measure. "You've still got plenty of time."

"Fine, but if we miss the previews you're paying me back."

He points his finger at me threateningly.

"How on earth did you get my sports-obsessed brother to see a feel-good, romance movie?"

Ellie leans toward the booth window and holds her hand by her mouth to block it from Max's direction as if she's about to share some major secret.

"It was actually his turn to pick."

She covers her mouth to hold in the laugh but I explode hysterically.

My stomach burns from laughing so much and I hold it with both hands. My big, tough brother secretly loves rom coms.

It's priceless.

"Oh shut up, Lyv. I just chose it because I know Ellie wanted to see it."

Ellie holds her hands up in defense.

"Don't blame this on me. We both now you wanted to see this more than I did."

Now we're both guffawing, much to Max's dismay.

"Alright, we're done here. Just for that you don't get any popcorn."

"We'll see about that."

She winks at me and Max shoots me the bird, which I pretend to catch like he did the night of my birthday party. I like Ellie. She seems like exactly the kind of girl that could keep up with my brother.

"Don't forget to use my family discount."

"Thanks. See you at home."

We wave our goodbyes and Max ushers Ellie toward the concession line.

Even my brother orders the Classic Combo.

Chapter Eight-Max

In hindsight, I remember overhearing a phone call between Mom and Reggie; one where they very plainly said Lyv would be working at The Cinema again this summer.

What a terrible time to forget that phone call.

Obviously I planned on telling Lyv about Ellie—eventually. I never really set out to keep this a secret from her and, considering how serious the relationship is getting, Lyv was bound to find out soon enough.

Unfortunately, it was just more of a sneak attack reveal than I'd planned for.

But I guess life rarely goes exactly how we plan for it to go.

"So, you didn't tell your sister about me?"

Ellie pops a piece of popcorn into her mouth and stares blankly at the movie screen in front of us. It's asked the same movie trivia question for the third time through now, but Ellie glowers at it as if it's the first time she's pondered the question.

It's a poker face, of course. Not that I blame her.

"Please don't look into this. I swear it's no big deal."

I try and fail to ease her mind and she pulls her hand away when I tug on it. She looks at me just long enough to say,

"Just because it's not a big deal to you doesn't mean it's not a big deal to me."

Then she's back to looking at the screen.

"Babe, please look at me."

A few seconds pass of me pouting at her profile until finally she caves.

Ellie sports her heart and soul on her sleeve and these stupid theatre lights still shine bright, so I see every ounce of hurt filling her baby blues.

To think I did that makes me sick to my stomach.

She gives me the silent treatment and I take that as my cue to keep talking.

"It has nothing to do with you. I swear. If it did I never would've introduced you to my parents. This has everything to do with Lyv."

Her nose wrinkles and she searches my face for any sign of lies. Finally, she gives me a   small smile and leans into me.

"What happened to you guys? I thought you used to be so close?"

Her voice drops to a whisper as the lights die down and the previews pop on.

"We just grew apart, I guess."

I don't know how to explain the distance that's grown between Lyv and I. Ellie couldn't possibly understand. Her sister is only a year older and they're best friends.

She intertwines our fingers and pulls my hand up to kiss the back of it.

My eyes focus on the screen but my mind wanders.

Lyv was actually the first person I wanted to tell when I asked Ellie out. She'd have known just what to say. She would've been honest, told me if I was way out of my league or aiming too high.

There was always so much I wanted to tell her.

But Lyv was more than a hundred miles away and had no time for my girl problems, or me.

So, I didn't tell her.

Then I told my parents not to.

I want to be the one to tell her, I'd said when mom asked why they couldn't say anything.

And then a week of waiting turned into a month, then a month turned into three months. Then before I knew it, summer was already here and I still hadn't told Lyv.

To be honest, I've been a little angry with Lyv the last few years.

Pissed, even.

It's a long time to hold a grudge, I know, but Lyv had no problem casting me aside when she was still here.

The movie in front of me carries on but I'm already checked out.

Up until a few years ago my sister and I were inseparable. Mom said I used to cry for hours when Lyv would leave for elementary school and I'd have to stay home, just because I missed having her with me.

I think back on all those times she used to bandage me up when I'd come in a bloody mess from skateboarding. Or when she'd make me sit with her through every one of crazy Nana Buckley's stories of old because no one   else cared enough to listen.

But Lyv was always there, which made me want to be too.

Now look at us.

I don't even know how to be around her anymore.

It's like she hit adolescence and was finished with her life here at home. She got a car and started staying out later, then went to college and barely came home except for a few holidays.

She was gone when Great Grandma Buckley died, which meant I had to suffer through Nana Buckley's reminiscing stories of her mother on my own. She was gone when mom and dad had that couple of months where they were fighting constantly about finances and I had to lock myself in my room to ignore them by myself. She was gone for my football games and first car and so many more monumental moments.

And I get it, life keeps moving and you have to move with it and all that.

But it's like Lyv couldn't wait to run away from it all.

She left me choking in the dust and sometimes I still feel like I'm choking.

"Max, you ready to go?"

Ellie shakes my shoulder and I blink through my haze to see the credits rolling. Her brows furrow but I smile and stand.

"Sorry, I was just waiting for that one actor's name."

She sees right through me, knowing I paid zero attention to that movie.

She rubs her thumb over my hand in that soothing way I love so much and we head toward the lobby. Lyv is nowhere to be seen when we walk out and I let out a small breath I didn't realize I was holding.

"Are you OK?"

Ellie moves closer in the light, summer breeze and I tuck her under my arm.

"I'm fine. Why?"

"You just seem distant. Is it what I said earlier, about you and Lyv? Ignore me. That was a stupid thing to say."

She pouts those perfect lips and frowns.

"Ellie, I'm fine. Seriously. I'm just tired. These two-a-day practices just wear me out," which isn't entirely a lie.

I kiss her forehead and she snuggles closer.

We're mostly silent during the drive to her house aside from her commentary on the movie. I chime in with an "mhmm" here or there and occasionally nod, but don't say much of anything.

The rain cloud is already over my head at this point.

We pull into her driveway and I move to open her door. When the door opens she doesn't get out right away. Instead she turns so she faces me, legs dangling out of the pickup and shoulder resting against the back of the seat.

Slowly she draws me close. First, with her hands, then with her legs, and finally with her eyes until I'm completely locked in.

"I wish I didn't have to work in the morning so you could stay longer."

She wraps her arms around my neck and pecks a kiss on the end of my nose.

I hug her tight and push her heavy, blonde hair aside to whisper in her ear.

"So call in sick."

She giggles as I nuzzle my nose into the crook of her neck.

"Only if you skip practice."

I breathe her in.

"Mmm. OK."

She pulls away just enough to see my face and call my bluff.

"Liar," she accuses. I sigh, caught red handed.

Her smile is soft and sweet, reaching all the way up to her eyes, and I wonder how I ever could've kept her a secret from anyone.

"Alright, I've really got to go now."

She pats my chest in an attempt to untangle us but I pile all my weight on her so she drops back into the truck.

"Please," I drag. "Just a little longer."

"C'mon, Max. You're too heavy."

She snickers and tries pushing me away.

This uncharacteristically giddy feeling bubbles up in me, like my heart doesn't know how to slow down. Like my lips can't keep from forming a smile, no matter how hard I bite down on it.

Finally, I move, but not without one long, slow kiss first. If I could only do one thing the rest of my life I'd stay right here, loving on Ellie until my last breath.

We pull apart and she looks at me under hooded eyes.

"You're one sweet guy, Maxwell McDowell."

"You make me that way, Eyebrow Ellie."

She throws her head back with a cackle and manages to push away from me.

"I take it back."

She yells out as she backs toward her house, smiling at me all the way.

"And Max?"

"Yeah?"

Ellie stops just short of her front porch, still within ear shot.

"Just talk to her."

Her meaning Lyv.

With one last kiss blown my way she steps inside.

Just talk to her.

As if it were that easy.

Chapter Nine-Lyv

After my shift I come home and crash on my bed, scrolling through TV channel after TV channel with little success at finding something good to watch.

You'd think with the TV subscription my dad has (fully loaded, because "we can't miss the sports") that at least half the channels would be worth watching.

A *knock, knock,* sounds at my door and I sit up to take a break from channel surfing.

"Come in," I call out and, to my surprise, Max steps through the threshold.

"Got a sec?"

I drop the useless remote and wave him in.

"What's up?"

He takes a seat on the floor and suddenly I'm twelve again and nine-year-old Max sits in his favorite spot on the floor. When he was little he'd sit there for hours listening to all the ghost stories I'd steal from Tilly's arsenal. Max would gasp and shudder in all the right parts. It was one of the few times in life *I* was scaring *him.*

Except Max doesn't quite fit in my room the way he used to.

Like many other things in my life, he's grown up and changed without anyone else realizing the difference.

His back is still against the wall by my vanity, straight across from my bed, but there's no room for his legs to stretch like they used to. Instead he hugs them loosely against his chest, silence unfolding while he gets comfortable.

Finally, he clears his throat and speaks.

"We started dating right after you left for second semester."

Just like that, he drops the bombshell without warning.

His sudden desire to confess momentarily throws me off track but I recover quickly.

"Why didn't you tell me? Or at least let me meet her?"

"Right, like how you so openly introduced me to what's his face?"

Touché. My family met Connor once and that was by accident. They came to visit and he was supposed to be out of town but stopped to surprise me when they were in my dorm. Connor actually tried to fist bump with my dad, except Dad went in for a handshake and got all confused and jumbled up. It was horrifying. I think the awkwardness of the whole encounter scared Connor away from ever wanting to meet them again.

"Besides, you're not exactly around, Lyv. Ellie actually comes over all the time; she's just been busy with an internship this summer. You're the only one who hasn't met her. Mom and dad are basically obsessed with her."

You're the only one who hasn't met her.

First the hurt sinks in, imagining my entire family having this secret.

Then guilt courses through me.

My brother has a girlfriend for almost six months and I don't even know it?

I ask myself if it's worth it, missing so much of Max's life just to avoid coming back here. Does the safety of distance really outweigh the fact that I'm missing Max grow up and move on with his life without me?

"Wow. I'm sorry, Max. I didn't even realize it."

He shrugs but his face turns down and he's suddenly very focused on an unraveling thread on his sock.

"No big deal."

"Hey," I snap my fingers at him and he finally looks up at me. "I'm really sorry. I mean it."

I repeat it, just to drive the point home.

"I know you do. It's OK, really."

His small smile seems genuine enough to ease some of the guilt, but not all of it.

A comfortable quiet falls over us. Max is in his own mind and I'm in mine, wondering just how much else I've missed. I want to ask him about dad and football, about what he actually wants to do with his life.

But, baby steps.

"Do you love her?"

The question comes almost accidentally. My mouth just couldn't catch the words from forming once I thought them.

So much for baby steps.

But I have to know, because if Max of all people can love someone, there really must be something wrong with my wiring.

142

"We've only been dating for, like, five and a half months."

He chuckles and picks at his sock again, avoiding any and all eye contact.

"That doesn't seem like a 'no' to me," I lightly toss a pillow at him to relieve some of his embarrassment.

Silly kid, thinking being in love is something to be embarrassed of.

"What are you, a love guru?"

He grabs the pillow from his lap and chucks it at my face. Still, he laughs and a glow paints his face.

My heart bursts for my not-so-little brother. I don't need to hear him confirm or deny the question when I can see the answer written so plainly on him.

It's there on his lips as he bites back the smile forming. And there, in the way his cheeks flush with the thought of her.

But, mostly, his answer rests in the twinkle of his hazel eyes.

It's a twinkle straight from a Polaroid moment. You know the kind, the moments where the subject shows emotion almost accidentally. Like they don't even realize they're expressing so much with just one look.

A true candid moment.

"Enough about me," he averts the attention away from himself. "What about you and lover boy? Things are all butterflies and rainbows, I'm sure."

"His name is Connor," habit forces me to roll my eyes.

Do I tell him about the break up or not? My initial response is no, don't make a big deal about it. But this night seems like a night of reacquainting.

I want to be open with Max again.

"And no, it's not all butterflies and rainbows," I cough out the words stuck in my throat. "We actually broke up."

If Max's sock were closer I'd pick at that loose string now, but instead I trace my name with my finger onto the fabric of the pillow in my lap.

"What happened?"

The question is simple enough but I don't answer right away. The response is a bit more complicated. How do you answer such a question when you can't even say the words in your own head?

He doesn't interrupt my thoughts. Doesn't make any move to speak up in my silence. It's excruciating, the silence that follows my hesitation to answer him. I finally look at him and the concern on his face pushes me on.

"He wanted too much from me."

Max squints, chewing on the inside of his jaw even after years of mom yelling at him not to do that.

"As your brother I'm sure I'll probably regret this question, but you don't mean he...?"

Max's voice falls away but where he's going with the next inquiry is too close for comfort. It puts my stomach in knots and sends my heart speeding.

"Connor never touched me," I mumble.

It's hard to put into words exactly how I felt right before I broke up with Connor. In my head it makes perfect sense.

He fell in love with me, like any normal human being would do after dating someone for months on end. He fell in love and wanted intimacy and compassion and relationship building. He wanted what anyone would want from someone they love. He wanted to know my secrets and inner workings, to know my past and what makes me the way I am.

That's more than I'm willing to give someone. More than I'm capable of giving someone.

But how do I put that into words without sounding like a self-sadistic maniac?

"He just cared about me more than I could care about him, is all. It seemed unfair to keep leading him on when I know we weren't going anywhere."

Max lets out a low whistle and shakes his head.

"I'm sorry, Lyv. That can't be easy. Don't blame yourself though. If you don't feel it, you don't feel it. You can't force someone to feel what they don't want to feel."

My lovely, naïve baby brother.

I don't correct him, though I guess maybe I should.

People force people into things they don't want to do all the time. That's the rotten part of life no one likes to talk about. The quicker Max learns that the better off he is.

I know he's only speaking out of brotherly duty, but I lap his words up anyway.

Sometimes you just really need to hear it's not all your fault.

"Yeah, well, life goes on I guess. I'm sure he's doing just fine with it."

I hope, anyway.

"Maybe. But that's a long time of being with someone to expect them to get over so quickly, though."

He means well when he says it, but I feel the backlash of the whip myself. Because truth be told it's hypocritical of me to say Connor should be over us. That's asking just as much from him as he did from me, only in a different way.

Tears well up at the corner of my eyes and Max sees them, despite my sleuth attempt at wiping them away with my shirtsleeve.

His eyes round and mouth gapes.

"Hey, I didn't mean it like that," he pauses. "All I'm saying is, sometimes I think you expect people to be capable of shutting off their emotions with the snap of their finger. It works for you. But it may not work like that for everyone else."

A snicker bubbles up through my self-loathing.

"It's fine. I know I'm a basket case."

He's shaking his head with a frown before I even finish the sentence.

"You're not a basket case. You're just wired different. There's nothing wrong with being different."

My heart warms at the sentiment.

"Thanks, Max. You're not so bad yourself."

"Yeah, well, I just watched you and learned what not to do with my life," he smiles and the atmosphere in the room feels less heavy than it did just a few minutes ago.

"Oh, before you go," I leave the sentence open-ended as he stands to his feet, hoping to keep him there for just a little longer.

The second I grab my camera from my night stand he protests.

"Not the camera again. Please, Lyv, no more."

I ignore him, of course, and square the camera up to see through the eyepiece.

I can't explain to him what it means to have him sitting there again. To have him here in my room, in his spot, talking like we used to.

Talking like we're kids and everything is right in the world.

Like home is home again.

And of course the picture ends up being him annoyed and flipping off the camera, but I didn't really expect anything less.

"Alright, now I'm going to bed. A.M. practices won't be pretty if I stay up any later."

"Goodnight, grandpa."

He barks a fake laugh and shuts my door behind him.

If today's taught me anything, it's this:

The little brother I left behind is not the little brother I've come back to.

⊙⊙⊙⊙⊙

After the heart to heart with Max last night I wake feeling more rejuvenated than I have in a long time. But reality crashes down when I look at my agenda to see it's only Tuesday and I have to work today.

It's an early shift, though, so by 3 p.m. I'll be home free and poolside. It's not until I'm in my car and pulling away from my driveway that I remember my workweek ends Thursday.

The day is already looking up.

That is, until I clock in.

When you spend so much time with a certain person or group of people, you become accustomed to weird habits or routines they may have. Like someone biting their nails or obsessively humming while they do a task—eventually all that is just normal.

After walking into The Cinema for my shift I've come to the realization that I've not been around Reggie enough yet to be used to his habits. The way he cracks his knuckles in a little pattern, for example, moving from pinkie to thumb in a quick rhythm before reversing back from thumb to pinkie—that habit's still annoying.

We've been staring at the same wall since I clocked in an hour ago; trying to decide which new movie poster should go where. All the while Reggie has cracked his knuckles enough that I'm sure they're close to breaking into tiny pieces at any moment.

"What if we move Ryan Gosling to the center and push Tom Hanks closer to the entrance?"

I scratch at the non-existent itch on my arm, an old habit of my own, while Reggie's knuckles crack on. I don't have the heart to tell him that I really don't care, not like him, anyway. Reggie thinks poster placement is some strategic marketing ploy that could make or break The Cinema.

But I can't focus on anything but the sound of bone popping against bone.

"You know that gives you arthritis, right?"

I think I remember an aunt or uncle telling me that once when they caught me cracking my own knuckles at a family barbecue. At any rate, I hope it will deter Reggie now.

"That's not true, actually," he pushes his glasses up by the bridge and I instantly regret saying anything at all. "Yeah, they did a study a while back on it and results showed there was no correlation between the two."

"Well, the more ya know," I mumble.

He stares into space for a seconds before muttering an "oh, right" and pointing back at the still empty wall in front of us.

Eventually and mercifully, we come to a decision. Gosling in left center of the wall, Hanks in right center, and me back to the concession stand.

Reggie follows close on my heels.

"So, your brother and Ellie seem to be doing good."

My itch resurfaces knowing even Reggie knew about my brother's girlfriend and I didn't. Hearing him talk about Max is a bit like seeing a fish out of water. The two just don't go together.

"It does seem that way, doesn't it?"

"Ah, to be young and in love again," he chuckles mostly to himself. "I remember that puppy-love stage. Once you're together for a few years that turns into an old-dog kind of love, you know?"

I don't, but what makes less sense than Reggie's metaphor is the fact that it sounds like he's saying he's in love. Which can't be true, because in all the years I've worked with him I have never seen him talk to a girl unless it's a customer.

"So you're with someone, then?"

It's hard to believe Reggie has a single romantic bone in his body.

"I am. I've been with Kelly for a while now. We've been married for two years, together for five. We're actually expecting our first child in a few months."

"Wow," I try and fail not to sound surprised. Completely dumbfounded, even. "I had no idea. Congratulations."

He smiles proudly.

"Thank you. It's actually our second, if you want to be technical. But our first baby girl was stillborn, so we're equal parts excited and anxious to get our little family going."

He says all this with a small smile, as if he's talking about the weather and not his stillborn baby.

"Oh, Reggie, that's awful. I'm so sorry."

He nods like he's expecting this response.

I'm sure by now he's heard "I'm sorry" a million times, though "I'm sorry" doesn't always fix the pain.

"I appreciate that, but I made my peace with it all a long time ago. But thank you anyway."

He walks away, still smiling to himself, and I wonder how someone can walk through the fire like that and come out on the other side with any peace of mind left.

The rest of the shift goes by in a blink of the eye, with me staying mostly to myself and replaying the conversation with Reggie over and over again in my mind. I'm still thinking about it when a *ding* pulls me back to the present.

Tilly's name pops onto the screen with a message following that tells me to stop by the city

153

pool on my way home from work. I text back a quick "on my way" and turn left for the pool instead of right for home.

Once I'm there I walk straight past the ticket counter—a perk of small towns and knowing basically everyone—and find Tilly in the lifeguard chair.

I stop in my tracks when I see Asher leaning against the lifeguard chair.

He stands there in a lifeguard uniform as if he works here.

I turn immediately and walk quickly back the way I came, all the while cursing Tilly under my breath for not giving me a heads up.

Maybe they won't see me. Maybe I can make it back to my car quick enough to get out of here. I'll just text Tilly and tell her something came up.

"Lyv, where are you going?"

Tilly's voice echoes across the pool and humor drips from her every word. Slowly I turn around and shoot daggers her way but keep a smile plastered on my face.

"I thought I forgot my phone but it's right here," I hold my phone up in the air to cover my lie.

154

"Well, isn't that something," Tilly grins like a Cheshire cat and I really contemplate pulling her off the stand and pushing her into the pool below.

I force my eyes toward Asher, knowing it'd be worse if I avoided him, and he's smirking that crooked smirk that makes my knees quiver.

"I didn't know you worked here," I wave and pray my voice is casual, despite my pounding heart.

"Tilly didn't tell you? I just started yesterday."

The humor in Tilly's voice seems to have transferred into Asher's as he continues leaning casually against the lifeguard-stand tower. Above us Tilly lets out a shrill blow of her whistle.

"No running!"

The kid in question speed walks the rest of the way to the diving board.

"Yeah, it must've slipped my mind. My bad," Tilly shrugs nonchalantly but she bites her lip and winks at me. "Asher, do you care to take over here while I talk to Lyv? It'll only take a second."

"Whatever you say," he salutes her and waits until she's completely out of the way to   climb up into the chair above.

Once Tilly puts her T-shirt back on we move to a section of empty, white lounge chairs. We're out of earshot but I'm in plain view of Asher on the stand.

The sprinkle of tattoos mix in more now that his skin is a golden brown, making it hard to see the faded, black ink. But still, I can see the leanness of his muscles constricting as he leans back to scan the crowd below him.

I swear lifeguarding was created specifically for him.

"Earth to Lyv. Anyone in there?" Tilly taps my forehead and I slap her hand away.

"Cut it out. You're going to get me caught.

We both laugh at my complete lack of denying I'd been staring. It feels good, laughing with Tilly about this kind of stuff again. I can't remember the last time we giggled about a cute boy like this.

"I swear, one of these days I'm really going to do it. I'm actually going to slap you. Why didn't you tell me Asher worked here with you?"

I pinch underneath her thigh and her whine mingles with a laugh.

"Would you have come if I told you?"

She nods in my silence.

"That's what I thought. Also, I just really wanted to see your face when I blindsided you."

"Right, I'm leaving."

She pulls me back down to the chair by my arm.

"Don't be such a baby. He didn't know you were coming, so he's just as blindsided as you. And I think what you meant to say was, 'thank you'"."

"And why is that?"

"Because I'm the reason you get to see that."

She nods in Asher's direction.

We both stare.

He blows his whistle and shakes his head at a small kid in the pool. With the beach umbrella open and his sunglasses now hanging by chums around his neck, I can see his honey eyes plainly. They roam over the crowd, scanning for trouble, until finally landing on Tilly and me. He smiles with a small wave and we quickly look away.

"Whoops," Tilly giggles.

"OK, so I'm officially embarrassed. Is that all you needed me for today?"

My black work capris get warmer with every minute we sit here and I'm sure my pit sweat has soaked through my yellow work shirt by now. The hideous theater visor probably would've come in handy right about now but unfortunately rests in the passenger seat of my car.

"No, that was only part of it," she nudges my arm but I look on humorlessly. "Mason's having a party Friday and you're coming."

If Mason's party is anything like my surprise party, I won't be there. Granted, I'm sure his will be much less PG than mine was.

All the more reason to stay home.

"You couldn't have just texted me that?" She shrugs again. "I don't know, Tilly. I kind of just wanted to relax this weekend."

Sometimes you just really want to stay in, you know? Snuggle under the covers and put Sex in the City on repeat while putting yourself into a food coma to finish the night.

And then sometimes you have friends like Tilly who don't believe in nights in.

"No way. You have all summer to relax. You're going, Lyvie."

She knows I hate that nickname.

"Who's going to be there?"

That's the determining factor in any social situation. People make or break just about everything, especially parties.

If it's all Mason's friends, I'm out. The last time I went to a party with just his friends the cops were called and I had to hide in some dirty laundry room until the cops cleared out.

"The usual," she ticks names off on her hand. But there's only one that stands out to me among the rest.

I pretend to contemplate with my finger against my chin and head titled up, but she had me the second she said his name.

"So I'll see you there then?" She gives me a knowing grin.

"Fine, I guess I can go."

Tilly claps her hands excitedly.

"But only if Max and Ellie can come. I think we're on the mend."

She nods happily and adds, "The more the merrier. That mending is long overdue   anyway."

We hug our goodbyes and I head toward the exit.

So there we have it.

Instead of a relaxing Friday at home I'll be at Mason's listening to obnoxiously loud music and small-talking with people I haven't seen since high school.

Too much has changed for me to enjoy small talk and I'm dreading it already.

But Asher will be there.

So it can't be all bad, right?

I take one last peek at him before pushing through the exit gate. He yells at another running kid, completely oblivious to me.

Chapter Ten-Asher

In theory, lifeguarding is a piece of cake. You sit in a chair all day, get paid to soak up the sun, and swim for free.

In reality, it kind of sucks. Your butt gets numb from sitting all day, you burn under the sun if you forget the sunblock, and you're forced to clean literal crap out of the pool after teenage twerps decide it'll be fun to take a deuce in the water.

If only people told you theory and reality rarely match up.

On the plus side, Tilly is all right company. I'd forgotten she worked here back when I applied for the job, but it was a pleasant surprise to see her here yesterday.

Even when she gave her little interrogation, it was enough to keep me intrigued.

Today her words replay, *don't break her heart.*

I don't understand what Tilly thinks I could possibly do to Lyv, but I still carry the obligation on my shoulders regardless.

"Asher, can I borrow you for a second?"

Considering my current task is to spray fresh ant-infested snow cone off the patio I'd love to be borrowed for as long as Tilly needs me.

I wrap the water hose up and walk the few short steps to the lifeguard stand.

"What's up?"

The sun is relentlessly blinding where I squint up at her, despite my sunglasses.

"What are you up to Friday?"

Tilly's mind always seems to go everywhere all at once. She can be in the middle of one story then branch off into five different stories, one right after the other, then somehow wind herself back around to the original topic without missing a beat.

It's hard to say where the current question is going to take us.

"I'm not really sure yet, to be honest. I don't think that far in advance."

She rolls her eyes. At this point I don't think she even realizes she does it.

"Seriously, Asher? It's summer. Everyone should know what they're doing on the weekend."

I open my mouth to tell her that's the exact opposite mentality to have. Summer means no agenda, no schedule. Do what you want. But she's already focused on something behind me.

"Lyv, where are you going?"

The name takes all of two seconds to register and when I turn around there she is in all her theater-uniform glory.

It almost looks like she's heading back toward the exit but she turns toward us with a tight-lipped smile and something about forgetting her phone.

Her steps toward us sync to the quick beating in my chest. A small smile creeps up on me.

She's got a power over me, that Lyv, and it boggles me. All she has to do is be there, be in my general vicinity, and suddenly I can't think. She's a fog that swallows me whole.

It's like the time in our second semester, when Mason, Tilly, and I were in the library studying. My mind kept wandering from the French words on my flash cards to the vacant seat next to me where Lyv would be sitting in if she weren't MIA.

I wondered if she were with that guy, the one from the party. I wondered if they were on a date or in her dorm studying by themselves. Then I remembered I wasn't supposed to care anymore. Except a minute later she rushes in, pulling all the air in the room toward her as she hurries to our table.

"Sorry I'm late," she'd mumbled. But it didn't matter. Because all I could do was think about the coconut smell she brought in with her and feel the body heat of her arm resting so close to mine on the table. And I knew all my avoiding her was for nothing.

Now, as her and Tilly talk I'm vaguely aware of some telepathic war going on between the two. Suddenly Lyv looks right at me and I'm hot from head to toe.

She stands there in restricting black jeans and a bright yellow shirt and I think movie theater uniforms aren't so bad when she's wearing one.

"I didn't know you worked here."

Part of me is surprised Tilly hasn't said anything, but the other part of me isn't so much. Tilly's exactly the kind of person to keep secrets until the last second solely because of the thrill.

"Tilly didn't tell you? I just started yesterday."

Tilly plays dumb and blows her whistle at a running kid, claiming with a wink that she simply forgot.

"Asher, do you care to take over here while I talk to Lyv? It'll only take a second."

Arrogance bubbles up in my chest. What will they be talking about? Could it be about me? I think there's a chance of my name coming up in their conversation but I push that thought—that hope—away for now.

"Whatever you say," and with a salute I'm in the chair and Tilly leads Lyv away.

As the only lifeguard on duty now, it's my sole responsibility to keep an eye on the entire pool below. But with Lyv here my mind strays from the task at hand. Instead of keeping an eye on the terrible swimmer inching closer to the deep end, my focus drifts back to Lyv sitting a few chairs away.

Her and Tilly have their heads tucked close to each other. With the glare of the sun reflecting back against the inside of my sunglasses it's nearly impossible to tell what they're talking about.

Like a proper sleuth, I eliminate the sun problem by raising the umbrella and lowering my sunglasses. With the glare gone I can see her face plainly; the way it scrunches and softens at whatever Tilly's saying. Her lips quirk quickly as she speaks. It's obvious she's heated about something. So many years I've overlooked those small things about her.

Those small things like her expressive facial movements and hand gestures, which add up to the bigger things.

How did it take so long for me to notice it all—to notice her?

And now in my peripheral is that stupid kid getting too close to the deep end again.

It's like he has some kind of death wish. When I blow my whistle he knows it's for him and all I have to do is give a quick shake of my head to make him move back to shallow water.

With one more glance around the pool I go back to my former position only to find both Lyv and Tilly staring back at me.

I'm done for.

Caught.

In an effort to save my pride I smile and wave casually.

When in doubt, play dumb.

But just to be safe, I stop staring as much.

Good move, too, because there's another kid running. He ignores my piercing whistle and runs to the diving board anyway, pulling on his falling swimming trunks as he goes.

Whatever. Fall and break something.

I tried to warn you, I think.

"So, about Friday," I jump when Tilly pops up next to me. I glance over to the now-empty chairs where they'd just been but it's too late.

"She's already gone."

Apparently Tilly's also a mind reader.

"About Friday."

I redirect her to take the heat away from myself.

"Right, Friday. You've got plans now."

"Do I?"

"You do," she says it so matter-of-factly as if any other answer is out of the question.

"What are my plans?"

It still doesn't make sense to me how someone so potent and demanding can be a best friend with someone like Lyv. That's not to say Lyv can't be a force of nature herself, but Lyv's nature is more of a subtle force that Tilly couldn't possibly pull off.

"There's a party at Mason's Friday and you'll be there. A, because Mase is your best friend and it's your duty to be there, and B, because important people will be there and it's in your best interest to show up."

She crosses her arms below me and raises her brows in a challenge.

But she won't get one from me.

Her message is loud and clear. My mind is made up instantly.

If Lyv's there, I'm there.

⊙⊙⊙⊙⊙

All my life I've been outnumbered with women.

Even when my dad was alive, it was three against two. When he was still here I at least had one person in my corner.

But now it's three against one and my mom has to cover us all, stand in everyone's corner.

Somehow we made it to Friday evening and mom spreads herself thin to accommodate for a knock-out-drag-out between two of her three kids, both of which are hormonal teenagers.

I want no part of the spat, so I mind my business on the couch with my giant bowl of Froot Loops. It's 8:30 and we've already had dinner, but I gobble down the cereal anyway.

"Mia, work with me here. You had the car last weekend. Your sister has her dance rehearsal practice tonight and I need the car to take her. So, unless you want to join us, I suggest you suck it up," mom sighs and pushes her bangs out of her face.

She barely holds onto her last shred of patience.

It's an old argument and I'm sure it won't rest until mom gives in and buys Mia her own car. Mia thought she'd get one the second she got her license, but now she's halfway through 17 and still without her own car. She's as distraught about it as any typical 17-year-old would be, despite my constant reminder that I had to save up and buy my own car when I was her age.

"But mom, I *need* the car today. The movie starts at 9 and I'm supposed to be at Tiffany's in, like, 10 minutes."

169

On days like today my dad came in handy. It's not in my mom's nature to address confrontation and with two teenagers under one roof you face confrontation almost every second of the day.

He was always the one to step in and give solutions. My mom's specialty is macro managing, which is why the thought of not being able to manage my sisters drives her a little out of whack.

My mind wanders to Lyv. She has a little brother. I wonder if they ever argue like this still? She claims they don't get along, but I find myself wanting to know exactly what it is that makes her tick with him.

Lately I've wanted to know every facet of Lyv's life there is to know.

Meanwhile, Cali, just two years younger than Mia, rolls her eyes in the hallway. Her babbling-hand gestures at our sister makes me laugh, which earns me a stink eye from Mia.

"I'm sorry honey, but I'm taking your sister to her rehearsals. I already told you. You can ride with me and have someone pick you up at the dance studio, or you can sulk here and miss the movie. It's your choice."

"It's so unfair," Mia mumbles and slams down into the couch next to me, jostling the milk in my bowl. "She's not even that good."

"Enough, Mia," mom barks. "I won't hear another word."

She flashes her wild eyes, the ones that go round and twitchy when she's about to lose it. She's always been a beautiful woman, my mother, with her crystal blue eyes and strawberry blonder hair—all of which I did not inherit. But since my dad died those bright eyes are a little more tired.

Mia wisely shuts up. Meanwhile Cali stands by the door now with tears in her brown, downcast eyes. Normally Cali takes a hit like a soldier, but Mia knows all the right buttons to push.

"I can take you," I volunteer before I really know what I'm saying.

Maybe it's the tension that's formed between Mia and Cali, or maybe it's because of mom's defeated face.

Either way, I know it's too late to go back now when I look at Mia.

Her eyes, which look identical to my mom's, light up and she grabs my arm. A drop of milk spills over onto the hardwood. Mom watches it fall but says nothing.

"I mean, it's on my way to Mason's anyway."

I didn't plan on leaving for another hour, but mom seems to be close to the edge today. My offer alone to take Mia already puts some life back into Mom.

"Oh, sweetie, are you sure? I don't want to disrupt your evening," she says, but her eyes silently plead with me.

"It's fine, honestly. He said it's on his way. Right, Ash?" Mia grins excitedly next to me.

Definitely no going back now.

"I've got it Mom. Get Cali to the recital practice. I'll get Bean to her movie."

The first time I saw an ultrasound of Mia I said she looked like a small bean in Mom's belly. The nickname stuck.

My mom holds one hand to her heart and blows a kiss toward me with the other. I pretend to catch it and her smile grows.

It's amazing, really, how small a gesture can be that makes someone else happy. A simple car ride, for example, makes all the difference in my mom's mood—or pretending to catch an air kiss even though I'm 21 years old.

Being kind is simple if people only put in a little effort.

"Thank you so much, Ash," she sighs once more before disappearing back up the stairs.

"I'll wait in the car."

Mia walks out the door without another word, brushing past Cali in a fury as if she hadn't just brutally insulted her minutes ago.

"I guess we're leaving now then."

I go bottoms up on the rest of the milk in my bowl and take it to the kitchen table. When I come back into the living room Cali is on the couch staring idly out the front window.

Out of all of us, Cali and I look and act most alike, resembling our dad all the way down to our dark scold when we're upset about something.

"Good luck at rehearsals."

"Thanks, I'll need it. Apparently I suck. Not that Mia's even been to any of my show's since I was seven."

Outside a car horn blows but I ignore it and focus on the sister in front of me.

"I don't want to hear that, got it?"

She mumbles something sounding like "whatever" and I lightly kick at her leg.

"I'm serious, Cali. You're the best damn dancer out there. Those other brats only wish they were as good as you."

Finally she smiles.

Small victories.

Mia blows the horn again, cuing me to leave, and I sigh.

"I better go. You gonna be OK?"

She nods and shoos me away.

"Of course I will be. I'm the best damn dancer out there, remember?"

My guffaw echoes against the walls around us.

"And don't you forget it," I point at her sternly and she giggles.

"Love you, Ash. Get out of here."

I place a kiss on top of her head.

"Love you too, kid."

Right before I step out the door I add, "and stop cussing."

I smile at the sound of her laughter before shutting the door behind me.

"C'mon Asher," Mia yells out the passenger car window. "You're going to make me late. If I miss this movie I'm blaming you entirely."

A brother's work is never done.

Mia barely gives me time to click my seat belt in before she reaches over and turns the key in the ignition.

"You're welcome for the ride, by the way."

I throw it in drive and circle the giant Maple where our old tire swing still hangs.

"Thank you," she smiles quickly then sees the time on the dash. "Now step on it."

My glare barely fazes her.

"Please," she adds with little conviction.

Once I'm on the open road and Mia has no escape except the double lanes speeding by below us, I approach a problem I'd been thinking on during the whole fight back home.

"You've got to start being nicer, Bean. Not just to Cali but to mom too. You have way too much attitude lately and always take things out on them."

Mia scoffs next to me   and her arms cross defensively.

"Cali's a brat too, Ash. She just hides it so she'll stay your favorite."

I can't help but laugh at her complete lack in denying that she herself is a brat.

"I don't have favorites."

"You so have favorites, and we all know it's Cali. You always take her side, you guys have inside jokes, and you've got this, like, private language or something."

Her tone turns from defensive to hurt in all of two seconds. I can't keep up.

"Private language? What does that even mean?"

She huffs and turns toward me.

"Don't play dumb. I see your looks," then proceeds to raise her eyebrows and make a face that apparently Cali and I make. "You just look at each other and somehow know what the other is thinking. It's annoying and kind of rude."

At first I think she's being dramatic again, but she seems genuinely upset. Guilt rises in my chest. It's been this way since Dad died. We're all playing this balancing act of trying to keep everything going in our lives like normal, but we're not doing very well at it. Surely Mia knows I don't have favorites, that I love both of my sisters equally.

I show that, right?

"Bean, come on. You know that's only because Cali and me are so much alike."

"Yeah, well, either way I feel like a third wheel with my own siblings."

It kills me to think I'd ever hurt either of my sisters. I'm their big brother. Big brothers are supposed to be the protector, the role model.

Role models aren't supposed to let people down.

"OK, how's this sound? From now on, Sibling Sunday is officially back on. Me, you, Cali, and The Cinema every Sunday. What do you say?"

And possibly Lyv if she's working that day, I think, but that's just a bonus for me.

Mia doesn't agree right away, just as I knew she wouldn't. She's too stubborn to ever give in right away. I let her pretend to mull it over as she stares at the passing houses. We've been to this particular friends house plenty of times before, so I know we're getting closer, but I still know better than to push her for an answer.

With Mia, the harder you push, the faster she pulls away.

"I guess that doesn't sound too awful," she gives me a smirk and slanted side eye. "But I get to pick the first reunion movie."

"Deal. But only if you're nicer at home."

She graces me with another eye roll.

"Whatever you say, dad."

Sarcasm laces her words and it takes a few seconds for either of us to really catch what she's just called me.

"I, uh, I didn't literally mean that. I mean, it was just a joke."

The more she tries to explain it away, the tighter my chest feels.

Whoever said time heals all wounds must've had a small wound, or maybe just loads of time. It's been six years since Dad died and I'm still waiting for the small sting to stop burning.

For all of us.

Cali was nine, just a kid, when it happened, so she forgets the pain pretty easily. But Mia was eleven and old enough to really get it; to get cancer and death and the agony of losing your dad to it. Me

178

being fifteen at the time meant I was plenty old enough to pick up the whole man of the house act.

I've got to say, I'm not doing the best job with it so far.

"It's OK. I know you didn't mean to."

She sighs and stares straight ahead, resting her head against the headrest.

"God, I miss him, Ash. So bad."

"Me too, Bean. Me too."

We get to the last stretch of houses before Mia's friend's house when she leans slightly toward me and sniffs. I can already see thoughts of Dad have been momentarily paused.

"Why do you have so much cologne on just to go to Mason's?"

She pulls back and eyes me from head to toe. "And why do you have your nice clothes on?"

She pokes and prods at my side until I swat her away.

"It's a party. Can't I look and smell nice?"

I guess my black jeans and grey t-shirt aren't as played down as I'd hoped.

"Will girls be there?"

179

"It'd be a pretty boring party if there weren't."

She's hedging toward the whammy question, and then it comes.

"Any *specific* girl?"

I hear the grin in her voice and she pounces on my hesitation.

Thank God we're at the house and I can kick her out before she cracks me open.

"Oh, so sorry to break up the bonding, but I don't want you to be late for your movie."

I grin widely and push on her shoulder to get her out of the car.

"Well," she leans into the open window for one last word, "I hope you have a great night with her, whoever she is."

She winks and waves me on.

I drive around some before going straight to Mason's, my mind already on Lyv.

Hats off to full-time party planners.

Between work today and setting up for tonight, I don't know how they do it. I'm partied out already and it hasn't even started.

"Babe, are you really napping right now?"

Mason's bed is quite literally the softest bed I've ever slept in and he's just successfully nap-blocked me.

"I *was* napping. You've had me running around like a madwoman since I got off work today Between this and mom's wedding planning at our house, I'm exhausted."

Especially after chasing down the only person in town who will sell alcohol to a minor, even if I am only a few months shy of being legal.

Mason pulls at the covers but I only cocoon myself tighter.

"Well, you better find some energy fast because people are already downstairs."

"What? Already?"

It can't be 10 p.m. yet, can it?

I look at the clock on his dresser.

10:15 p.m.

"Fiiine," I let him pull me to my feet. "But know I'm waking up under protest."

"Noted," he laughs.

Together we leave the comfort of his room and greet the first guests. Of course it's Emily and her cronies from her college.

We lucked out, Lyv and I, in leaving Emily behind. I was never really a fan of her cookie-cutter routine, but Lyv always liked her so I dealt with it. Em was always the one getting on the parents' good side growing up, always the one brown nosing the teachers.

It was always exhausting to watch.

"Em, hey! Who've we got here?" Mason asks.

She kisses me in that French way she's been doing lately and steps back to introduce me to her friends. There are four of them, two guys and two girls.

"This is Alice, Jenna, Chris, and Alex."

Alice, the petite blonde directly next to Emily, holds her hand out.

"Hi, it's so nice to meet you. This house is incredible."

182

Blondie compliments the house but sizes Mason up while scanning the extravagant entrance to his house. She's automatically on the "No thank you" list. (That's a list Lyv and I made years ago when we started weeding out the bad friends in high school.)

The lavender-haired girl, Jenna, waves slightly.

"Thanks so much for having us."

The two guys just nod hellos.

"Oh, our pleasure. I'm Tilly, by the way. This is my boyfriend, Mason."

I pull him close, snaking my arm through his with eyes locked on Blondie.

She blushes and nods slightly.

I didn't get my nap out completely, so I'm feeling even feistier than usual.

"Right, so who wants a drink?"

Mason leads the group to the backyard where the party is stationed but I hang back.

"Tilly, you coming?"

Emily calls back for me but I wave her on.

"Just have to make a   call."

183

An urgent call, I silently add.

Lyv answers right away.

"What's up?"

"What's up? I'll tell you what's up. Emily's here with her little posse and one of her blonde bimbos is trying to make a move on Mason. I need back up. Where are you?"

My breathing comes out in short bursts as I spill everything out in basically one sentence. As I'm talking, Seth and Johnny come in. They're old friends of Mason's, older even than Asher, and I wave them toward the backyard before focusing back on my phone call.

"Calm down, Tilly. We're on our way. We had to let Ellie get changed out of her work clothes first, but we're leaving now."

"And how far away is that? Are you leaving your house, her house, where?"

I'm being beyond childish and I know it, but can't seem to stop myself.

"My house. We'll be there in ten minutes, at the most."

"Ten minutes is an awful long time," I mumble.

"We'll be there with guns blazing. Don't worry."

"You better be. See you in a few."

"Later."

We hang up and I feel a little better knowing my backup is on its way. If college has taught me anything, it's that people have zero respect for other people's relationships.

Vows and promises be damned.

I really don't want to face the crowd alone but I trek on toward the backyard anyway.

"I heard there's a party going on around here."

In my inner turmoil I didn't notice Asher come in with his keys swinging carelessly in his hand.

"Boy, am I glad to see you."

I wait for him to catch up to me and punch him lightly once he's close enough to reach. He rubs the spot on his solid stomach where my fist connected. Since we've been working together I'm starting to feel like Asher is more of *my* friend instead of Mason's. His presence here gives me the same ease and calmness as Lyv would if she were standing next to me.

"You've got a funny way of showing that."

"C'mon," I laugh. "You can save me from Emily's little monsters while Mason plays   host."

185

"Where are his parents this time?"

"Somewhere in the Bahamas I think."

I know my mom is always preoccupied with my sister and my dad is completely nonexistent, but somehow they look like The Joneses compared to Mason's parents. The Williams think they can buy their way out of or into anything, which includes their son. Buy him something and maybe he won't notice they're never around.

It sounds nice in theory, but no one wants to be bought, especially with someone who's supposed to love you unconditionally.

Mason's parents are both lawyers and take month-long trips every time one of them wins a case.

Luckily for us, Mrs. Williams just cracked her recent case wide open.

We walk outside and there's a small group formed near the stone fire pit. Much to my approval, Alice has moved onto Seth while everyone else is in their own circle.

"Asher, my man, glad you could break away from that little sister of yours to join us," Mason breaks away from the group to meet Asher.

"Ah, you know, brother duties call and I answer."

He jokes like he has a choice in the matter, but I know Asher well enough to know if it comes between his sisters and anything else in the world, he'd burn everything else to the ground to be there for them.

"I can't relate, but I'll take your word for it. Let me introduce you to some people. These are some of Emily's friends from CSU."

Mason lists them off again. Alice waves, but focuses back on Seth. Meanwhile, Jenna with the lavender hair steps up to the plate.

"Asher was it? That's a great name," her hand lingers in Asher's until he finally pulls back.

"Thanks, I was born with it."

It's probably in the top-5 worst jokes of all time, but Jenna laughs like she's never heard anything better.

"That's so funny. I bet you were the class clown, then, huh?"

She smiles while she flips her ridiculously luscious purple locks.

"He was actually the dorky one. You know, constantly reading in the corner while everyone else went out. Definitely the nerdy type."

I have this sudden urge to step between Jenna and Asher.

This is Lyv's place, not Jenna's. And while the reading part isn't a lie, the rest is entirely. Asher was anything but nerdy in high school. Intelligent, yes, but in that 21st century kind of way where the smart guy in the room is the brooding, sexy guy everyone wants to be friends with.

And this brooding, sexy guy is supposed to be with my Lyv.

There's a plan here, I want to yell at Jenna.

"No way," she says now. "I love to read. I want to own my own bookstore someday."

"Wow, that sounds great," Asher smiles but Asher always smiles, so I can't tell if it's carrying any kind of flirty weight.

Where the hell is Lyv at, anyway?

She should be here complimenting Asher on his corny jokes.

I grab myself a drink from the patio island and mope over the now freed-up bonfire.

My attitude is precisely why I needed to finish that nap earlier.

Even from here, a dozen feet away, I can still hear Jenna's nagging voice.

"Yeah, it's going to be, like, this boho chic kind of book store. It'll have coffee, muffins, reading nooks—the whole thing."

Asher nods but something at the door catches his eye.

Or, more accurately, someone.

He turns completely away from Jenna, eyes and attention solely on Lyv as she steps onto the back patio.

Max and his girlfriend follow behind her, but it's Lyv who holds the power. Lyv, who smiles slightly and waves bashfully at some people in the crowd. She has just a hint more makeup on than usual, and high-waist jeans that showcase her curves perfectly beneath her pastel-striped tank top.

She looks stunning, and it's Lyv who pulls Asher away from Jenna and everyone else, drawing him into her like a moth to a flame.

I smirk over the rim of my cup as Jenna slouches in defeat.

"You're sure it's not too much?"

I stare over Ellie's shoulder into the passenger side mirror I'd asked her to pull down on our way to Mason's. It took a while, but she finally convinced me to put on more makeup than my usual natural look.

But don't touch the hair, she'd said, *leave it wild.*

And so, here we are, almost to Mason's with my hair flying out in loose curls and makeup beyond the norm.

But, looking in the mirror now I have to admit, I don't look half bad.

After the phone call from Lyv, we rushed out of my house before she could call again or send out a search party for us.

Max turns a ten-minute drive into a five-minute one and I holster in my speech about speed and driving recklessly. It's Ellie's car, anyway, and she seems perfectly fine with my brother's terrible speed.

Besides, tonight is a night for fun, not lectures.

Technically speaking, Mason's parents are in the picture and completely in Mason's life. They provide for him and leave him with plenty of money to take care of himself, but in actuality they're about as present in his life as Tilly's MIA dad is in hers. So, I never spent any time in Mason's miniature mansion growing up.

My parents are strong believers in parental supervision of minors.

Once we pull into the driveway Max stops as we all stare with wide eyes.

"Wow, this house is gigantic," Ellie leans forward toward the dash as we circle around the fountain in the middle of the brick driveway.

Houses like this don't belong in small Colorado neighborhoods like ours. No, this house belongs on the corner of Beverly Hills with Range Rovers and security gates. But, here it is, complete with a turret rooftop, half-moon staircase leading to the front door, and massive windows spread all across the front of the house.

It's hard to say whose house is bigger, Mason's or Tilly's.

"Maybe I should change my major to law," we step out of the car and walk up the steps. I'm half joking, but the expensive wooden door does tug at my greedy heartstrings just a little.

"Yeah, right. You wouldn't last a day as a lawyer. One argument would send you packing with a silent treatment."

I laugh but he's definitely not wrong.

I assume it's too loud inside to hear a knock, so I step through the door with no announcement. Max lets out a low whistle and Ellie gasps. If I thought the outside was extravagant, the inside is otherworldly.

A giant chandelier hangs from the center of the ceiling and a staircase winds its way up from the middle of the entryway. I'm consciously aware of the loud clicking and squeaking our shoes make against the checkered, marble floor below us.

"I knew Mason was loaded, but I didn't know he was this loaded."

Max swipes his hand across the raised wall paneling as we follow the sound of music through a back room that closely resembles a dazzling ballroom from one of those old black and white

'20s movies. Since the back wall is mostly glass there's a clear view into the backyard, dimly lit with torches and lanterns.

There's Tilly frowning into the fire by herself. Mason plays host to a crowd, talking animatedly to Emily, Seth/Sean, Johnny, and some people I don't recognize. Then, finally, I find who I'm really scanning the crowd for-only to find him talking to a long-legged girl with gorgeous purple hair.

Of course Asher is talking to a long-legged girl with gorgeous purple hair. Why wouldn't he be? He's handsome. She's pretty.

They look good together, not that I care if they look good together or not.

Even as I think this, my heart sinks and face warms with some feeling of rejection.

I lead the way into the backyard and all eyes fall on us. With the backyard so grand and open, I have nowhere to hide.

Max, on the other hand, basks in the attention.

"Mason, dude, this place is sick," Max yells. He walks away towards Mason, leaving Ellie and I to stand behind awkwardly.

"Look who finally decided to show up," Tilly sneers as she saunters over with a goofy grin that could be a tipsy grin. Then again, with Tilly it's a tossup on if she's tipsy or simply in a bad mood.

"Yeah, yeah. You're the one who always says it's best to be fashionably late."

She rolls her eyes and waves my comment away.

"Since when did you ever listen to me?"

"Touché."

"El, could you come here a second?" Max beckons Ellie over and she nods a goodbye to us. Just as she moves away, Emily steps into her place.

"Who's that?" She stares after Ellie with a sour look on her face. Envy certainly is an ugly color on Emily-or anyone else for that matter.

"That's Ellie, Max's girlfriend."

"Bummer," she pouts, as if she's talking about someone else besides my underage brother. "Is it super serious?"

I laugh uncomfortably.

"He's pretty infatuated with her. Not that you should worry about it anyway."

"Gross, Em," Tilly scrunches her nose. "It's Max. He's practically a little brother."

"*Your* little brother, maybe," Emily mumbles into her red cup.

I'm officially done with the conversation.

"Anyway, who's who here?"

"Oh, right. So you know Seth and Johnny."

So it's Seth, not Sean. Got it.

Emily takes over for Tilly here.

"And then there are my friends from school. Alex is over there with the sexy tan, Chris is the one with the spiked blonde hair, Alice is there talking to Seth, and Jenna is the one talking to Asher."

Ah, so purple-haired girl with the long legs has a name.

"And, just between us girls, I think they're getting pretty cozy."

She bumps Tilly's hip and stares proudly at her friend and Asher.

"I wouldn't say cozy," Tilly scoffs. "Unless you're meaning the lighting out here. That's pretty much the only thing 'cozy' about it."

Tilly looks at me with narrowed eyes, mouthing, "who invited her" when Emily turns away.

I stifle a laugh.

Still, the thought of Asher getting "cozy" with anyone puts me on edge almost involuntarily. It's as if my heart races without me telling it to.

And now he's coming this way with the purple-haired girl following after.

"I'm starting to think you're stalking me, McDowell."

"Yeah, McDowell," Tilly teases behind the rim of her cup. "What's that about?"

I ignore her.

"Obviously I'm not stalking you very well since you keep catching me."

He laughs a full laugh, eyes dancing with the warm lighting around us.

It's the kind of laugh that echoes long after it's finished, reverberates around in your mind so that all you hear is its deep, raspy tone.

"You're definitely the worst stalker I've ever met."

"You meet a lot of stalkers?"

We go back and forth, Tilly smiling ruthlessly next to us while purple-haired girl half-scowls with arms crossed next to Asher.

"Hi, my name's Jenna. And you are?"

She puts her hand out for me to shake, moving herself ever so slightly in front of Asher so she's between us.

Tilly doesn't even try to hide her "hmph" of disapproval.

"Nice to meet you. I'm Lyv."

"Lyv. That's a nice name. Is it short for something?"

She smiles, but her honey-filled words are a bit too sweet for me to really believe they're sincere. I grind my teeth together and force a grimacing smile.

"Nope, it's just Lyv. Short for nothing."

There's a moment of silence filled only by the cutting edge of a girl-on-girl stare down. She's marking territory that's not hers to mark and I'm defending territory   that's not mine to defend.

We eye each other a few seconds longer before she puts a hand delicately on Asher's arm.

"I'm dying of thirst. Anyone else?"

But before any of us can answer she adds, "Want to help me grab some drinks, Asher?"

He hesitates, glancing back and forth between Jenna and I before agreeing to help. They retreat, Asher following behind her, and whatever hope I had leaves with them.

He followed her. He actually followed her.

"Bitch," Tilly barely mumbles under her breath.

"Could you be any louder? Besides, we don't know that she's some evil wench. We just met her."

But in my head I'm chanting right along with Tilly, which only infuriates me more. This is not me-petty, jealous, and territorial. I am not that girl.

And yet...

"She just stepped onto *your* turf, challenged you to a stare down, beat you in said stare down, then dragged your handsome devil off into the moonlight. What exactly would you call her, if not a bitch?"

My mouth opens and closes like a gapping fish.

"Right, now that we've settled that, let's go get you a drink."

She grabs my arm and pulls me toward the drink table where Asher and Jenna now stand.

"Let go, Tilly. I'm not doing this."

"You don't actually have to drink if you don't want to, Lyv. I'm just trying to get you closer to Asher."

She charges on despite my constant pulling back. My heels dig into the ground beneath us.

"Right, and again, I'm not doing this. I'm not playing your dumb cupid game tonight. Let go."

In a huff she drops my arm and spins toward me so fast I stumble back.

"Fine," she spits. "But don't come crying to me when you decide to change your mind about him."

She storms off toward Mason, leaving my chest burning in her absence.

Since when have I ever cried to her about my problems? Not with college stress, not with breaking up with Connor, not even with-but I push that one to the   back of my mind.

Now it's my turn to storm off, but instead of going to the crowd I wander back into the house.

After nosing around, I find my way to the kitchen. It's immaculate and almost entirely white. White backlash spreads behind the counters above white tiled floor. The only things that aren't white are the dark pots and pans hanging above the oven in the middle of the kitchen.

It's peaceful in here, despite the soft thud of the music outside.

But in here alone I can actually hear myself think, can actually calm my heart rate down from the entire encounter I just had with Asher, Jenna, and even Tilly.

I find my way to a bar stool against the tall island and rest my head against the cool tile of it. White tile, of course. Just as I'm starting to completely relax a voice sounds behind me, making me almost jump off the stool.

"Is the party that boring that you need to escape in here all alone?"

Mason smiles his lopsided drunk smile and flops down onto a stool next to me. I try my best to give a genuine smile back, but

Mason irks me. He tries his best to get on my good side. I'll give him that.

But what Mason doesn't know is that many years ago he opened the gateway to my greatest nightmare in life, and for that I just can't forgive him.

Even if he has no idea he has something to be forgiven for.

"Just loud, is all."

I lie.

Loud, suffocating, crowded.

Those are all on the list of why I'm in the kitchen, among many more.

Then, to top it all off, Asher walks through the kitchen doorway.

"Mase, man, what's taking so long on the water?"

He slows when he sees the two of us sitting there.

"And that's my cue," Mason sings and walks out, leaving the water and whatever else he was supposed to get behind him.

"Hiding out?" Asher sits down where Mason just sat.

I start to lie, but find it difficult to muster the words with him.

"Is it that obvious?"

We laugh, and the two sounds mix together in perfect harmony.

"I don't blame you. Parties aren't all they're cracked up to be."

He leans forward on the island, pulling his gray t-shirt taut against his back. No matter how much I try to focus back on the white counter in front of me, his brown, inked skin is such a contrast that I struggle to look anywhere else.

"I never realized you had so many tattoos," I blurt before I can even think about it.

Why I decide to be so blatantly obvious about staring at him, I don't know, but I just can't seem to control my thoughts or words around him.

"Yeah," he laughs. "That's what my sisters say. They're not fans."

"Why not?"

I know of Asher's sisters, but I've never actually had a one-on-one conversation with him long enough to talk about his personal life.

"Oh, you know, the usual stuff. I'll regret it when I'm older, my skin is too nice to ruin, blah, blah, blah."

He rubs absent mindedly over fading ink just below the crook of his arm. It's made of random triangles with an eagle head connected to the top of the largest triangle. It looks like a bird, only with a triangle body, and is easily his largest one I've seen yet.

Out of bravery, or possibly stupidity, I reach out and brush my index finger across it.

"What's this one mean?"

I try to ignore the small chill bumps that rise as my finger brushes across his skin. My breath hitches when his dark eyes flicker up to mine.

"That's the first one I ever got. It's a Native American symbol for freedom," he leans closer as he speaks. "I got it when my dad died. He was half Navajo, and I thought it would kind of symbolize him finding his freedom-you know, after he died."

I let out a small huff of air I'd inattentively been holding onto.

"That's beautiful, Asher."

Surprisingly my whisper reaches him and he glances at me with a small smile.

"You really think so?"

Closer and closer he leans toward me.

"There you are!" Jenna bursts through the kitchen right at that very moment. "I've been looking everywhere for you."

And just like that, the moment's gone. I lean back with a quick snap.

How dumb of me to get so wrapped up that I lose this much focus because of him? I'm starting to see a pattern with myself where Asher's involved, and I don't like it.

"Sorry, we just needed to take a break from the noise for a second."

Asher has now stood from the bar stool, leaving me craving a few minutes ago when it was just us two.

"Well, time's up. Let's go back out to the party."

Jenna grabs Asher's arm, almost exactly where I'd just touched him. Seeing her hand there makes my vision blur with irritation.

"Care to join us?"

Asher asks as he expertly pulls his arm out of her grasp.

"Yeah, I'll be out in a minute."

I muster up a fake smile and let them walk away. The only sliver of joy I get in seeing him leave with her is when he turns back with concern in his eyes before he disappears around the corner of the kitchen entrance.

All too soon, I'm ready to leave here. I'm ready to crawl into bed under my warm blankets and binge watch whatever Netflix show I can randomly land on.

When I find my way back out to the party, Tilly storms over toward me with fire burning in her eyes.

"Why is *she* with him and *you're* over here? You should be over there getting your guy."

She crosses her arms, but I can say with complete confidence that my annoyance is greater than hers right now.

"Enough, Tilly. Enough," I snap. She steps back as if I'd just smacked her. "Please, just give it a rest. I don't want to do this right now."

She looks at me then in a way I haven't seen before and I squirm under her harsh glare.

"So what do you want, then, huh? You want Asher or not? Please just make up your mind, for God's sake."

I'm not sure where all of this is coming from. She's like a freight train dozing over me with every word she spits out.

"What are you talking about? Could you keep your voice down?"

She's not actually yelling, not even stage whispering, but Max and Mason are close enough to hear us anyway. They glance over warily and Max takes a slight step towards us, but I shake my head at him. He stays put.

"I'm talking about your complete inability to make a move toward something you actually want and drop the shit you don't want."

My face warms and breathing hitches. Tilly's never attacked me like this before, never questioned my way of closing off to people.

"You're drunk," I croak. "You're not thinking straight."

"I'm not that drunk," she retorts. The look she gives me is worse than any eye roll she's ever thrown; worse than any sneer she's made. She looks at me now with arms crossed and eyes dull, as if

I'm a child she has to reprimand. Like I'm too dumb to understand my own head.

"I'm sober enough to know you wasted all that time with Connor because things got too serious for you. I'm sober enough to know you're completely into Asher but won't act because you're scared. Tell me I'm wrong."

She arches her brow in a challenge but I now better. Challenging Tilly only stokes her fire.

And on some level, deep down I can't say it.

I can't admit she's wrong.

With nothing else to say, I speed walk out the side gate without turning back. It's not until I get to the car that I remember Max has the keys.

I mumble under my breath and start walking.

Home isn't too far away if I walk fast enough. My feet carry me but it's a heavy load. Heavy from Asher's rejection when he followed Jenna away from me. Heavy from Tilly's humiliation with the complete truth.

Heavy from a memory of long ago, during a moment in my past that breathed life into the   monsters that still haunt me.

My phone dings with a text from Max but I shoot him a quick, "I'm fine" and he leaves it at that.

My feet drop one after the other, my steps resounding against the concrete sidewalk below me with an agonizing thud.

Every word Tilly spoke replays in my mind.

"Scared" and "wasting time" float around, like some buoy that refuses to just sink already.

I'm not scared, or wasting my time.

I know what I want.

I want to be happy and free of the pain that follows me around like a dark cloud.

For too long I've danced with the demons of my past and I can't figure out how to let them go; how to get over what's held me down all this time. And who is Tilly to say I wasted time with Connor?

It wasn't a waste of time.

We're still friends, Connor and I, right? It's not a waste of time if I came out on the other side with something to show for it, is it?

Just to prove myself right I pull my phone and dial his number.

It's a mistake in the making, I know, but I ignore the warning signs and go with it anyway. It's a Friday night so I'm sure he has a gig, but that doesn't deter me.

The phone rings and rings and I almost hang up, but on the last ring his voice replaces the ringing.

"Lyv?" His voice is raspy. That means he's probably just finished a show.

I have no plan for what comes next now that he's actually answered.

"Uh, hey. Hi. How are you?"

He breathes a small laugh.

"I'm-um-I'm alright, I guess. Lyv, why are you calling me?"

It's not hateful, his tone, but it's not kind either. Just--tired. I guess he's not as over us as I hoped he'd be.

"I just wanted to see how you're doing, you know? See how your summer's going. Are you still doing shows?"

This is a train wreck and all I can do is suffer through it. The familiarity of his voice stops me

209

from pushing the red button to end this dreadful phone call. I'm more comforted than I imagined I'd be talking to him, but not comforted enough to ever think about going back to us.

There's rummaging around on the other side of the line. Loud voices blend with the background music.

"Hang on a second."

I can't make out his mumbling, but in an instant the background noise gets quieter. How could I ever be so stupid to call him? All feelings beyond platonic for Connor are gone, but I still torture us further by staying on the phone instead of just hanging up.

"Sorry about that. We just finished with a gig and it's kind of crazy in here."

I swallow the lump that's suddenly rising in my throat.

"No, it's fine. I need to get going anyway. I shouldn't have called. I'm sorry."

"Wait, Lyv. Just wait," he clears his throat. "It's nice to hear your voice again and I, uh, I hope you're doing good."

Tears prick my eyes as I keep moving forward down the uneven sidewalk to home. His kindness only heightens the guilt I feel inside.

"I've been better, but I've also been worse," I laugh quietly.

I wish so badly that I could be who he needed me to be. I wish I could take back all the bad things that have happened to me to create this rift between me and anyone who tries to get close. I wish we were different people and that life had treated us differently. But we aren't different people, and I can't take back the hand life has dealt me. It's this reality that pushes me to my next question. "Can I ask you something?"

"Anything," he breathes.

My voice is weaker than I want it to be.

"What's wrong with me? I mean, we were good, right? So what's my problem?"

It's hard to say how many times I've asked myself that.

Other people get through worse than me and move on with their lives just fine. But me? I let this dark stain from years ago fester until it leaks out into every crevice, consuming me and destroying any chance I have to be happy.

"There's nothing wrong with you, Lyv," he sounds sad, but keeps going. "You just have your own mountains to climb, is all, and you seem to prefer climbing   those by yourself."

He's taking it easy on me, I know, but I lap the words up anyway.

"Thanks Connor. I'm sorry about how it all turned out."

I don't wait on a reply or goodbye.

I hang up, staring out at the dark skyline in front of me, coming to the realization that I'm a destructive person. I destroyed my relationship with my brother, my relationship with my family, and my relationship with every guy who's ever been remotely interested in me. On top of that, I'm destroying my relationship with my best friend.

I don't know how to fix it.

I don't know how to fix *me*.

My house comes into view 15 minutes after I'd set out on my little walk. I run the last few steps it takes to get there, reminding myself to breathe.

In.

Air fills my lungs like a balloon.

Out.

I let it go, busting that balloon as air falls away in a puff.

My mom sits on the couch reading when I come through the door.

"Hi sweets, how was your night?"

I don't reply.

Then there's dad, staring intently at the TV. He pauses long enough to give a wave but I keep walking.

Up the steps.

In.

Into my room.

Out.

My door slams behind me as I fall to my bed, burying my head in the heap of pillows waiting for me. The dam breaks before I have a chance to breathe in again.

And for the hundredth time in my life I cry over a life I can't seem to control.

⊙⊙⊙⊙⊙

The next morning is a morning for apologies.

I apologize to Max for leaving without an explanation. Max apologizes to me for not coming

213

after me. I even apologize to mom and dad for coming in without stopping to acknowledge either of them.

The biggest apology, though, comes when I'm still in bed, wrapped up in my covers, as Tilly bursts through my door near tears to say how sorry she was for all the "shitty, awful, unbestfriend things" she said last night.

But, I make no apology to Connor. I'm burning that bridge here and now. No more late night calls. No more regret or questioning it. It's done and over with.

"I swear, next time I see you two fight like that I'm going to smack your heads together cartoon style."

Somewhere between my accepting Tilly's apology and beginning the story of my embarrassing late-night call, Max wanders into the room and now threatens both of us to an inch of our lives. As if he has nothing better to do on a Saturday morning.

"Down, boy. I started it and I owned up to it. It won't happen again."

Tilly pats Max's arm but still, he shakes his head like a disappointed dad.

"Though, I have to say, it's pretty entertaining seeing you storm around trying to figure out who hurt Lyv's feelings."

I laugh around puffy, post-crying eyes at the image of it.

But, unlike last night, I now have Tilly curled up under the covers with me and Max sits in his spot on the floor. I find comfort in the familiarity of the two.

"I really am sorry though. I don't think I've ever been so sorry about something before. I was way out of line."

Tilly pouts beside me.

"It's fine, honestly. Yes, I was mad last night in the heat of it all, but you weren't completely wrong. I think that's what made me the maddest."

Tilly frowns.

"What are you talking about? I was drunk off my ass, Lyv. Nothing I said was even remotely true," she pauses. "Unless you mean the part about you secretly being into Asher, because that's totally true."

I laugh with her, mostly because I don't feel like explaining myself. She was right on so many levels.

I am scared of getting   too close to people.

I am interested in Asher, at least I think I could be eventually.

I am all of these things and more.

Tilly picks at the broken button nose on my childhood teddy bear, Max stares absently at the ceiling fan, and I glance out the window at the sprinklers going of in the neighbor's yard across the street.

"I've got it."

Max's shout echoes around the room, causing Tilly and I to jump.

"I think little bro's taken too many hits on the football field."

Tilly's wide eyes look from me to Max and back again before he shoots her the bird. It's like a breath of fresh air to really laugh this much.

"No, seriously, I've got the perfect pick-me-up idea."

I'm wary, but Tilly's focused now. She sits up in the bed with eyes trained on my little brother.

"Keep talking."

"The pool. Let's go to the city pool."

Tilly's shoulders slump and she sinks back into the pillow mound behind her.

"That's it? That's your grand idea? I'm not going to my place of employment on my weekend off, even if it's to cheer up a friend. Forget it. Sorry, Lyv."

I shrug. The idea doesn't sound that appealing to me anyway.

"I don't mean right now," Max scoffs. "I mean later, after it's closed. We could sneak in and have our own little private pool party."

Tilly's right, he's taken too many hits. I see the wheels turning in my best friends head. It seems I'll have to be the voice of reason here.

"We can't sneak into the pool, Max. There are cameras and a security guard on duty. We'll get caught for sure, right?"

But one look at Tilly says she's sold.

She taps her chin and stares into the distance through squinted eyes.

"No, I think Max is onto something. Those cameras are phonies. They're only there to scare people. They don't actually work," she smiles broadly, as if this lack in security cameras is a good thing. "It's also Saturday. Security isn't on duty during the weekends."

217

She nods just as I shake my head in a firm no.

"No way, guys. I'm not breaking into the city pool. That won't make me feel better. I'm anxious about it already."

Max and Tilly glance at each other, likely already scheming ways to get me to go.

It's two against one.

I take the loss under great protest.

"So, how'd it go last night?"

Mia and Cali burst through my bedroom door with no regards to my privacy.

"Sure," I sneer. "Come on it."

They slam onto my bed, Cali at my feet and Mia at my side. I cover my head with my pillow. But Mia, being the feistiest of all us Brooks children, pulls it off immediately with a swift smack against my back.

I turn on my side and look at Cali for backup but she crosses her arms, eyebrows arched nearly to her hairline.

"I see how it is," I sit up, shaking my head at the two terrors. They're like pesky gnats constantly buzzing around my ear. "I force you guys to makeup and you turn on me."

I make that "tsk" sound Mia hates so much.

"Stop stalling," this from Cali as she punches my leg. "Answer the question."

They're obviously not going away anytime soon, so my only real option is to cave.

So I do just that. I tell them about last night and how it started out great, but then turned into a colossal waste of time. I tell them about the conversation in the kitchen, sans her brushing my arm of course, and about Jenna giving all her uninvited attention. Finally, I tell them about the crushing disappointment of Lyv disappearing halfway through the night.

I don't know where she went or why she left, especially when it seemed like we were hitting it off so well. That's the most I'd ever talked with Lyv in the many years of knowing her. I finally felt like our moment was coming when Jenna decided to interrupt it.

And then, just as I was ready to find Lyv again and try to get that moment back, she was just gone.

"I guess she's just not into me. Whatever. I'm sure I'll get over it eventually."

I shrug nonchalantly, but my scowl speaks for itself.

"You're so clueless it's cute," Mia notes snidely.

"Oh? So, enlighten me then."

"She's totally into you," Cali lays down so that she stretches completely across the foot of my bed.

"I guess you two missed the entire story I just told."

"Again I say you're clueless, except it's a little less adorable the longer you go with it. She was jealous, Ash. Another girl was hanging all over you in front of her. Why would she stick around to see that?" Mia says.

Jealous?

I try to picture Lyv as the jealous type.

"I doubt it. How would you know, anyway? You weren't even there."

I hate how my voice gets all squeaky and accusatory, like I'm 16 all over again and have no clue what women think.

As opposed to now, at 21, when I still have no clue what women think.

"Because we're fluent in the language of subtext," Cali chimes in. "And you, my sweet, big brother, are not. If it's not as obvious as a semi-truck smacking you in the face, you're oblivious to it."

My phone rings, interrupting me from their assault.

Tilly's name flashes across the screen.

"As much as I appreciate our early-bird therapy session, I'm going to need you two to go now."

Finally they leave but not without complaint.

Just before I answer the phone Mia pokes her head around the door, Cali's coming in just under Mia's.

"Remember," Mia states. "Don't screw it up."

They both dodge the pillow I throw and slam my door shut.

"What's up?"

I blame Tilly for the entire mess of last night, since she is the one who coerced me into going when I didn't have plans to in the first place.

"Don't make plans for tonight."

Here she goes again.

Despite my gut feeling to hang up and never answer to Tilly's crazy antics again, I stay on the line and pray whatever she has planned includes her beautiful, mystery of a best friend.

"What do you have in mind?"

Excitement laces her every word.

"How do you feel about   night swimming?"

Chapter Fourteen-Lyv

I'm not even a little surprised to see Asher's navy blue jeep pull up to my house late Saturday night. It's just past 11 p.m. and our break-in excursion begins soon. Max, Ellie, and I sit on the front porch, waiting for the rest of our friends to pick us up.

When the jeep pulls up to the curb, Tilly hangs out of the back window grinning wildly.

"Let's go," she drags, smacking her hand against the outside of the backdoor.

"She's insane," Ellie smiles next to me. Thrill gleams in her eyes and I wonder if she's ever gotten in trouble a day in her life.

"That's the understatement of the century," Max walks ahead of us, Ellie falling in line behind him and me bringing up the rear.

There are two seats open in the back next to Tilly and only one seat up front between Asher and Mason.

Somehow I know which seat will be mine.

"Lyv's the smallest. She's upfront," Mason lies. Ellie is two times smaller than me and that's easy to see. Still, Mason gets out and moves over so I can squeeze into the middle of the long front seat.

There's no seat belt, but Mason assures me he'll put a "mom-arm" across me if anything happens and I start to fly out of the windshield.

"Everyone ready?"

Asher speaks up and his voice alone sends shivers up my spine.

"Ready," Tilly shouts from the back.

Asher grabs the gearshift between us, accidentally brushing against my knee in the process. My skin burns where he touches and he coughs out a "sorry" before propelling us forward.

The touch sends me reeling for more reasons than one. Instinct pulls my leg as far from him as possible; distance my constant go to.

We get to the pool shortly but instead of parking close, we stop about a block away to leave space between the getaway car and the scene of our trespassing.

Mason and Asher get out first, followed by the three in the back. I'm the last to move, mostly out of fear, but the sight of everyone waiting on me gets my limbs moving. It's like my feet drag me forward against my will—against my mind screaming at me to stay put.

"Let's do this," Max calls.

He runs ahead and Mason chases him with arms flailing and legs flopping around haphazardly. Asher follows after them, but much calmer than the other two. He walks with his hands tucked into this pockets and a goofy side-grin in place.

He's always the calm, collected type.

"I'm beginning to think you have a death wish."

I shoot Tilly my hardest glare the moment we're out of earshot of the guys. She only loops her arm carelessly through mine.

"You wouldn't dare, Lyvie. I know you better than that. There's a little part of you in there thankful I set this endeavor up. Thankful I got you and Asher in the same spot so you can redeem yourselves from last night. Even more thankful, I believe, than before now that you and Connor are totally and officially dunso with last night's little stunt."

"Stunt? What stunt happened last night?" Ellie's eyes widen.

"Lyv here decided to make an embarrassing late-night, tear induced phone call to her old boy toy," Tilly answers for me, but I silently thank her so I don't have to go through the story all over again.

"Regardless, everything is fine in the world again. Because there are three guys here and three girls, and only two out of the six are single," Ellie smiles when Tilly throws her other arm over Ellie's petite shoulder.

"Now, I know I'm no genius, but add those numbers up and it seems to me like one gorgeous, hazel eyed girl plus one drop-dead-handsome man equals match made in heaven. Am I right, El?"

Ellie giggles hysterically.

"Sounds right to me."

"I hate you both," but I don't mean it. While the past 24 hours haven't been ideal, I'm feeling better already as we follow behind the rest of our rowdy group, arm in arm. Like some misfit team of trespassing delinquents.

"So, how are we doing this?" Max asks once we finally catch up.

"How am I supposed to know?" Tilly shrugs. "This was your idea, remember?"

"Yes, but you work here, remember?" Max retorts.

We listen to the two bicker as if they were the siblings. There's an outdoor light that almost reaches us where we are to the side of the entrance, but the light falls just a few feet away.

Darkness creeps around us as we deliberate a way into this mess.

It's unnerving, standing here in the middle of the night with nothing but blackness around us. The nearby street lamps and pool safety lights cast shadows against the ground around us, creating dark, stretched out arms as the light hits the branches of trees above us.

Flashbacks threaten to come up from the deep abyss I've thrown them into in my mind, but I take deep, long breaths until they fall back to the bottom.

"Maybe this is a sign we should just go back," I whisper as if we're going to get caught if talk at a normal volume.

"We're already here," Mason says. "We're doing this."

He can't see me roll my eyes at his stubbornness. He pulls his phone from his pocket and taps the screen until the flashlight shines. Max, Tilly, and Asher follow suite.

"We just need to find an opening somewhere," Mason mumbles, already searching the perimeter of the fence as he walks away from us.

He obviously doesn't take into consideration how city property isn't likely to be surrounded by lousy protection—unless, of course, you live in a small town like Carter Springs where lousy protection is exactly what city property is surrounded by.

"Found one," Asher shouts from a few feet away.

The "gap" sits at the back corner of the fence and is barely wide enough for a child to fit through, let alone grown people.

"I'm supposed to fit through that?"

This coming from Ellie, the tiniest of us all.

Her lack in confidence does little to help my own. If she can't get through, none of us have hope.

"Oh, we'll be fine," Tilly brushes past Asher to examine the entry. "We'll just have to move slow. Easy peasy."

The jagged wire sticking out at every angle of the gap screams anything but "easy peasy". I can already imagine the colorful threads of my t-shirt catching in the fence's sharp teeth. Of course, this would all be solved if Tilly or Asher would just use their keys to get in the front, but apparently that's just too obvious of a way to get in.

"C'mon, don't be such a baby," Tilly shoves Ellie playfully and heads into the jaggedness that is the broken fence.

She sticks her right leg in first then slides her hip in after until the lower half of her body is almost completely in. Next, she puts her shoulders through before dragging her head in like she's balancing under a limbo stick.

A sharp, spikey limbo stick.

With one last shimmy, Tilly pulls her last leg through until she stands on the other side like some escaped fugitive in an alternate universe where the inside means freedom.

"Who's next?" She calls. Her hands rest proudly on her hips and she smiles.

Mason steps forward.

Tilly made the maneuver look somewhat effortless, but Mason struggles to push his larger body through. His jeans catch when he steps through and I stifle a laugh as he stumbles to the other side.

Tilly smacks a noisy kiss on his cheek before clapping her hands excitedly.

"Alright, I'll see you suckers on the other side," Max winks and steps through with even more struggle than Mason, thanks to his newly enhanced physic. Ellie follows, graceful as ever.

And then there were two.

"You're up, sis," Max stage whispers from the inside.

Why I have to be next is beyond me. My mind finally outwits my body, stopping my feet from moving toward the fence.

It'd be so easy to go back to my warm, cozy bed surrounded by a mountain of pillows and blankets; just go home where I'm safe and sound. No dangers of what might be lurking in the dark. No worries about what all could go wrong here.

And all I'd have to do is walk away.

Easy peasy, as Tilly said.

But that means the monster inside wins, right? He gets under my skin. He controls my every move. He breaks me down until there's nothing left but a scared little girl.

If I walk away now, the monster wins—and I can't let him win.

"Hey," Asher reels me back in. "Don't sweat it. We're all here with you. If you get caught, we get caught."

He gives me a reassuring nod and his kind smile momentarily chases my doubt away.

We're all here with you.

The idea pushes me forward, stirs some courage I've struggled to find on my own thus far in the evening.

I step cautiously through the fence without a single thread ripped and, as promised, Asher follows so that they all surround me on the inside.

"Now what?" Asher asks.

"Now," Max says with a dark glint in his hazel eyes, "we swim."

Without another word he strips off one article of clothing after another until he's left in   nothing but his briefs.

"Cannonball!"

He hurls himself into the pool, tossing water into the air around him. Tilly follows, of course, disrobing to her bra and underwear before strutting toward the diving board.

"I dub this the Black Swan," she uses her terrible British accent she thinks is perfect, then dives into the murky water below.

By the time Ellie steps up I almost lose my courage. Comparing myself to Tilly is something I've grown used to. I've compared myself to her all my life, since growing up with a best friend as flawless as her becomes sort of routine.

But Ellie is a fresh person to compare myself to, no matter how much I tell myself not to.

Being almost bare in front of all these people puts me on edge, but I've been completely bare before in worse ways than this.

So that's not what really stops me.

It's Ellie, with her slender waist and model thighs. My stomach looks twice the size of hers and suddenly I feel surrounded by girls much prettier than I am.

For the millionth time in my life my mind goes in a whirlwind of all the reasons I should just walk away.

Then I glance at Tilly and she stares straight through me with encouragement in her gaze. She shakes her head slightly, just enough that if you weren't really paying attention you would've missed it—almost as if to say, "don't go there."

She beckons me with a wave of her hand, tempting me to put my worries aside and just enjoy the moment.

It's the same look she gave me during one of our first weekends at college when we went out for the first time. I was content with people watching from the corner of the room quietly but Tilly wouldn't have any of it. The people around me were beautiful and exotic beyond what I was used to, and maybe that was just because I'd never really been away from home before. Regardless, I wasn't willing to move from my cozy corner spot.

But Tilly refused to let me hide away. She pulled me into the crowd, introduced me to people she'd already met within the first 20 minutes of the party, one of those being Connor.

She'd ushered me into groups of people so I had no choice but to feel comfortable in my own skin.

Standing there at the pool's edge I realize I am my own worst enemy and no one on earth could judge me as harshly as I judge myself.

I drop my arms I hadn't realized I covered my stomach with, pull my shirt and shorts off in quick motions, and jump into the pool before I lose every ounce of bravery I've mustered.

I don't think about how Asher makes me feel standing so close or how Connor made me feel so far away. I don't think about the monster that always tries clawing his way back in. I don't think about what I may look like in the bathing suit I sensibly put on under my clothes in case something like this would happen.

I think of nothing else except for how the air feels rustling through my hair as I plunge into the water below.

I think about how the water feels pulling me under, then pushing me back up again, leaving me gasping at the surprising chill the water carries.

My laugh echoes with the cheers of my friends around me.

That laughter catches in my throat when Asher starts undressing in the same spot I've just left.

He's magnificent in every way.

It's not really the fact that he's almost naked that gets to me. I've seen him shirtless before in nothing but swimming trunks. I've seen those little random tattoos littering his smooth, tanned body—seen his lean muscles once before.

No, that's not what gets me.

It's the way he undresses so slowly.

Seductively. Sure of himself.

One article of clothing at a time.

First goes the shirt over his head where it tangles up with the gold chain around his neck. Next goes the shoes and socks. Then the pants where they slide down and tug his boxers just enough to spot the v-line outlining a happy trail downward.

He takes it all off with a smirk on his lips—and his eyes locked with mine.

Like he knows exactly what he's doing to me.

I knew I'd have to hold my breath under water but I never imagined it'd be worse up above.

With a mischievous manner to his movements he jumps in. When he comes back up out of the water he does so smiling wildly, dark hair shaking the excess   water away.

By then everyone else has already jumped in. We laugh and splash, feeling like we're nine-year-olds getting away with something we know we shouldn't be doing.

We swim and compete for the best dive off the diving board. We play Marco Polo and chicken, where my heart races with Asher beneath me, his hands on my thighs.

Then we all float, gazing up at the stars cascaded above with the moon hung high.

The water roars in my submerged ears.

Resting this way makes it easy to forget my sorrows; to forget the ache in my chest from that feeling of dread that never seems to completely go away. My mind focuses on the water holding me and the people surrounding me.

It hits me all too fully that I'm not the same as I was before I left here a year ago. I'm different. This place is different. The people around me are different. I don't have to worry about making the same mistakes twice because nothing is the way it was before in this moment.

I've never trusted this place as much as I do now with the water holding me and the stars lighting me up.

I've never laughed this much here.

Smiled this much here.

Felt this much here.

It's all so new in a place I've known my whole life.

"I hate to break up this illegal pool party, but my fingers are pruning. I need out," Tilly breaks the roar in my ears as she paddles her way to the nearest ladder.

"I'm with Tilly," Ellie echoes, rubbing her wrinkled fingertips together.

The rest of us follow and grab towels Tilly finds in a nearby towel rack.

"You know what I used to love about the city pool as a kid?" Mason gives no time for an answer. "The nachos."

"Yes, the nachos! Those were the bomb," Max rubs his stomach longingly.

"Lets go make some then," Tilly suggests as if there couldn't possibly be consequences for that.

They walk off toward the concession stand with Tilly's work keys that she finally decides to use, but I hang back.

"I'm not really hungry, so I'm going to sit out here a little longer."

"Are you sure?" Ellie's eyes scrunch with concern.

I want to tell her I'm fine and just want to enjoy the view a little while longer. I want to enjoy it before I wake up in the morning and despise the night all over again.

But instead of all that I smile with a thumbs up.

"Positive. You guys go enjoy your nachos."

Tilly puts out some extra towels and I grab one to dab against my knotted hair.

I'm already by my clothes when Asher speaks up.

"Actually, I think I'll pass on the nachos too."

Of course, no one questions him when he says it. Instead Tilly and Ellie eye each other with a grin and follow an oblivious Max and Mason toward the concession stand.

My stomach twists around and around until it feels like one tangled ball inside.

Once again, it's Asher and I left standing there alone together.

Don't ask me why I stayed back instead of joining in on what I'm sure are great nachos. Scratch that, I know exactly why.

It's because Lyv, with all her quiet beauty, reels me in no matter who else is around us. I've done nothing but think of her all summer, so when the opportunity arises for me to spend one-on-one time with her, I'm going to take it.

For the first few minutes we're alone, no one speaks. My mind races with images of her in her bathing suit, of the peach hue against her slightly browned skin—I want so badly to sneak a peak just one last time before she's fully dressed again, but fear that would be disrespectful of her somehow.

There'll be no shaking that image of her jumping in the water earlier tonight from my head. It's engrained and will be, I'm sure, until I take my last breath. It was mesmerizing to watch her battle with herself about whether to jump in or not. I wanted to tell her, to shout it for everyone, that she's the most beautiful one here tonight—whether she's in a bathing suit or not.

She's always the most beautiful one in the room, mind and body, and it kills me to see her ever doubt herself.

But then when she found that courage, it brought out something animalistic in me. Lyv jumped in and every fiber of my being told me to follow her.

After minutes of excruciating silence, Lyv speaks up.

"So, how was the party after I left?"

The question catches me a little off guard, but I'm glad she brings up the party. If nothing else maybe I can get answers for her disappearing act last night.

"Pretty lame, if I'm being honest. Tilly was crabby the rest of the night, which bummed Mason out. So basically, you ruined it."

I mean it as a joke, but when she whips around with her ever-changing eyes squinted, I see it hit some nerve I didn't realize it would hit.

But I laugh with my hands up in surrender.

"You're a real comedian," she scoffs as she tosses my wet towel towards my head. I catch it easily.

Even in the barely lit night, I can see the colors dancing in her eyes. I'm floored by her effortlessness; how easy it seems to be for her to be her honest and strong self without even trying.

"Care to join me by the pool?"

She nods when I gesture towards the pool with one wide sweep of my arm.

"Only if you don't throw me in. I deal with that enough from Max."

Images of her birthday party flash in my mind, of her cheeks flushed with anger and embarrassment when she came out of the water. I didn't think I'd ever seen someone so stunning.

That was just the beginning of it for me.

"Pinky promise."

Just to show her my commitment, I hold my pinky out for her, which she then wraps her own around.

The contact is soft and gentle, much like her hand brushing against my arm the night of Mason's party when she traced over my tattoo.

She'd sent chills over me that night, and I hope she didn't see what she was doing to me. It's not just about the physical contact with her. It's the thought-provoking questions, the curiosity she has, that pulls me in so much.

We put towels down at the pool's edge and sit. Water from my boxers soak through my jeans, despite the towel, while Lyv sits with another towel wrapped around her still semi-wet body. The heat of her thigh pours out of her high-waist shorts, warming up the part of my leg where we touch.

Maybe people like Lyv exist solely for the purpose of enchanting people. Maybe that's why they captivate people so much. Like they're here to remind us that, at the end of the day, we're still capable of hope and happiness.

I'm convinced it's that way with her, at least, if no one else.

And I find myself wanting to know every single thing I can about her in my own hope of breaking down the walls she so obviously puts up with people.

"Let's play 20 Questions."

I can see before she even answers that she's hesitant.

She hugs her knees to her chest and chews on the inside of her jaw.

"But with 100 percent honesty," I add. "No bullshit answers."

Twenty questions, I silently plead. *Just twenty questions, then you're free.*

She continues to chew on her jaw but says, "You go first."

And since we were already on the topic of Mason's party,

"Okay. Why did you leave the party so early?"

I want to add that I felt betrayed when she left; like we were having a great time and she just vanished on me. But I know that would only make her cave further into herself so I leave it alone.

She stares out at the rippling water in front of us.

"Because I got in a fight with Tilly."

A simple response, but I think there's more to it than just that. I've seen Lyv and Tilly "fight" before and it's never something serious enough to make one walk away from the other.

"About what?"

She hesitates for what feels like eternity.

"Basically, she called me a scared little girl with no backbone."

Anger courses through me at her words. How dare anyone say something so wrong about her, least of all her best friend? Red blurs my vision and I hold myself in my spot to keep from finding Tilly right this second to yell at her.

She laughs a sadistic, robotic laugh.

"She's not entirely wrong, I guess. But it still stings to hear it out loud."

My heart rips open.

How can she say these things about herself? Can she not see the person I see? She's strong and courageous. She's beautiful and funny. She's talented, loyal, and brave. She's all this and more, so how on earth could she and everyone else she meets not see that?

When I look away from the darkness of the tree line past the pool fence, she's already looking at me. Her rounded eyes search mine for some kind of response, good or bad.

"Well, I have to say I disagree entirely with both of you," I say unblinking.

"That's something I always remember about you," she whispers then straightens as if she hadn't meant to say anything.

"What's that?" I taunt.

"Nothing."

"C'mon. What do you   always remember about me?"

I'm curious now to know what it is that she remembers about me from growing up. We grew up at a distance, really, so it's nice to know she noticed something about me from that distance.

"Your eyes," her cheeks heat even in the dark. "They're so dark and relentless when you focus on someone or something. I feel like you can see right through me."

It's the most honest and vulnerable answer I've gotten from her since knowing her.

Again, she laughs that shy laugh of hers and changes the subject before I can comment further.

"That's, like, ten questions all at once. Don't I get a turn?"

I shake my head in a laugh and say, "I guess, but before that you have to promise me you won't say something like that about yourself again, at least not in front of me."

I'm not sure if I can handle anymore of her degrading herself.

"Fine," then for the third time tonight she catches me completely off guard. "My question is, what do you think about the girl from the party? Em's friend with the purple hair?"

If I didn't know better, I'd say there's a hint of jealousy behind her tone.

I guess Mia and Cali were right after all.

My nose scrunches at the thought of that girl who tried so desperately to distract me from Lyv, as if it were ever possible.

"I think she doesn't know what personal space means in the slightest," my laugh comes out stiffer than I meant it to. "I also think purple hair doesn't work for everyone."

Her cackle breaks through the air as I eye the hand she's just used to cover her laugh.

"That laugh is too good to cover up."

When she bites on her lip to keep the smile at bay, my insides twist at the loveliness of it.

"Your turn," she whispers.

We go on for God knows how long in this exact way. We talk about siblings and parents. She brushes her hand against mine when my voice catches about my dad and the cancer; the sympathy-sorrow in her eyes matches the sorrow in mine. We talk about dream jobs, ones we would do if money and stability were out of the equation (me an author, her a National Geographic photographer). And then we talk about what we plan to do instead. She smiles sweetly when I say a pediatrician because of my love for kids and the medical field. I'm impressed when she says a college professor because of a class she took this year about inspiring young photographers.

On and on we go, question after question.

I quickly realize I've shared more of myself with Lyv than I ever have with anyone else before, even this girl, Becky, I tried dating for a while in college. It's freeing and terrifying all at the same time.

To let someone in so far, to share so much of yourself with them, both feels like a weight has been lifted while simultaneously feels like your very being rests in the palm of their hand.

But, if I had to let anyone have this much of me, I'd want it to be Lyv.

"If you could live anywhere in the world where would it be?"

Thirty minutes later our game of "Twenty Questions" morphs into a much longer game and, if my counting is accurate, we're somewhere between question number 37 and question number 42.

I try not to dwell on just how much I've let Asher know about myself. It's more than anyone else knows, besides Tilly, and it came from absolutely zero tugging on his end. But instead of feeling weighted down by that realization, I feel like I can take a deeper, fresher breath because of it.

"Hmm, that's tough, but I think I'd pick LA."

Asher cringes as if he'd just caught a whiff of something awful.

"What? What's so bad about LA?" I ask with a laugh.

It'd be easy to be offended by his blatant disapproval if it weren't so much easier to adore the way his nose wrinkles up when he's unhappy.

"I'll pass."

"And why is that?"

He doesn't answer right away but instead gazes up above us. At what, I'm not sure. But it's serene and pure in the moment.

Movies and art paint these flashes of life beautifully; make these small moments so vivid they seem real. But they have nothing on the actual moment.

See, in the movies there'd be a song in the background to amp up the way Asher's eyes go soft with the stars reflecting back in them. Paintings would catch the way his jaw clenches under the weight of his thoughts with vivid imagery.

But right here, right now in this moment, Asher is real.

I don't need movies or art or anything else in the world to tell me that.

This moment is beautiful and I only need my own eyes to see that, my own heart to feel that.

Finally, he answers.

"You can't see the stars in LA. You look up out here and it's like God got bored and decided to litter the sky with them. You can't do that in a big city like LA. All the city lights snuff out the real light."

I follow his eyes and try to see what he sees, imagine the sky the way he imagines it.

I've always had a bad relationship with the night. Bad things can happen in the dark of night that wouldn't be as easily done in the daylight.

But tonight the stars outshine even the full moon.

Like they're trying to prove themselves to me.

Remind me why they're important.

"Alright, my turn."

Asher brings me back down to earth.

"What's your biggest fear?"

My pulse quickens at the question. He smiles light-heartedly, but it's the question I've been hoping would not come up during this little game of 20-plus questions.

But, just before I have to answer (or more likely decline to answer) a flashlight catches his small smile.

"Hey! Who's over there?"

It's not Mason or Max's voice yelling at us in that gruff manner, and it's definitely not Tilly or Ellie's.

"Looks like we've got   company."

Before I can comprehend what's happening Asher pulls me to my feet and drags me behind him. We're running through the offices Tilly opened, weaving around desks and lockers until he pulls me through another open door.

It's like a maze back here and my only anchor is Asher's large hand pulling me through the confusion.

This last door he pulls me through leads to the inside of the concession stand, which is completely void of any of my friends who were supposed to be in here. Our only cover from the searching security guard is the tall cubbyhole to the right of the giant opening where patrons get their food.

Asher leads us into the spot. My back presses against the wall and he stands close in front of me.

"Was that the police? Are we going to get arrested? We're going to get arrested, aren't we? Asher, I ha—."

He stops my words with a hand gingerly placed over my mouth.

He does it out of good intentions but I quickly pull it away before that old, familiar panic rises up in me.

The shine of a flashlight breaks around the wall hiding us but doesn't hit our bodies directly, thanks to the way we're squeezed into the hole in the wall. Darkness covers us and I'm distinctly aware of Asher.

Of his chest heaving against mine.

Of his other hand resting on my waist.

Of his eyes now locked with mine.

He's everywhere.

And there I am, my hands on either side of his solid waist, my heart racing no matter how much I scream at myself to chill out.

My lips perch so close to his, I can almost feel them already.

The beam of light fades into the night but we stay there.

Asher slides his hand to my jaw, caressing its edges. In the pale moonlight I can only catch half of his expression, but I can still see the way he quickly licks his lips in anticipation.

I'm locked in.

In another world this move sent me running. Years ago, demeaning hands controlled my body in a way so different from now. Back then they were hands connected to a boy undeserving of anything he could take from me.

But here and now, under Asher's tender touch, it's gentle in a way that makes me want to trust him.

Or at least try.

His eyes are focused and lips are parted just slightly.

My breathing quickens as my vision dances from his shadowed eyes to his plump lips. He leans in. I go to meet him halfway.

His other hand stays on my waist but I move mine, sliding them over the fabric of his t-shirt covering his taut stomach.

My eyes drift shut as our faces move closer and closer until—

"Guys, where are you?"

This time it is Tilly's voice stage whispering in the darkness.

Surprise jolts me and in my shock I pull back too far, smacking my head against the wall behind me with an audible thud.

I gasp and check for blood. Luckily there is none.

"Shit, are you OK?"

Asher pulls back to get a look at my face before reaching behind me to put his hand over mine on my head.

"Yeah, I'm fine, just a concussion. I should survive, hopefully."

He laughs softy, shaking his head.

"Always the mishaps with you, McDowell. What am I going to do with you?"

"I'm sure you could think of something."

I've never been one to blatantly flirt, but something about Asher makes me want to do what I never could or would be willing to do before. Or maybe it's just the concussion talking.

Tilly's head pops around the door then in the perfect timing she has.

"Hellooooo? Can we go now? I'm not trying to get fired or arrested because you guys want to play tonsil hockey. We should be outrunning Larry the Security Guard right now, not making out."

Asher steps away, leaving a cool draft in his absence.

"I thought he wasn't working tonight?"

"So did I. Obviously we were wrong. Let's go."

Tilly walks ahead while Asher shuts the concession stand and office doors behind us.

We go back to the gapping fence we'd come in, but I won't be leaving the way I came in. Not really.

It's as if a piece of me was chipped off back there and I feel its vacancy like a dropped weight.

Once we're on the other side Asher hangs back without a word, without hesitation, arm brushing mine as the others walk a few feet in front of us back to the jeep.

Asher and I stay silent the whole drive home.

We're all buzzing with excitement, my friends and I, but all for different reasons.

It's a new feeling, what's bubbling up inside.

And when Asher's hand brushes against my knee again, I don't pull away this time, and it's then I put a name to the feeling.

Hope.

Chapter Seventeen-Asher

There are two days we Brooks avoid like the plague: January 22 and the third Sunday of every June.

One being my dad's birthday and the other being Father's Day.

It's strange, I'm sure, to dislike both of those days so much. Wouldn't you want to celebrate then more than ever? Celebrate your loved ones' memory and think happily on the life they lived with you?

But we don't.

It's one of the few things I resent my mom for, even though I'd never say that out loud.

It's all too much for her, my dad being gone, so instead of talking about him she carries on like nothing's different. She walks around the house doing her usual routine as if it's not the day he was born, or the day fathers are supposed to be celebrated.

Usually I'm able to deal with our family's complete shut out of these two holidays, but this

Father's Day has me wound up more than usual and for no particular reason at all. At any moment I'll be ready to fly off the handle.

There's only so much channel surfing I can do before I combust.

Even the thought of Lyv and our 20 questions last night can't distract me from the tension building in my chest.

"Would you stop fidgeting?" Cali lightly smacks my chest.

She sits next to me on the couch, controlling the remote and my impatience in the palm of her tiny hand. Her eyes stay glued to the TV as she flips from one screen to another. I glance over and can't help but pity myself with how lucky Cali is when it comes to our dad.

She was pretty young when he died, so she remembers him, but not like the rest of us. She was barely seven when he was diagnosed, nine when he actually died. Mostly she just remembers what he was like when he was sick, barely able to hold himself up to get from place to place. In Cali's head our dad is far away from the strong, capable man I knew him to be before the cancer.

Cali doesn't remember him like my mom, who's outside cleaning out the shed to keep her mind and hands busy. She doesn't even remember like Mia, 11 years old when dad died and currently upstairs locked away in her room like she always does on Father's Day—or any other day she wants a good cry by herself.

Then there's me—the child who remembers the most.

And I can't stand another second in this house pretending I don't miss him. Pretending I don't understand what today is or how important it should be.

My sudden jump from the couch jostles Cali and her eyes crinkle at the corners.

"Are you OK?"

No, I want to scream. *I'm not. None of us should be.*

"I'm fine," I say instead. "I'm going for a run."

I don't wait on a reply as I grab my headphones off the entryway table.

I don't even answer my mom when she pops her head out of the shed door to ask where I'm off to once I'm outside.

I take off in a dead sprint with no idea of where I'm headed. Two minutes into the run is all it takes for me to know which way I want to go.

There's only one spot   I *could* go right now.

My lungs scorch with every breath that fills them. The adrenaline coursing through my veins barely dulls the aching stretch of my lengthened stride. I push my feet to go harder.

To move faster.

They comply and in 10 minutes I find myself doubled over and panting at my destination.

My knees give just in time and I drop to the ground below. The fresh cut grass sticks to my sweaty kneecaps and the summer breeze fills my senses. Luckily this place is empty of anyone who could catch a glimpse of my breakdown.

The tears brimming my eyes burn worse than my labored breathing but I don't even try wiping them away. It would be useless. I let them mix with the drops of sweat falling from my forehead as I stare blurry-eyed ahead.

My chest aches at the sight of the engraved words "Beloved father, husband, and friend." My head throbs when I look at the bright, fake flowers arranged on the sides of the tombstone. My pulse quickens when I finally let my eyes fall onto the background picture we'd had inscribed to the lump of cold stone.

There's my dad holding a child-sized Cali in one arm as Mia climbs on his back like a monkey. His other hand rests on my shaggy head as I stare up at him with a bucktoothed grin. As if he were the world's greatest hero to ever breathe. He smiles down at me, dimples deep in the sides of his cheeks.

The picture was taken days before Doctor Nelson gave us the news.

You have about 6 months, by my estimate.

The words haunt me still.

But dad pushed for us.

He pushed and pushed until his death sentence looked like it wouldn't come from cancer after all.

But everything in life has an end, I guess, because two years after his diagnosis he died.

That picture was the last time I remember him pre-cancer.

It was the last time I remember knowing my dad without his dark cloud hovering over him. The last time everything was normal and good and easy.

I don't try to stop the sob bubbling up inside.

I let it come up and break over the surface, shaking me to my

core until I'm sure I'll dry out for good this time.

Chapter Eighteen-Lyv

All my life I've been told I look just like my dad.

"She may have your quick wit, Ginny, but she's her father made over," people always say.

We couldn't go anywhere without someone telling me I look more and more like my dad as I get older, or act so much like my mom it's scary. As a kid I hated it.

I'm just me! I'd shout in my head over and over.

It was like, no matter where I went or what I did, I was compared to my parents. Then Max was born, and I was compared to him too. I couldn't just be Lyv with my own looks and my own personality and my own self.

But I'm older now.

Wiser.

More mature.

Knowing I have bits and pieces of my parents, knowing Max has bits and pieces of all of us, reassures me. I'm not alone. I'm not isolated. I'm the best and worst of them, but I'm part of something beyond just me.

It took years of experiences, sometimes awful, horrendous experiences, to appreciate that fact for what it is. But I finally got there.

It's what keeps me glued to my seat now, even after my dad's tenth Dad joke (and counting). Our matching hazel eyes meet across the patio table and his crinkle in the corners.

"No, but on a serious note," he dabs his napkin against the water forming underneath his red plastic cup. Father's Day is one of the few days of the year when you can get my parents, Max, and myself all in one spot. With just us four I feel like a kid again, gazing at my dad like he's hung the moon.

"On a serious note," he starts again, "I've started reading this book on anti-gravity recently and it's phenomenal."

My mom nods, completely hooked at the mention of anything astronomical. She begins piling up paper plates and burger-greased napkins but keeps up the conversation.

"That's sounds fascinating. Is it any good so far?"

While my mom is oblivious to the oncoming punch line, I catch Max's eye just as he snorts a preluding snicker before the line hits.

"Definitely. I can't seem to put it down."

Biting my lip does little to keep the smile off my face.

There's this world my dad lives in where nothing's ever really *that* bad or bleak. A world where everything has a chance of turning around for the good; where the sun always ends up shining again, eventually.

Then, of course, there's the world I know and see, where things are usually exactly as bad and bleak as they seem.

But sometimes, like now, it's still fun to jump into his world and laugh even when you know things can't and probably won't stay as bright as he paints it out to be. I laugh, despite myself, because in the end he tries so hard to keep us all happy—and he really can be funny sometimes.

My mom doesn't think so, however, and she rolls her eyes toward the bright sun above the back porch.

"Oh, honestly, Alan. Could you ease up on the corny jokes?"

"Never."

He glances my way and shoots a wink, giving me a small smile in the process. He looks at me with so much love, like no one else in the world could measure up to his little girl, and when he puts his arm around the back of my chair to pat my back I feel tears prick in the corners of my eyes.

I'm not that innocent little girl anymore, daddy. I think it but don't dare say it.

It'd be nice, really, if what we wished for always came true like it does in fairytales. If they did I'd wish for 10 years old when we had whiffle ball games in the backyard every Father's Day because it was dad's favorite and that was his one day to sucker us into it.

I'd wish for childhood and innocence and I'd never let it go.

Unfortunately that's not how life works.

And now I have to look away from his kind smile.

"Well, I think it's time for a swim, don't you?"

He moves from the table and completes a perfectly executed belly flop. The sound of skin cracking against water has me laughing before he's even been fully submerged by the water. I watch him come back up with his face scrunched, but can also feel eyes on me too.

Max has already followed dad to the pool, so that leaves only mom as the staring suspect. Sure enough, when I glance her way her twinkling eyes rest on my face. A serene smile washes over her. Her hands pause over the napkins she'd been using to clean up a stray ketchup spot on the patio table.

"What?" My cheeks heat from the attention.

She laughs lightly.

"I'm just happy to have you home," she whispers. "You made it through the year and I'm so proud of you. It reminds me of that bible verse your grandmother was always harping about, the one about leaves remaining. Oh, what was it?"

She taps her manicured nail against the table in thought.

"Jeremiah 17:8," I reply without hesitation.

I remember it clearly. We would go to church with Nana Buckley all the time as kids and Jeremiah 17:8 was her favorite verse. She'd talk about its symbolism and message of resilience in tough times. I didn't really understand her obsession with it, but it's been engrained in my head for   life nonetheless.

"That's the one," mom snaps her fingers and her smile grows. She reaches for my hand and holds it tightly. "You remind me of that verse. You've been through a tough semester but you came out on the other side still standing strong."

Her confidence in me is definitely one sided. I feel anything but resilient or strong. She couldn't be more wrong, and the realization only reminds me of just how broken down I still am even after all these years of trying to stand up under the weight of all these secret terrors I've faced in my life.

Terrors that no one knows of except for me and me alone.

My arms shove me upwards out of my chair and away from my mom's warm smile and gentle hand.

"I'm sorry, but that food really upset my stomach. I'll be back in just a minute."

I don't give my mom anytime to react before racing back into the house.

When I was younger I had these God-awful panic attacks. Sometimes they were so bad I wouldn't be able to move. I'd drop into the fetal position, chest heaving and mind spiraling. Panic attacks are worded so because the panic strikes like a cornered cobra, swift and stinging at a speed you couldn't possibly expect or outrun.

People don't tell you how the smallest of things—a crowded room, thoughts of future plans, memories from the past (good or bad)—can trigger anxiety.

My mom never knew how to handle my attacks, though she tried, so my dad was always the one to calm the storm. He would run to me, coaching me to breathe. In and out, in and out—over and over again he'd breathe with me, keeping me focused on the air circulating from my nose, through my lungs, then back out of my mouth.

But life changes and what used to pacify just doesn't anymore.

When that old familiar storm stirs in my chest I excuse myself, rushing to the bathroom before anyone can see me break.

I wish my dad could fix me like he did all those years ago.

I wish my parents could've protected me like they wanted.

I wish and wish but it's no use.

The panic still comes, even as I lock myself in the bathroom. The solid door holds me as I slide down it, staring at the bathtub Asher sat on just weeks ago.

Focus, I coach myself.

But my chest rises and falls in quick spurts. Images of childhood days with my parents and my brother flash through my mind and the panic only doubles. It only reminds me of days I can never get back.

My eyes slam shut so tightly I see stars.

Pick something else. Anything else.

My eyes drift back open, landing on that stupid, overly done bathtub again. I try to picture Asher sitting there like he did only a couple of weeks ago. He starts flashing through my mind like a slideshow. I see his watchful stare that first night of summer. That quickly morphs into his smile, so bright and genuine. I even think about the whole Daisy fiasco when I helped create his small injuries.

Like a dying engine, I feel the fright fall away little by little.

My legs shake as I stand slowly and saunter toward the double sinks. Looking in the mirror isn't the greatest idea I've ever had. Tears stream down my flaming cheeks and I splash cold water on my face.

Once I'm calmed down and back outside my mom has joined the guys in the pool.

"There she is," my dad floats on his back, rounded belly breaking above the surface.

Max cannonballs into the deep end and my mom cradles a float in her arms.

"Come on in," she beckons. "The water's great."

She smiles up at me while my dad squints into the sky.

"Actually, I really need to go pick up next week's schedule from Reggie."

I lie, knowing full well that Reggie is off today and wouldn't even have my schedule ready anyway. My mom frowns before I even finish the sentence.

"Well, hurry and you can get back in time to swim before we lose the sun."

I swallow the lump in my throat. Lying to my parents has never come easy, even now as an adult. It's never felt good and I venture to guess it never will.

273

"I was thinking I might walk. It's close enough and I need the exercise," my mom pushes her sunglasses on top of her head and wrinkles her forehead.

"If dad doesn't care," I add. "It's his day, so I don't want to spoil it."

I look away from my mom's hawk stare and to my dad still floating on his back.

"Go on, get out of here," he says with eyes closed and small smile in place. "I've been spoiled all I can handle for the day. Just be careful."

"Well, then, I'll get going."

I'm almost free but I hear my name just as I start to back away.

"Lyv," I turn back to my mom. "Is everything OK?"

"Everything's fine."

This lie tastes just as bitter as the first one.

But she says no more and frees me up with a simple nod.

I've no idea where I'm going when I leave the safety of my front yard.

All I know is I want to put distance between myself and my mom's questioning eyes. I take a left at the end of our street, then another right at the end of Berkeley Street. By the time I've stopped 15 minutes later I find myself staring at a graveyard.

More specifically, I see a vaguely familiar back hunched down in front of a tombstone two rows into the cemetery.

Slowly and quietly I lurk closer. The dark hair at the nape of the neck looks recognizable, then I see the black X tattoo on the back of his tanned bicep and I know it's Asher. I should be feeling anxious, considering I'd only been using him to come down from a panic attack 20 minutes ago.

But instead I feel guilty for intruding on such an obviously personal moment.

It's his dad's grave.

It has to be.

My stomach knots with regret at letting myself creep this close to him. Thoughts of our intimate conversation last night only tighten those knots.

Just as I back away a branch snaps beneath my feet, echoing far beyond the rows inside the cemetery. The sound reverberates against the surrounding trees and tombstones, bouncing back at me and ensuring I have no way of a quiet escape now.

"Lyv?"

I hate myself more and more once he turns around to look at me.

The shadows under his eyes are darker than usual and his brown irises sparkle with the remains of fresh tears. He lifts the bottom of his shirt to wipe away any snot that might be lingering at the base of his nose, but I'm locked in on his wounded eyes.

"What are you doing here?"

It's not cruel, the way he asks it, only genuinely confused at seeing me here, like two of his worlds have collided. The day his dad died, half the town showed up to the funeral. Mr. Brooks was a well-respected man in town, so everyone felt the blow.

Not as much as Asher and his family, of course. I still remember the way he held his shaking mom that day, stone face and solid, as if he were the parent instead of her.

When he speaks now it comes out deeper and more hoarse than I've ever heard. It's the voice of someone who's just let out a sea of emotions and I thank God I've only come up on the tail end of it.

"I was just going for a walk and somehow ended up here," I chew on my lip so hard it might start bleeding. "I didn't mean to disturb you. I was just going."

He moves quickly toward me with his arm outstretched, like it'll keep me in place.

"Don't go, please."

His chin quivers just barely. It's enough that if I'd blinked I would've missed it. But I saw and my heart clenches in my chest. He looks away for a few more breaths before looking back at me.

"I mean, I was just leaving anyway."

I shuffle from one foot to the other and watch as he carefully comes to stand next to me.

"I just had to get out of the house for a bit," his eyes stay glued to the broken up concrete a few inches in front of our feet. "But I don't really think I want to stay here any more either."

He doesn't say it outright, but I catch the hidden question there. I've been there before, wanted to get away from a certain place but had no idea where to go to get away from it.

In high school I felt that almost every day of my life. It's how I began to get into photography in the first place. I'd start walking, wandering around our little town until I found something worth getting lost in.

If it's an escape Asher needs, I know just where to go.

"C'mon."

With a surge of courage I lace my hand through his and gently pull him along side me.

"Where are we going?"

With this close proximity it's difficult to look him in the eye. I crane my neck just a bit to get a good look. His hair has grown since summer started but I don't mind the length. It hits now at his eyebrow line and he pushes it back so it's not so far in his eyes.

His sharp jaw line frames his clenching and unclenching jawbone.

And finally, I find myself staring into those notoriously dark, unblinking eyes of his. The left over tears are gone, but eyes still

278

sparkle in the sun with tiny specs of gold littered throughout the irises.

They search mine, questioning me.

"Do you trust me?"

"Yes."

There's no hesitation. No wavering to his answer.

He trusts me.

Even more surprisingly, I think I'm beginning to trust him too.

"We're going to get lost."

And he follows me without another word.

Chapter Nineteen-Asher

Flakes of rusted metal stick to my palms as I climb higher and higher. Apparently Lyv's idea of getting lost is climbing to the top of the old water tower on the edge of town.

I'm not necessarily afraid of heights, but the creaking of the worn-down ladder is an unsettling sound.

"Are you sure this is safe?" My voice wavers.

"Too late now, isn't it?" Lyv replies with a small laugh and continues to climb.

I pause, however, gazing out around me. I've stopped in the middle of the ladder and look up to see it shake with each step Lyv makes upward. It's the only motivation I need to keep going, to get off the ladder before it disintegrates beneath me.

The pine trees and bushes get smaller and smaller below until I'm at the top, a sea of green resting below us.

"Take a look," Lyv whispers.

I look, but not out at the skyline.

Her hands rest delicately on the brown and white rusting rail around us. The light breeze picks up strands of hair from her shoulders, tossing it back away from her face. She smiles into the horizon like it's some old friend and I don't think I've ever seen her so serene before.

So at peace.

"Beautiful," I breathe.

She only glances at me out of the corner of her eye with a small smile before taking a seat.

I follow, cautiously leaning back against the bowl of the water tower.

The scene in front of us can be described as nothing else but magical.

The sun just begins to set, painting the sky in orange and pink hues. Birds soar through clouds and trees' leaves rustle in the wind.

"This is heaven," I whisper and Lyv nods quietly.

Her voice comes out quiet, so quiet I almost don't hear her.

"When I'm feeling really anxious, I mean *really* anxious, I come up here and scream it   out."

Her admission surprises me, but when I look at her now, see the smirk that so rarely comes out on her, I am more than intrigued by the confession. She inhales deeply, pulling a breathe deep from her stomach, then lets it out in one loud, echoing yell.

Her "ahh" rebounds off the trees around us. Birds fly away from their perches near us.

I'm mesmerized.

She turns to me then with flushed cheeks and teary eyes.

With one small nod, she urges me to go now. To let all the anger and sadness fly out of me.

And when I bellow louder than I've ever done before, I feel it. I feel the tension leave my shoulders. I feel the knot loosen in my chest.

It all disappears with the wind.

"Feel better?" She whispers, but her full smile pulls me in and threatens to never let me go.

"Much better," I croak.

She leans back next to me with legs crossed in front of her. Mine dangle off the edge, but it's more freeing than I imagined it'd be.

"It's just so peaceful up here," she looks away from the skyline long enough to give me a full smile, bright teeth shining and all. "This is my escape spot. It's where I come to when everything down there is too much."

She focuses back on the ground and the smile fades slightly.

"Anyway," she continues and looks back up at the sky. "I thought maybe you could use it too."

I rest my head back, eyes closed and breathing slowed. I need it more than I even know. We sit in silence for what feels like forever.

No one speaks.

No one tries to break the silence.

It's comfortable and welcome.

My family problems feel small up here. They feel insignificant in a way I've never felt before. After so much time, who knows how much, I speak. Not because I feel like I have to, but because Lyv's made it feel so easy now.

"When my dad was diagnosed I didn't really believe it," I almost cut myself off when I feel Lyv's gaze turn towards me, but I can't stop now.

I have to say it out loud to someone.

"I felt like I was watching a movie or something. It couldn't be real, you know? It couldn't really be *my* dad. He's too strong for that, I thought."

The words tumble out despite the burning in my chest.

"Cancer definitely doesn't discriminate," Lyv quietly chimes in. She gives me a moment to try and cool the ache rising up.

When I finally muster up the nerve to look at her she has glassy eyes. I want to smooth the wrinkle between her brows. I want to lift her mouth out of the downward tilt it's taken on.

But I just keep talking.

"No, it doesn't. He lasted longer than they thought he would, though. I think it was out of sheer will power. He stayed until he knew we could handle life without him."

Lyv's frown deepens.

"What do you mean?"

I share something I've never shared with anyone then. Something I've locked inside the moment he died.

"That night, before he was gone, he called me into the bedroom. He died in our house, you know. A lot of people don't know that. He wanted to be home and not in a hospital his last days," I push through the break in my voice. "So that last night he made everyone get out of the room, everyone but me. At this point he'd already made it years past what they expected with cancer as advanced as his. He waved me toward him but I really didn't want to get too close. He looked so different that it kind of scared me."

At some point Lyv's hand slipped its way into mine and she gently squeezes it now, encouraging me to go on.

"He looked at me so serious, more serious than I'd ever seen him, and said 'it's your job to take care of them now. Promise me you'll take care of them.' I was a teenager at the time, so of course I promised. He died that next morning and I swear it's like my promise was the last thing he needed to hear before letting go."

Tears fall warmly down my cheeks but I leave them there.

"For years I was so pissed at him. How could he put that on a teenage kid? How could he ask that of me? But eventually I wasn't pissed at him as much as I was at myself. Because I feel like I have no idea what I'm doing here. I have no clue how to be the man I promised him I would be."

Lyv sniffs next to me but I keep my eyes on the sun, now just a half-circle against the horizon.

She clears her throat.

"I think you're every bit that man," she gently turns my chin so I have no choice but to look at her and hear her evenly spoken words. "You're that man, and so much more."

And when she says it that way, so sure and solid, I actually start to believe it.

Chapter Twenty-Lyv

Rain pelts my face as I lie on the cold ground. Puddles of water form around my eyes until they burn.

All around me is darkness.

There's so much darkness that I can't see my hand right in front of my face.

But what am I doing outside in the rain? Why am I here? Where is *here?*

Then a voice. Just one chilling voice.

"Don't back out on my now."

My body freezes in place. I'm paralyzed as footsteps come closer and closer.

"Those curls."

A hand runs through my soaked hair.

"Those lips."

Fingertips brush my trembling mouth.

No, no, no, I cry out to the air around me.

But it's no use.

Nothing can save me now.

Nothing can stop him as he moves closer until—

There in the distance I see Asher standing in the rain.

I sigh in relief.

Asher is here. Asher will stop this. He will protect me.

But when he moves closer to stand above me, he doesn't speak or pull me away from the nightmare controlling me. I thrash on the ground, calling Asher's name but he makes no move to show he even hears me crying out to him. His face is blank and emotionless and so unlike his usual joyful spirit as he stares down at me, my monster holding me down all the while.

But it doesn't matter that my captor has me in his clutches, because the cold, unaffected Asher standing above me hurts worse than my monster's grip on my arms.

My chest heaves up and down in heavy spurts and the vile beast pinning me goes in for the kill.

"Lyv, wake up!"

Someone shakes my body, rattling my mind until I realize it's not real. It's just a dream. A terrible, disgusting dream.

Max hovers above me with panic in his rounded eyes.

"Are you OK?"

His voice shakes.

I don't trust my own to stay steady so I nod through leaking tears. Max looks as if I'm a ticking time bomb, so I force words out past my burning throat.

"I'm fine," I croak. "It was just a bad dream."

Liar, I accuse myself.

Max's hands still cling to my shoulders. I'm convinced he'll keep them there if I don't physically remove them myself.

"You're sure? That was a pretty bad one."

I don't have the nightmares often, but enough for Max to know they exist. It's the same dream every time. The same memory, same moment in time my subconscious brings back up. But each time the memory adds a new detail, a new piece to the puzzle.

This time happened to be Asher, looking down at me as if he couldn't care less about what was happening. That was the worst of it all; the thought that Asher wouldn't care about what happened.

A little part of me begs to tell my brother everything. Just spill it all out so I'm not carrying this weight all on my own.

The bigger part of me   says keep quiet.

289

"I promise. Everything's good now. Thanks for waking me up."

He hesitates but eventually leaves me alone.

When the dreams started a few years ago I had a post-dream routine down to bring me back out of that nightmare state. First, I'd get a drink of water and walk the dream off as much as possible. Then, after I'd walked enough to tire out again, I'd go back to bed and sing a song in my mind—something long and soothing. I'd sing it over and over again until finally drifting back to a peaceful sleep.

But tonight the song doesn't work. Tonight I'm on round three of the melody and miles away from sleep.

It's like the dream knew my life is going good right now. It sensed the happiness brewing inside me and jumped back in front of me to remind me that, at the end of the day, my past will always be here to haunt me.

To strip away the hope that I so badly want to hold onto.

Out of desperation I grab my phone, hoping it can distract me even a little.

Two unexpected texts glare up at me in the darkness of my room.

I can't stop thinking about you.

It's Asher, by the way. Hope you don't mind I got your number from Tilly.

The time on the texts say he sent them a few hours ago, just after I'd fallen asleep. Right before the nightmare sunk its cold, sharp teeth in.

My heart soars at the contrast between this real-life Asher and the nightmare Asher. It's just after 1 in the morning and before I can talk myself out of it, I send back one quick text.

Are you awake?

A couple minutes pass where I wait for his reply. The screen tells me he's read the text and seconds later his name pops up.

I answer on the second ring.

"Were you asleep?" I ask as soon as I hit the green button.

"No, were you?" He laughs and it's rougher than usual. "That was dumb. Obviously you weren't since you texted me."

A giddy feeling rises; both because of the obvious sleep sound still resting in his voice and at the image of him choosing to call me despite his sleepy state.

"Sorry for calling so late," I whisper through the darkness surrounding me in the night creeping into my bedroom. "I just couldn't sleep."

"Me either. Not very well, anyway."

We keep talking until slowly but surely a smile creeps its way in, despite it all.

And in the end it's not a song that calms me back to sleep, but instead a vision of Asher's sleepy smile and unruly hair on the other end of the phone call.

"Another coffee, dear?" Charlotte comes by my table a third time, coffee pot in hand.

"That'd be great, thank you," I hold my cup up for her and she fills it to the brim.

Eddie's Diner has been around since I can remember, and Charlotte along with it. She's the only 70-year-old I know who can still carry an entire tray full of hot, steaming food with complete grace.

Up until this past year I only came into *Eddie's* with my family for dinner or those legendary milkshakes that melt in your mouth.

But junior year is rough and those milkshakes are a drug that keeps me going.

No one really tells you just how bad junior year can be.

It's the year of ACT testing, of the long awaited prom privilege, getting your license, and looking ahead to colleges you want.

That's a lot of pressure to put on a 17-year-old's shoulders.

But here I am at *Ernie's* studying for the math portion of my ACT because it's a Sunday and mom's doing her "Zumba Sunday Funday" session in our living room. Ten middle-aged women dancing to "Despactio" in spandex is something I'd rather not see so early in my day. Or at any time of day, really.

It's just past noon and the lunch flow picks up, but I carry on in my corner booth with my headphones tucked in my ears. Charlotte's general rule is I can stay as long as I need to so long as I stay in the back and out of customer traffic.

I try to focus on studying but Lyv's sweat-soaked, thrashing body from last night distracts me.

That focus, or lack of it, is interrupted when someone pulls one of my ear buds out in that way that makes you want to throw something. I'm only more annoyed when I see Tilly standing above me, ear bud still in her hand.

"That's a good way to lose a hand," I snatch my headphones out of her hand but she only laughs and slides in the booth seat across from me.

"Nah, you're all bark and no bite, Maxine."

294

She steals a fry off my plate and smirks at my annoyance.

Annoyance at the dumb nickname, annoyance at ACT prep, annoyance at feeling like Lyv straight up lied to me about her nightmare.

And now, annoyance at Tilly stealing multiple fries from my plate.

"You do know this is a restaurant, right? You can order your own food.

Her eyes widen and my cheeks flush in embarrassment at my obvious overreaction.

"What's with you?"

I flip the ACT study textbook over so she sees the cover and she lets out a slow "ahh".

"The ACT. That's a bummer," she eyes my plate but doesn't take anything. "But it's summer. Why are you studying for the ACT in summer? You won't even take that until the end of the school year."

I close the book entirely and shove it to the side, knocking a ketchup bottle over in the process. If I had the choice I'd burn the book entirely.

"Because my dad's been kind enough to sign me up for an early practice test to see what I need to work on most this year."

A bitter taste fills my mouth.

"'Pass the ACT and you get to college,'" I put on my best imitation of him, deepening my voice as much as possible. "'Get to college and you get football at the next level. After that, who knows what could happen!'"

I stuff the last fry into my mouth harshly.

"Lyv had it easy with dad. He always treated her like a little princess. She never had to deal with the hovering dad I've had to deal with."

Tilly's faux pout only reiterates the fact that I'm whining like a baby.

"You're right, she didn't have to deal with the hovering dad. But she did get the hovering mom, which in its own way is worse."

By this time Charlotte spots Tilly and makes her way back to the booth.

"Hi dear, what can I get for you?"

She flips her order booklet out and pulls the pen from behind her ear.

"I have an order to go for "Tilly". I just ordered it a few minutes ago, though, so it's probably not out yet."

"I'll go check and be right back," Charlotte leaves with a smile.

"Speaking of Lyv—," I start but Tilly interrupts me.

"Her and Asher? Match made in heaven, right?"

One thing that's always awkward for me is relationship talk about my sister. No matter how old I am or how old Lyv is, talking about her flings with other people is uncomfortable.

Though, to be fair, she hasn't really given me too many chances to be uncomfortable, considering she's only dated a few guys over the years.

Tilly winks, despite my scrunched forehead.

"That's not at all where I was going," she shrugs and waits for me to get to the point. "Lyv had a nightmare last night, and I think she lied to me about the whole thing."

Tilly's brow furrows as she chews on her fingernail.

"Strange. She hasn't had one in, like, almost two years, right?"

When Lyv was in high school she started having bad dreams occasionally. Not all the time, but enough that mom tried to take her to see someone about it. Lyv refused, of course.

I nod.

"What makes you think she lied about it?"

I take a minute to think about my response. If I'm not careful, I'll sound just as overdramatic as I was about the headphones or fries earlier. This isn't something I want to describe wrong.

"I don't know how to explain it exactly, but it just felt different last night. She seemed more shaken up with this one than the others. She was screaming and literally shaking in her bed. When I woke her up she looked like she was ready to hit me or something with this crazed look in her eye."

A million emotions cross Tilly's face in just a few short seconds. Her creased forehead straightens out as she leans forward to rest her elbows on the table. She taps what remains of her chewed nails against the table and stares out the window next to us. Finally, she focuses back on me with worried eyes.

"What do you think it was about? Did she say?"

Her questions come in waves but I catch each one easily. I've already run through all of them and more in my head by now.

"When I asked about it she said it was nothing, just a bad dream. But it didn't look that way. Whatever she was dreaming about looked like she thought it was real. Regardless, she screamed loud enough to wake me from a dead sleep."

Tilly's jaw drops open.

"You're serious?"

It's rhetorical, but I still come back with, "Why would I lie about that?"

I shake my head at her with the same squinted eyes from earlier. "All I know is, I ran in thinking someone was mugging her only to find her tangled up in her sheets screaming no over and over again."

There's one more part, and I almost hold it back, but curiosity gets the better of me.

"Do you know someone named Jackson? I'm racking my brain but can't think of anyone."

The seemingly change in direction makes her hesitate.

"I know one Jackson," Tilly says. "Mason's cousin. Why?"

Her face twists and she leans forward, even more interested than before.

"She kept mumbling that name. That's weird, right? I'm not just overreacting about it?"

Please tell me I'm overreacting, I silently plead.

Because I'm putting two and two together here and Lyv screaming no to a guy named Jackson in her nightmare has me picturing the worst-case scenario.

I need someone to tell me everything's fine.

"No, that's definitely weird."

My last shred of hope goes up in flames.

Charlotte comes back to let Tilly know she has another five minutes on her food and I order a chocolate milkshake while she's here. She leaves us again to go back to the dreadful mystery in front of us.

"Would Lyv have met him before? Jackson, I mean," I rip through the empty straw wrapper Charlotte already left behind until there are only tiny paper squares left. "I've never even heard of him before."

"You wouldn't have. He's only been here once and that was a few years ago when you were still in middle school," she picks up the paper squares and rips them into even tinier pieces. "If I remember right him and Lyv hung out a few times that summer, but not a lot that I can remember. He left right before we were supposed to go back to school, so nothing came of it."

A few minutes later Charlotte places a tall glass of chocolate milkshake in front of me.

"You don't think—" I start the question but can't finish it. If I finish it, if I put that worst-case scenario out there in the air, then it actually has the potential to be real.

"No way," Tilly jumps in, not needing me to finish in order to know where I was headed. "She would've told me. Maybe it was all just a random coincidence."

But even as she says it, I see the doubt on her face and hear the uncertainty in her voice.

Still, my hope clings to her tentative words.

Maybe it is all just random.

Lyv's bad night could be exactly that—a bad night.

Nothing more and   nothing less.

I'm beginning to think studying for the ACT sounds like less of a headache than this conversation.

Thank God for Charlotte, because at that moment she comes up with two heaping bags of fried food. A grease spot pools at the bottom of the bags as Tilly grabs them before standing.

"Here you are, sweetie. You have a good day."

Charlotte leaves with a smile but Tilly hovers at the table.

"That's my cue. Good luck with all that studying," she nods toward my discarded textbook. "And remember, you don't know the full story. Don't jump to conclusions just yet."

She waves a paper bag of food at me in goodbye and walks away.

Her advice goes perfectly with my plan to stay out of Lyv's nightmares, but I still find myself dumping my notebook and textbook into the backpack at my feet.

I take one long slurp out of the extremely delicious milkshake and pray the chocolaty goodness can distract me from my worries.

Chapter Twenty Two-Asher

The night of the water tower I thought I'd go insane with thoughts of Lyv.

She was all in my head and in the stirring in my chest. She made talking about my dad feel so normal.

Less painful.

More free.

I can't help but wonder what I would've been like all those years ago if we'd actually talked then. I imagine how much easier it all would've been if I'd opened my eyes and saw Lyv when she was actually right there in front of me instead of just seeing her as a familiar stranger.

My fingers hovered over the keys of my phone for hours after getting home from the water tower. I debated whether to go for it or not; whether I should put the truth out there or just leave it. If it weren't for the tossing and turning, leading to a sleepless night I may have chickened out.

But I couldn't sleep, so   what else was there to do?

I told her honestly that she's all I've thought about and now here we are, two days later and about to go out to eat—as a group.

It'll be just about everyone from Mason's party crowd, but I still go about getting ready as if it's just Lyv and myself.

And then of course there are my two terror sisters to take into consideration. They pestered me enough until finally I mustered up the strength to actually text Lyv and now they coerce me into looking my absolute best tonight.

Even if it is just a group outing.

My heartbeat won't slow down and I'm sweating buckets, no matter how much deodorant I put on.

It'll be the first time I see her in person since my little late-night confession—and of course I can't pick a decent-looking outfit.

"No, the army green tank top wins for sure," Mia tosses the shirt from my closet towards my chest and I grab it before it hits my bedroom floor.

After struggling to find something to wear on my own I roped Mia and Cali into helping. An hour later I'm regretting my decision.

"You can't be serious," Cali scoffs. "That shirt has holes in it, Mia. He can't show up on a date with *holes* in his shirt. Go with the yellow one, Ash."

Cali hands me her choice of shirts, which is a yellow cotton one with a solid, black stripe across the chest. Meanwhile, Mia rolls her eyes and I flop back onto my bed, already tired of their bickering.

"It's not a date," I remind them, but I'm basically talking to myself.

"It's supposed to have holes in it. It was made that way," her voice goes high and she twists her face up as if Cali were the dumbest person she's ever met. "Besides, it's a tank top and shows off his muscles."

She turns to me.

"Wear the tank top, Ash. You'll thank me for it. I swear."

She winks and Cali mumbles a defeated "whatever" as I grab the shirt back from Mia's hands. She gives a "ha" Cali's way and crosses her arms triumphantly.

"Now get out. I only have 10 minutes to get changed."

They both scurry from the room giggling and leave me alone with my nerves. I do all the last minute checks.

Deodorant (again).

Cologne spray.

Fingers through my hair.

With one last look in the mirror I see Mia's point. The tank top shows off the arms I've been working so hard on this year, but the holes *are* a bit much and I'm starting to wonder why I ever bought this in the first place.

I walk down the stairs a couple minutes after I'd planned. Only one sister is to be found on my way out. I give a quick wave and smirk as she grins brightly at my last-minute outfit change. She eyes it with a nod of approval.

"Good choice," Cali says. "And good luck."

My stomach flips.

I'm thinking I'll need every ounce of that I can get tonight.

***

There are only a few times in my life I've ever been breathless.

There was that one time in the seventh grade when I ran cross-country and attempted to place first in the entire event. I did it, but crossed the finish line feeling like I had zero oxygen left in my body.

Then there was this family vacation years ago when I was just 12. We went to Busch Gardens and my dad and I thought I could handle the 90-degree drop on the 200-foot tall Sheikra rollercoaster ride. My inability to breathe the entire way down the drop said otherwise.

But right now seeing Lyv stand in her doorway—my breath vanishes altogether.

I happily volunteered to pick her up on the way to the restaurant and I told myself over and over again that this was not a date the whole way to her house.

Her hair falls like a curtain over her shoulders. She's tucked her black tank top into those notorious high-waist shorts of hers that fit so well. The white, rolled up cardigan contrasts with her dark hair.

I have to remind myself to breathe.

To speak.

307

To do or say *anything*.

"Wow, Lyv. You're stunning."

"Thank you," she blushes and I don't think she could get any more adorable.

"Are you ready to go?"

She nods just as Max pops around the door.

"Have her home by nine and not a second later. You hear me, boy?"

He points at me around a half-eaten apple and gives me a mock-stern face.

Though, somewhere just beneath the surface I get the feeling he's a little more serious than he's letting on. There's a brotherly warning there in the harshness of his eyes.

I've given it myself a dozen times to any guy that comes near my sisters.

"Seriously Max? Go away. It's not a date," Lyv shoves him back so she can shut the door.

The comment stings just a little.

"Behave kids!" Max gets out just before the door slams in his face.

"Sorry about him," she scratches absentmindedly at her shoulder with a small smile playing on her lips.

"No worries," I laugh. "He's not a good brother if he's not trying to embarrass you."

She scoffs.

"Then he's the best."

I open the passenger door of the jeep and she climbs in. I have to admit, I'm bummed she doesn't slide into the middle seat like last time.

"So who all is coming?"

She asks as soon as I'm in the driver's seat.

Those hazel eyes point my way and I really wish it was just us two going.

"The usual, I think. Us, Mase and Tilly, and then Emily is coming with her friends we met the other night."

The car ride is mostly silent. Lyv stares out the window thoughtfully. Her bottom lip tucks under her teeth and she squints at the objects passing by.

I try my best to keep the glances to a bare minimum but I'm failing miserably.

"So, have you taken many pictures since you've been home?"

She turns her eyes toward the windshield and sighs.

"Unfortunately no. I need to, though, because I have a big project due the first month we go back to school."

"That's got to suck. What's the project for?"

"It's a program entry project for the university's photography program. We have to come up with some central theme and turn in a portfolio of photos to sort of try out for the program."

Lyv turns toward me then, positioning her leg so that her knee is bent in the seat next to me. Her kneecap brushes my thigh but she's so focused on her project now that she doesn't even notice.

"Problem is," she continues, "I have absolutely no idea what to use as my theme. No clue at all. Well, except that I want it to deal with people. But that's pretty vague."

Growing up I never noticed Lyv to be much of a talker. That was always Tilly's forte, but this summer I've been proven wrong. Lyv talks, but only when she's passionate about something.

I shouldn't be surprised.

Lyv is exactly the kind of person to only use her voice for things she deems worthy of it.

"What about home? You could take shots of landmarks around here, or something like that."

She hums curiously.

"Maybe," she faces the window again. "I don't know. I guess I've got a little more time to think about it."

And then all is quiet again.

"What about you?" I jump at the sudden sound of Lyv's voice after minutes of silence.

"What about me?"

I sneak another glance.

"Anything exciting happening this summer? Any passions you've had time to do, besides running?"

She smirks.

The image of her bandaging me up replays vividly in my mind and there's no stopping my smile that reaches from cheek to cheek.

"There's been loads of running, yes." I laugh. "But also a little bit of writing. I work for the school newspaper so I've been writing on their summer edition."

She nods.

"Impressive. Does a summer issue of a college newspaper get much traffic?"

"A little, but not much. Mostly it's just for the online platform."

"Is that the kind of writing you want to do when you graduate?"

It's a thought I've had multiple times. The idea of writing at a newspaper for the rest of my life is pretty boring, but it's the most plausible way to write for a living.

"Maybe, but I'm leaning toward no."

I look over and her eyebrows are practically in her hairline.

She waves her hand, ushering me to explain more.

"I don't know. It's just kind of boring already and I've only been into it for a couple of years. I love writing though, so I don't really want to give it up. I like writing for me, like fiction, you know? But that sounds crazy to say it out loud."

My cheeks burn and I silently beg the driver in front of us to speed it up so we can get to the restaurant and away from this embarrassment. I've never talked this much about my writing to anyone. It's unnerving and freeing all at once.

I give up all pretense of trying to keep from looking at Lyv at this point.

What I find when I turn my attention to her can be described as nothing short of angelic. Her cheeks glow and her smile reaches all the way to her eyes.

"I don't think that's crazy at all."

I try not to focus on the complete contact she makes with me. Or let my eyes linger on the full curve of her smiling lips. I try to push my eyes away from the pulse I can see thumping at the base of her throat.

As I try all these impossible tasks, Lyv turns her glittering eyes back to the windshield, leaving me in a struggle to breathe— and that's when I realize this is Lyv's game and I'm perfectly OK with losing it.

By some strange twist of fate I find myself at dinner sitting right next to Asher, which after our drive here I wouldn't mind as much—if Jenna with the lavender hair weren't sitting on the other side of me.

I'm not sure why she was invited, but after Asher's obvious lack of interest I'm not so worried about her presence, just mildly irritated by it.

After my recollecting nightmare a few nights ago, it doesn't take much to get me even slightly irritated.

"So, do people ever call you Ash or is it always just Asher?"

Jenna leans across me, almost pushing my menu out of the way to talk to Asher just to my right. Across the table I catch Tilly eyeing me over the rim of her cup. Her dark eyes move from me to Jenna where she shoots daggers with each sip of her water.

If Jenna notices Tilly's glare or my pull away from her she shows no obvious sign of it. Instead she only leans closer into me to get closer to Asher.

He clears his throat and taps his wrapped up silverware against the table.

"My family does, but that's about it other than really close friends."

"Well, I think Ash suits you perfectly."

She leans her elbow on the table and smiles while Asher's leg bobs up and down under the table, hitting me with each movement. Everyone else at the table is engaged in their own conversations. Tilly and Mason now chat with Sean and Alice, who apparently have went out a couple of times since meeting at Mason's party a few weeks back.

But my focus remains on Asher; on his clenched jaw and shaking leg and the poor girl next to me who's missing all the signs screaming at her to stop trying.

"I don't know," I jump in. "You look more like a Carl to me. Or maybe a Phillip."

Jenna gives me a side eye as if she's just remembered I'm sitting there between them. She half rolls her eyes and turns away, back toward Alice on the other side of her.

When I look back at   Asher my palms clam up.

His smile reaches just one corner of his perfect mouth and the restaurant lights shine in his typically dark eyes.

He stretches his arm to rest on the back of my chair, eye contact never broken.

"Thanks for the save."

He whispers with a hint of a laugh.

"Anytime."

Hopefully my obsessive drinking from my cup distracts him from my fumbling voice.

Friendly banter leads us to plans for the rest of the summer.

For the most part, I fade in and out with the conversation. Random sentences catch my ear here or there, but I struggle to put the image of that dark night I'd dreamed about out of my head. I fight against the ghostly feeling of the rain crashing down on my skin and have to remind myself I am not there.

I'm not in that moment anymore, but instead I'm in this moment surrounded *mostly* by people I love, people who love me back.

Somehow the conversation leads to a timeline of just how little time we have left before everyone goes back to their usual, post-summer lives. It's Ellie who finally suggests we all go mini golfing "immediately."

"We can't waste a single second of summer," she chimes.

"Hear, hear!" Tilly raises her cup and the rest of the table follows.

We clink plastic glasses together before paying and venturing out to vehicles.

"I'll ride with Ash!"

Jenna skips toward Asher with a perfectly white smile in place but he quickly tosses up an excuse.

"Oh, actually I told Lyv she could right with me, right Lyv?"

His eyes widen as Tilly gives me a slight push in his direction.

"I remember you saying that," Ellie chimes. I roll my eyes at the three of them. "Something about putting the top down or something like that?"

Her cheeks flush and she bites down on her terribly executed lie.

"Whatever," Jenna scoffs. "I'll just ride with Em."

She calls for Emily to wait on her and jogs toward the car.

"You're welcome," Ellie sings.

Then it's just me and Asher walking toward his jeep.

"You know you have to put the top down now, right?"

He shrugs with a lopsided grin.

"That's better than the alternative."

I'd always imagined riding with the top down on a vehicle would be a nightmare, what with the hair blowing all over and the possibility of bugs getting in my face.

But it's actually really nice.

Once we get going toward Suzy's Mini Golf (Colorado's finest, according to their sign), I drop my head against the headrest and let my eyes drift shut. The wind blown hair is easier to control once I ball it up and push it between my head and the headrest.

My hand glides in the wind, reminding me of that scene in "The Watson's Go to Birmingham" that we read in sixth grade. I think of brushing my hand through God's beard like Kenny. I didn't understand it then, but I get it now, that feeling of the air drifting between your fingers with the peaceful breeze.

My smile is overwhelming when I glance up at the clouds passing above us.

It's all enough to temporarily vanquish the memories that have been gnawing their way back into my mind over the last few weeks.

"You should put the top down all the time," I half shout above the sound of the wind and when I tilt my head over to look at Asher, he's already looking at me.

Maybe has been for some time now, who knows.

But when the blush creeps up across his cheeks I surge with confidence. It disappears quickly, since Asher Brooks is not the kind of person to be easily embarrassed, but I bask in the fact that I'm the one to get his pulse pumping.

I watch him a little longer than I probably should.

One hand clutches the top of the steering wheel while the other rests lazily on the gearshift between us. He's slouched, but just slightly so that he leans a little toward the center of the jeep.

There's some untapped beauty in the way his jawline clenches and unclenches as he maneuvers around the curved road ahead of us. In the way his veins snake out underneath his already sun kissed arm outstretched toward the wheel. His eyes stay locked ahead but after a few seconds too long of me gawking, the corner of his mouth turns up.

It's that slow smirk that sends me reeling. Now it's *my* face burning with embarrassment.

"Looks like we're here."

He breaks the now-awkward silence as we pull into a giant parking lot half filled up. Once we're all into the mini-golf complex, we split up into makeshift teams to avoid such a large group playing one game.

The only team I'm really focused on is mine, which consists of Max, Ellie, Asher, and me.

I haven't been on a technical date since I was with Connor, so I don't know how to act on what feels like this double date.

"Alright," Max claps his hands together. "Let's do this."

Our little group follows behind him.

"I have to warn you guys," I say as I put my bright pink golf ball onto the Hole One green. "I'm a pro at putt-putt."

And because I believe actions speak louder than words, mixed with a new sense of confidence around Asher, I hit the ball in with just one swing.

"She's just showing off, aren't you Lyvie?"

Max winks and my hand twitches against the golf club that I could easily throw at him.

But there's no need, because after the first hole Max and Ellie fall behind, basically making it a game of just Asher and me.

By hole eight I know I've been hustled.

The game started out as an obvious blow out against Asher but shockingly turns around on me. The rest of the game goes with Asher hitting his golf ball in with two shots or less. I'm still shocked an hour after the game's ended.

What's even more surprising than that is the fact that Asher asked me to get ice cream before taking me home—and I actually said yes.

Still not a date, I remind myself.

"I thought I had you! You played me," I point my spoon at him as we walk down Agnes Lake Pier, cups of ice cream in hand.

It's not much of a pier, really, just about 500 feet down the town's biggest lake. But, with the sun setting behind the trees, shades of orange and red reflect onto the rippling water and I see the allure.

"You are the last person I would ever play," Asher smiles around the spoonful of Rocky Road but I'm too scared to trust his words just yet.

"I almost had you though," I try to lighten the mood to ease the overdrive in my chest.

He's always doing that, catching me off guard with his intense words and praises. He's more in tune with his feelings than any other man I've ever met.

I don't know how to react to that.

We reach the end of the pier and Asher takes both of our empty cups to dump them in the trashcan. He comes back to my side, leaning against the wooden railing next to us.

"Did you know I almost asked you out, back at college this year?"

If I'd been eating my ice cream still, I'd probably have choked on it. Instead I gulp down a gust of air at this new revelation.

Asher peers out at the lake and keeps talking.

"I'd been thinking about it for months but never had the nerve," he laughs to himself and leans slightly over the railing, cheeks growing pinker and pinker.

"Why didn't you?" I croak.

He looks at me then with the smallest smile.

"Someone beat me to it," he shakes his head. "That night I thought to myself, tonight's the night. If I wait another second I'll go mad—and then that guy, the one with the blonde, spiked hair, he walked up to you, said something, and you laughed. That's when I knew it was over. Because I'd only seen you laugh a handful of times, so for this guy to get one out of you meant I'd missed my chance."

My heart beats wildly in my chest.

"I hated him and respected him all at the same time. It's like, hats off to him for being able to make you happy, even for a minute, but also screw him for taking my chance away, ya know?"

Funny thing was, I did know exactly what he meant.

Oh, how different life would've been had he beat Connor to the punch. Maybe I'd have actually let someone in. Maybe I'd have been more comfortable with myself and laughed a little more. Smiled a little more.

Or maybe I would've pushed him away then, just like I did Connor, and we'd never be where we are right now.

The pressure of his words threatens to weigh me down. Hastily I find someway to throw some comic relief into the situation.

"Well, tonight you had me laughing for sure at that mini golf. I still say I would've had you in two more rounds though," I raise my eyebrows in a challenge.

"Two more rounds and I would've smoked you even more than I already did."

He smirks, inching closer until I can feel his cool breath brush across my face. Once again I find myself questioning how I could've possibly gotten to this point with him. One minute we're at dinner with our friends then the next we're face to face, fighting against the undercurrent of tension coursing between us.

Unlike last time when we were this close by the pool, I have space to move away if I want to.

But I don't.

I'm not sure who's more taken by aback by it, Asher or me.

I gnaw on my lip and feel my pulse jumping frantically at the center of my throat. Finally I look up to see that heavy gaze unceasing in my direction.

"But we can rematch if you want," closer and closer he gets. Slowly, like he's waiting for me to back away—waiting for me to stop him.

I do neither.

"That is, if you're up for it."

My eyes drop from his. The dice tattoo on his hand is suddenly fascinating to look at.

"Like a date?" I whisper.

My soft laugh distracts me from the pounding in my chest. I swear I can feel it all the way up to my ears. Surely he can hear it by now.

I can't bring myself to completely hope for the response I want.

Because if I hope in Asher that means I have to trust him, and if I trust him, that means I have to be vulnerable with him.

I'm not entirely sure I'm ready to be vulnerable again with anyone just yet.

He takes so long to answer that I finally look back up. His smile is so soft, so pure, that nothing in this world could taint it. He's unlike anyone I've known.

That much I'm sure of.

"I think I'm ready for a real date," he takes one last step closer.

"And a second," he leans in slowly.

"And a third," he whispers.

"And a fourth," he mumbles before completely closing the gap between us.

I've kissed a few guys before. Some I try not to remember, like Dennis Cooper from 4th grade. Others I've blocked from my memory entirely. Then there's some that were just OK, like Connor.

With Connor everything was safe and sound. I never got chills when he looked at me or felt butterflies when his skin brushed mine. He was a safe space I could lean on at a time when I didn't want to let my guard down.

But this feels different. This feels new and risky.

It's a slow kiss, sultry and sensitive.

I've never felt a kiss all the way down to my toes, or felt it ignite every cell of my body.

He's hesitant at first, or maybe that's me, but after a few seconds I take a leap of faith and respond to him against me.

Asher gently cradles my face so tenderly that I almost don't realize his hands are there. He fills me up and I drink him in, fitting to him like a mold.

When we finally come up for air he holds me in place, touching his forehead to mine and grinning like a mad man.

"You have me, Lyv McDowell. Hook, line, and sinker."

My eyes stay closed. If I open them now it might all disappear or turn out less perfect than it feels. But I at least let a small smile loose so he knows I feel it too.

Despite my every intention not to, I feel him creeping into my every thought and emotion.

He doesn't wait for me to respond, which is all the better. I don't trust my voice right now anyway. Instead he grins stupidly at the ground as we start back the way we came, gently rubbing his bottom lip like it'll keep our kiss locked in place.

We walk back to his jeep, not holding hands but arms still brushing all the same.

The air blows through my hair the whole way home. I keep my eyes happily on the sky above me. My hand swims through the breeze.

And I try ignoring the ugly monster budding its head up in the back of my mind, reminding me I've been in this similar predicament before.

He whispered sweet nothings too, remember? The monster taunts.

But that was a different person from a lifetime ago.

I was a different person then.

And Asher is not that guy.

"I just don't understand why *I* have to go, Mom. Why can't you go? Or, here's a thought, why can't her actual maid of honor go?"

I can think of a million other things I'd rather be doing on my lunch break than arguing with my mom over the phone about my sister. Like stand in the middle of traffic, pluck my eyebrows with dull tweezers, watch paint dry—literally anything.

But argue about going with Mona to pick up her wedding dress? That's at the bottom of the list. Scratch that. It doesn't even make the list, period.

"Not that again," I can practically hear Mom's eyes rolling around in her head. "So your sister didn't choose you to be her maid of honor. The world keeps spinning, Matilda."

I hate when she full name-drops on me.

"Besides," she continues, "she's choosing you now to go with her to this significant milestone in the wedding process. So you're going."

She uses that no-nonsense tone I loathe. It leaves no room for anymore arguing. No room for a last word. It means what she says is the final word and, as much as I don't want to, I know I'll do what she says.

Growing up with a single parent means she's taken on the role of two parents in one. That's double the authority in one tiny, fiery woman.

I've learned when to pick my battles and this isn't one I'm going to win.

"Fine," I sulk, throwing my banana peel into the trash on my way out of the break room. "But I go under protest."

She sighs.

"I'd be more surprised if you went any other way. I love you, have a good rest of your shift."

As if I could possibly have a good day after this phone call.

She makes a smooching sound to signal her goodbye and hangs up before I have a chance to add any other complaints.

Once I'm back outside I watch Asher blow the whistle at two kids dunking each other under the water. I sigh with zero hope for the day to turn around. Even Asher, with his quick humor and bright smile, can't pick this day up. He's easily the best coworker to share a shift with, but today even he can't fix my mood.

"So, anything you can share to lift spirits? I'm in serious need."

I lean against the lifeguard chair as Asher gazes out at the pool below.

"Well, since you ask," he smirks in that way that makes the girls weak in the knees. I'm madly in love with Mason, don't get me wrong, and I'd never give him up for anyone or thing. But I'm not blind either.

"Last weekend went great."

Last weekend? Am I supposed to know what that means? I was there last weekend and it was fun having everyone together, but I don't know about great.

"Lyv and I went to the pier for some ice cream after mini golf."

He scratches the back of his neck in a rare show of nerves.

"That's amazing! I had no idea"

I reach out and swat his leg excitedly.

He smiles around another whistle blow at a little girl running toward the diving board.

She giggles then speed walks to her friends all lined up and watching Asher like little schoolgirls. There's always that one group that comes just for him; his faithful groupies, though he never seems to notice.

He never seems to notice just how many people stop and stare when he's around, which is one of many things him and Lyv have in common.

He drops the whistle back to his chest to show all those perfect white teeth.

"It was amazing," he's completely incapable of keeping the grin off his face and the excitement out of his voice.

His joy is contagious and for a moment there I forget about Mona's stupid wedding-dress shopping. I've known Asher for years, as long as I've known Mason, and this is the first time I've seen him get this worked up over someone.

He's not the kind to screw around and leave a girl after. He's picky about who he sees and, up until this point, has yet to really show any real significant interest in someone (even with Becky Hampton).

But, if anyone can meet his incredibly high standards, it would be Lyv.

"Tell me more," I know I should be asking my best friend about all the little details, but I need the pick me up now rather than later.

And so he spills it all.

He tells me about their mini-golf game and how "adorably competitive" she is. He tells me about her surprise when she figured out he'd been hustling her the whole game so she wouldn't lose too bad, then about how she'd gotten frustrated because she didn't want him to take it easy on her. Then, to my surprise, he vaguely tells me about their kiss at the pier.

I rack my brain wondering why I've never thought of matching them up before now. Clearly the chemistry between the two is insatiable, no matter how much Lyv tries to fight it, yet it's taken this long for anyone to really see it.

"I swear, a wall came down, Tilly. I saw it. Something got through to her and she wasn't as guarded—as cautious," he stares off into nothing and I know he's miles away from here.

"I'm going to break through them all," he looks at me straight in the eyes then and his honesty makes my heart race for Lyv.

***

Asher's words stay with me days after he speaks them. Words about Lyv's walls and her caution and guarded eyes.

It's all too familiar, like they're recurring when it comes to her. They're the same kinds of words Max used in the diner that day, and even some I've come to use when describing her myself.

Thinking about Lyv and Asher and just about anyone, really, takes my mind off me now sitting shotgun with Mona on our way to pick up her wedding dress. Somehow we've made it to the end of June already and Mona insisted we pick the dress up now, even though we have until the middle of August until the wedding hits.

The store for her final fitting is in the same town as my university, CU Denver, which explains the real reason Mona wanted me to come along.

Basically I'm the tour guide.

I watch trees zoom by while Mona hums along to her wedding playlist. She explains each song's place in the wedding, telling me which will play during what part of the ceremony, but I tuned her out about 20 miles ago.

My mind travels instead back to Lyv.

She's been haunting my thoughts ever since that stupid talk with Max.

Lyv wasn't always so closed off, and to be honest I can't pinpoint the exact moment it all changed. Sometime just before college, I think, when we were still in high school. It's like one day she was spontaneous and ready for whatever I dragged her into, then the next day she just wasn't.

No explanation. No reason for the change in heart about everything around her.

She started questioning where we'd go and who we'd be hanging out with. Instead of her willingly charging into social events with a smile on her face, I had to beg her to come out with a grimace. It was strange, but I didn't know how to fix it because I didn't really understand what *it* was.

All I knew was she started acting more isolated.

335

When asked about it she always replied the same way, "I'm fine."

Lyv's been my best friend since preschool. I know her better than anyone in the world, and not to be able to help her out of her funk crushed me. It's a strange experience watching someone you love and care about cave in on themselves right before your eyes without any clue as to why it's happening or how to help.

I think I just eventually got so used to her new self that I kind of forgot what she was like before.

"OK Sulky Sue, we're getting off the exit, so I need directions to the store."

Mona pulls me back to the busy highway exit in front of us.

"Sorry, just turn right at the light up here. You'll stay on this road for the next few miles until you get to Main Street."

I feel her eyes boring into me.

"Everything alright up there?"

She nods toward my head curiously.

"Of course," *not,* I silently add. "Why do you ask?"

"Because you just voluntarily apologized to me without batting an eyelash."

I laugh.

"Well, take what you can get because it won't happen again."

"Whatever you say, Altoid," a small smile brushes across her lips before it quickly vanishes again.

Nostalgia stirs in my chest at the old nickname. When Mona and I were little Mona had a seriously severe speech impediment and when she said my name it came out more like "altoid" than "Matilda". The name stuck, but she hasn't called me it in years. I've almost forgotten the name completely.

Hearing it now makes me wish I were seven again, giddy over my big sister still playing Barbie's with me because she knew how much I loved to play, even though she was considered too old to still be playing with them.

Unfortunately, people grow up and things just don't stay the same, no matter how much you wish for it.

After a few more minutes of driving we arrive at the dress shop. Mona puts the car into park and I open the passenger door. I've got one foot out before I realize she's still sitting, door closed and hands tightly gripped on the steering wheel.

"What if the dress doesn't fit? What if I'm too big for it? I mean, there's not enough time to get it altered again this close to the wedding and I can't look big in my wedding dress, Tilly. I just can't."

I want so badly to roll my eyes and leave her there to complain over her first-world problem, but instead I pull my leg back in, shut the door behind me, and put a supportive hand on her arm.

"You're joking, right? Because you are actually the most beautiful person I've ever seen."

While we have our ups and downs, that much is true. Mona is a level of physical beauty very few could reach (granted, physical beauty isn't all there is to a person). Her long, dark hair falls down her back like a waterfall and her black eyes sit perfectly above her strong, tan cheekbones.

She smiles and literally stops people in their tracks.

"If anyone was made to fit into a wedding dress, it's you. Don't cut yourself short before you even put it on. Besides, you know Dylan is going to love you regardless."

With a slow nod she steps out and we make our way into the shop.

A chirpy "Leslie" leads us to a back room surrounded by floor-to-ceiling mirrors.

"Your dress is magnificent, by the way." Leslie gushes. "You just wait here and I'll bring it out."

Leslie leaves us alone in the mirror room. Mona claps excitedly. She looks like those pageant moms whose daughter just finished her grand talent set.

"How great is this, Tilly? I can't believe I almost chickened out."

Leslie comes back a minute later with a large, white plastic bag draped in her arms.

"Shall we try this beauty on?"

"Of course!" Mona squeals.

Leslie smiles widely before ushering Mona into one of the mirrors, which apparently doubles as a dressing room door. The dress bag still hangs limp in her arms. The two go into the dressing room without me, pulling their bubbling personalities in with them.

I find my way to one of the many faux leather chairs scattered about the room and for a few minutes I sit in peace and quiet, awaiting the final unveiling with my eyes serenely shut. When the mirror/door swings open Mona steps out, I reluctantly open my eyes, and my jaw hits the floor.

I stand in awe at the splendor that is my sister.

When I said Mona was made for wedding dresses I didn't actually mean it, as bad as that sounds. I really just wanted to get her out of the car. But seeing her now in the flowing white lace—there's no doubt she was made for this dress.

Or rather, this dress was made for her.

"I'll just give you girls a moment," Leslie smiles proudly, as if she handcrafted the dress herself. When she leaves I move toward Mona.

I gently slide my hand against the dress, tracing over the intricate lace carefully sewn together.

"Well," Mona whispers hesitantly, "what do you think?"

The fabric hugs her like a second skin. White blends with her caramel skin and she runs her hands nervously over the flowery lace.

"I've never seen a more beautiful bride in my entire life."

To put this compliment into perspective, I watch "Say Yes to the Dress" religiously, which is something my mom and sister have teased me about since I can remember. I've seen my fair share of beautiful brides.

But my sister tops them all.

I'm even momentarily distracted by the whole sting of not being the maid of honor.

Mona's eyes glisten and she smiles through her nerves.

"Oh, you're just saying that."

She's phishing, I know, but I indulge her anyway.

"You of all people know I wouldn't say that if I didn't mean it."

We laugh and Mona wipes at the tears while I choke back my own.

"We have one more thing," Leslie returns just in time to stop us on our road to a bridal breakdown with a veil in her hand. She heads toward Mona with a medium-sized black jewelry box in hand. "You'd asked us to get this ordered and it's taken some searching, but we found an authentic version from a seller in Utah."

Leslie opens the box once she gets to us and my breath falters.

"If you turn, I'll clasp it   for you."

"Um, actually, can I?" I ask, nodding toward the delicate jewelry.

"Of course," Leslie hands the box over and Mona looks like she's about to lose it again.

"Don't freak out," I laugh. "It's just a necklace."

But we both know it's more than just a necklace.

We aren't extremely invested in our family's Navajo traditions, but we were raised by a mother who was adamant on teaching us about where we come from.

It reminds me of years ago, when we were kids. I was 9, maybe 10, Mona a few years older than that. We were at our grandparents' house and found an old box of Granna Ward's stuffed back in her closet. We weren't supposed to snoop in Granna Ward's house; there were too many precious items we could break, she'd always said. Too many family heirlooms she claimed were hundreds of years old and passed down through generations of our Navajo ancestors.

But that never stopped us from doing it anyway when she'd take her afternoon naps.

So there we were, with an old tattered box, which, we found out, was a box of old wedding treasures. We pilfered through the trinkets, one of which was a rare photo (rare, because traditionally speaking, photos at weddings were a big no-no) of Granna Ward in her traditional wear. Beneath the photo was a beautiful, vintage squash blossom necklace that perfectly matched the one Granna Ward wore in the sepia-colored photo. I was too afraid to touch it, afraid I might mess with the energy Granna Ward always told us was in turquoise gems.

But Mona wasn't afraid.

She picked it up, sliding the stunning gems and silver chain through her tiny fingers.

"When I get married some day, I want one just like this," she'd said. Leave it to Mona to dream about her wedding day at just 14 years old.

She then made me promise that when the day came, I'd be the one to put the necklace on her, helping her get ready for her big day.

Mona always talked in such a wistful way; like the whole world was her playground and she could have all she dreamed up. I was never like that, but that didn't mean I couldn't still get caught up in her moments from time to time.

This turquoise and silver necklace in my hands now isn't Granna Ward's and we aren't those rosy-cheeked little girls anymore. But that old promise remains all the same.

Even if she didn't choose me as her maid of honor.

"Well, ladies," Leslie clamps her hands together with her pointer fingers resting against her chin, "are we satisfied?"

I spread the gems along Mona's collarbone and raise my brows at her in question.

"Absolutely," she chimes.

By the time we bag the dress back up and make the final payment, my stomach rumbles like a hungry beast.

"I need food ASAP," I declare once we're back in the car.

"This is your area. Lead the way."

"Green's Bar and Grill it is. Their cheeseburgers are mouth watering and I'm in serious need of some greasy food."

The bar and grill is close enough to walk, so we get back out of the car and trek the couple of blocks it takes to get there. Music flows from the open door at the front of Green's. People bustle in and out, just as I knew they would be. It's a popular place, even in summer when college is out of session.

There's a vaguely familiar voice coming from the live stage just inside, but we're seated on the outside patio before I get a chance to catch who's on stage.

"So, what's good here?"

Mona flips through the menu, gazing at words through squinted eyes.

"Literally everything, but if I had to choose I'd say their Extra Cheesy Goodness burger."

She pulls her menu down just enough to shoot daggers at me from over the top of it.

"Are you kidding? Were you not just there with me trying on my *wedding* dress? It's less than two months away. I can't be eating extra cheesy anything. I'll just get a salad."

And the normal, non-sentimental Mona is back.

I almost tell her their salads are just as fattening as anything else here after all the add-ons, but it's not worth the fight.

Our waiter comes back with our drinks then leaves again with our food order written   down.

My family's never been the small-talk kind, so we sit in silence for a while. I scan the street near the patio people watching. I'm just about to get seriously invested in an old man attempting to finish his large, melting ice cream cone across the street when someone steps up to our table.

"Tilly?" I turn at the sound of my name and see none other than Lyv's ex, Connor, standing there with a small smile.

"I thought I saw you come in."

"Connor—hey," I'm caught off guard and that's the most elaborate greeting I can think of. "Um, this is Mona, my sister. Mona, this is Connor, Lyv's, uh," I catch myself before finishing the awkward sentence.

"Lyv's ex," he finishes with red cheeks.

"Ahh," is all Mona can muster. The tension suffocates us all. Then, "Oh, I think this is my fiancé. I better take this."

Mona points to her obviously black phone screen before standing up and walking away. She ignores my wide, pleading eyes begging her to stay and save me.

Once she's far enough away to avoid the whole interaction about to ensue I motion for Connor to sit down in her place.

To my dismay he does.

"How've you been?"

"I'm good, thank you. Just doing some wedding stuff with Mona. And you?"

"I've been great, actually," he smiles and nods like he really means it. "I've got a gig here a few days out of the week and am working at the radio station in town the other days, so I'm pretty busy. Not that I'm complaining."

I ooh and aww like I'm impressed with his gigs even though I hated when Lyv used to drag me along to his band's shows. They're not a terrible band, per say, but their alternative sound is not one I'd find myself listening to on my own accord.

But that does explain the familiar voice when we first came in Green's.

Just as I think he's about to cut our conversation short and go back on stage, he clears his throat.

"And Lyv? How's she been?"

Don't ask me why I say it. Maybe I just want to stir the pot, or maybe I want to dig deeper into the whole psyche of Lyv's emotional walls.

"She's doing good," I take a long drink of my Dr Pepper. "She's actually seeing someone. It's a guy we grew up with back home."

I play with my straw a few seconds, swirling it around in the cup like I used to as a kid when I'd pretend to be a witch spinning her spoon in a cauldron. I peak up at Connor from my twirling straw.

His forehead wrinkles and those shaggy blonde locks rustle as he nods again. He doesn't seem particularly surprised by the news.

"Is she happy?"

I pause.

Is she happy? She seems to be. But with Lyv, sometimes you just never really know if what's going on internally is actually what shows on the outside.

"I think so," I say just above a whisper.

"Then I'm happy for her."

Because I'm me, I push instead of leaving it alone.

"What happened with you two, anyway? I mean, it looked like everything was great from where I was standing. Then it just ended."

All concerns of stepping over boundaries have completely slipped my mind, despite his scrunched up face.

"Hasn't Lyv talked to you about all this?"

She hasn't, but I won't tell him that.

We're best friends, practically sisters, but every time I pushed her about Connor she shut down.

"Yeah," I lie. "I just want to hear it from your perspective."

He rubs his hands roughly over the small stubble growing on his jaw. The crystal blue of his eyes meets mine with sadness coursing through them.

"I loved Lyv, and still do, despite it all." He shakes his head tiredly. "I wouldn't take back any of it, but she didn't really give me a chance to get to know her. I tried to get through to her but no matter how hard I tried, she just wouldn't budge."

It's like déjà vu; only instead of Asher talking about tearing Lyv's walls down Connor reminisces about struggling to get over them.

"What do you mean?" I push my drink aside and give Connor my full attention. This day is already way out of my expectations for it. "You guys were together for, like, eight months. Surely she let you in during that time."

That's a long time to shut someone out, especially if that someone is your boyfriend. Connor and Asher couldn't be that different to strike such a different reaction from Lyv, could they? According to Asher she's finally starting to open up a little, so I'm struggling to understand the "why" of all of this.

Connor sighs. It's obvious he regrets ever bringing her up. But that can of worms has already been opened. It's too late for him to try and stop my interrogation now.

"It's like this. We could be having the best day where she'd actually be laughing and just generally enjoying herself," he plays with the corner of a napkin, folding it and unfolding it to avoid eye contact. "But when things got serious—too touchy or affectionate or deep in the conversation about our history and all that—she'd shut me out every time."

He pauses and I wish he'd stop altogether.

I wish I'd never pushed it.

I wish I'd never come into this stupid bar with their stupid live bands and their stupid greasy cheeseburgers.

Connor paints a picture of Lyv I don't enjoy looking at.

"She never wanted to talk about love or past relationships or where we were headed."

Pieces of the puzzle come together. Little tidbits add up and I hate where the math is leading me.

"Did she ever mention a guy named Jackson?"

My voice comes out weaker than I intended and Connor doesn't catch the name the first time.

"Jackson," I whisper urgently. "It's random, I know, but it's important. Did she ever mention him or have nightmares about him?"

"Um, I don't think—wait, there was this one time, actually," I wave him on impatiently when he pauses. "She'd just got off the phone with her mom and they'd been fighting about her going home for the summer. She was crying, which threw me a little because she'd never cried in front of me before like that. I stayed over that night to comfort her and she had a bad dream that night. She didn't say anything about a Jackson, but she did scream not to touch her. I remember that part vividly because I thought she was yelling at me, but it was just in her dream."

351

Red flags fly in my mind.

My stomach turns and a vile taste fills my mouth.

Connor looks at his watch and pushes his chair back from the table.

"As much as I'd love to keep talking about Lyv, I've been doing really good at burning that bridge. So I think I'm going to head back to the guys."

He stands but before he walks off he adds, "Sorry if this was weird. I really just wanted to know she was doing OK."

He gives a wave as I nod, my smile barely there at all. Connor goes back the way he came, almost running into our waitress with a tray full of food I'm not even hungry for anymore.

Mona conveniently reappears just as the waitress puts our food on the table.

"That looked intense," she says. "What were you guys talking about, anyway?"

She's already biting into her salad, moving past the question.

But no matter. I don't make an effort to answer anyway. I barely even enjoy my extra cheesy burger.

My mind races as things start building up. I'm starting to connect the dots of Lyv to see warning signs that weren't there before.

Or maybe I just never paid attention.

Mona tries talking the entire way home, but I'm checked out.

I don't like the dark and dreary place my mind goes to when I think of the terrible thing that's possibly pushed Lyv over the edge.

Chapter Twenty Five-Max

A few summers ago my parents went through this remodeling stage. They started "upgrading" everything around the house, including the entire backyard. It looked like something out of an HGTV special. I'm talking screened in porch with the built-in hammock, stone fire pit surrounded by a fancy L-shaped couch, streamed lights hanging from one side of the yard to the other—the works.

I'd always thought it all was a little too much, too gaudy for my taste. And, if I'm being honest, probably too much money. It looked like a Pinterest board came to life and jumped from the phone screen and into our backyard. But then I napped in the screened in hammock the day after they put it up and I was a believer.

No matter how gaudy.

No matter how expensive.

That hammock made it all worth it and became my new favorite spot.

Especially on rainy days like today.

As the hammock squeaks and sways beneath me I feel my eyes drift shut. I dream one of those small nap dreams, the ones where you're fully aware it's a dream but you carry on with it anyway because it's impossible to make your limbs move or get your mind to wake up.

I dream about Lyv and it's all Tilly's fault.

Her frantic phone call earlier in the day echoes in my mind; her worry about Lyv soaks into my every thought. I try forgetting the entire conversation she'd had with Lyv's ex and only focus on the way the rain sounds against the porch roof, but dream Max can't let it go.

The image morphs to another rainy day during the summer before my freshman year. Lyv was about to be a junior. Up to that point she still liked hanging out with me.

But that summer changed and I guess it wasn't cool anymore to be around your little brother. I understood it, I guess, but her distance from me still stung a lot.

Dream Max recalls all of this, rewinding back to that one rainy night when Lyv came home soaked to the bone.

It was Fourth of July but our town was under a no-firework rule, courtesy of the months-long drought we'd been in. But that night we were forecasted to have rain. I came outside to catch the storm rolling in. It was well after that midnight rainstorm started when Lyv burst through the new screen door. Her pink dress (or was it a skirt?) dripped with water. Mud streaked the ends. She'd been so focused on getting inside that she didn't even notice me as she passed through the porch and into the house.

At the time the moment didn't seem important.

Just a small, insignificant snippet in the grand scheme of it all.

I didn't stop her to ask why she was out so late or who she'd been with. I didn't try to ask the real reason for why she was so upset. I'd even teased her the next morning about ruining her favorite outfit.

But I didn't notice she hadn't laughed—she didn't even crack a smile.

But now—now it feels heavier somehow.

It's like that moment in time was something I should've paid more attention to.

"Knock, knock," Ellie opens the screen door and I jump, eyes shooting open at the sound of her voice. Her water-soaked hair and smeared makeup looks so much like Lyv did back then, except for the different hair color.

It stops my breath.

I feel the familiar worry Tilly talked about stirring in my chest.

"Earth to Max," Ellie snaps her fingers with brows raised high. I shake the dream and memory from my mind.

"Sorry, my nap is still hanging around," I pull her by her arm until she's squished next to me in the hammock. It kills me to lie to her, but I don't think I have it in me to put my chaotic thoughts into words, even for Ellie.

"You look like Harley Quinn in that scene from Suicide Squad."

I laugh and she scrunches her nose as I wipe the black away from her cheek.

"You're so sweet," she rolls her eyes but smiles still. "I was just talking to Tilly on the phone. She said we're invited to The Beach on the Fourth."

She runs her hand up and down my arm absentmindedly and I sigh irritably. Now she's going after my girlfriend too? After all the stress Tilly's given me lately, I'm already dreading any kind of Fourth of July party where she's involved.

"I'm not sure I'm a fan of you and Tilly being so close lately."

Ellie reads my mind.

"Don't freak out. She's your sister's best friend, not mine. I'm not going to start ditching you for Tilly. But she is fun to be around."

"That's one way of putting it," I huff.

Ellie laughs in that intoxicating way of hers.

"I love you, but you annoy me sometimes," she whispers. "I swear, you are so spoiled and it's mostly my own fault."

I lightly poke her side.

"Easy, or I'll ditch you."

She guffaws.

"Right, as if you'd even try. You love me too much."

I bite the inside of my jaw to hide the smile coming. We've officially said our first "I love you", but hearing it out loud still catches me off guard.

"And," she drags out, "you pretty much have me to thank for you and Lyv reconciling this summer, since I basically attacked her at the theater that night with my excitement."

And we're back to Lyv.

"Her and Asher seem to be hitting it off pretty well, don't they?"

But I don't answer. I'm already too far gone in the Lyv mystery.

Maybe Ellie's right. Maybe Lyv and Asher will keep seeing each other and he will sweep her off her feet soon and she'll become an emotional dam busting over so that it's impossible for her to hold anything in anymore.

Maybe by the time summer rolls to an end everyone and everything will be back to normal and I can stop worrying about what, or who, has drastically damaged my sister.

***

Ellie's prediction proved right since, exactly one week after our hammock conversation and just days before the Fourth of July festivities, Lyv is going out with Asher on an official date.

It's a new phenomenon seeing Lyv actually interested in someone. I know I only met the punk guy, Connor, once by accident in her dorm room. But even in that one quick run in I could tell Lyv wasn't into the guy.

It's like she just went through the motions, standing robotically by his side as he awkwardly chatted with my parents.

But with Asher, I don't think she's going through the motions of it at all. I see her smile with him, even when she tries to hide it behind her hand. I hear her laugh more when he's around, even as she tries stifling it behind a fake cough. She opens up with him in a way I haven't seen her open up with any guy.

I'm happy for her, or at least I'm trying to be. But every time I get to the point of feeling hopeful for her, Tilly's conspiracy theory and mine plays through my mind and my stomach knots all over again.

I'm scared for Lyv.

Of what, I'm not sure, but after her dream the other night and Tilly's conversation with Connor, I'm struggling to let her out of my sight the past few days.

No matter how great it is to see her start to be happy, I still feel the need to protect her. I still want to give Asher a lecture about treating her right.

Just in case he has any plans to do otherwise.

Of course, Lyv isn't having any of that.

"Seriously, Max, give it a rest. We've known him for almost our whole lives," she rolls her eyes on the couch and sifts through photos on her camera, ignoring my dozen questions about where she's going today and what she'll be doing with him.

I'm still in shock she's letting Asher go with her on this little photography adventure of hers, and even though she swears it isn't a date, it looks a whole lot like one from where I'm standing.

"You haven't known him that long though," I remind her from my spot in the recliner across from her. "He's been around for a while, yes, but you haven't *actually* known him or talked to him until college."

I lean forward so my elbows rest on my knees with purpose.

"Plus, you only broke up with Connor a couple of months ago. I just don't want to see you get hurt."

Her head snaps up then with so much force I practically hear it crack. Her eyes cloud and for a second there I'm sure she's not even in the same room with me anymore. She's in a different place, looking at a different moment in time.

It's gone as quick as it came, that distant look in her hazel eyes, but she smiles through it.

"I've been hurt by much worse, baby brother. I think I'll be okay."

The comment doesn't ease my paranoia, but I don't have time to ponder on it any longer because a knock sounds at the front door. We stand in unison but I get to the door first. Asher stands on the other side with a smile plastered across his face.

"Max, how's it going, man?"

We clap hands before Lyv steps into the doorway next to me.

"Ready?" She asks with a small smile.

My palms grow sweaty at the thought of her leaving.

"I'll walk you guys out."

Her eyes round in warning but I give my best "I'm not up to anything, I swear" shrug.

The three of us walk to Asher's jeep in silence until Lyv breaks.

"Well, thanks for walking us to the vehicle, Max. Have a good night," she pats my shoulder in dismissal.

My pulse quickens.

Asher opens the door for her but not before giving me a confused glance. Lyv jumps into the passenger seat with a wave.

But when Asher closes the door behind her I grab his arm firmly. He looks slowly from my face, to my hand griping his arm, and back to my face.

"What's on your mind?"

He's too damn perceptive.

There are a million words I want to say right now. I think back to that Fourth of July, the one where the drought finally broke and Lyv came crashing past me in the hammock. That moment was bigger than it seemed at the time, I just know it—feel it in my gut.

This moment feels like it could be just as important, but I struggle to find the right words to say to him to express that importance.

"You hurt her, I hurt you," is what finally comes out. I cringe at them, but it's the best I could come up with.

He searches my eyes for any hint of humor.

A frown cascades his face when he comes up empty handed.

"I would never hurt her, not purposefully."

It's not enough. His promise doesn't ease the panic in my chest. When I picture Lyv tangled up in her sheets, covered in sweat and tears as she shouts into the dark of her bedroom, Asher's words just aren't enough.

But before I can give any other warnings, explain to him how important it is that he's good to my sister, his arm is out of my grip and he circles around the jeep to the driver's side. The two of them drive away, leaving me on the sidewalk with worry falling heavy on my shoulders.

Chapter Twenty Six-Asher

I can't shake my nerves, not after Max's bizarre warning about hurting Lyv.

Hurt her? As if I could ever purposefully hurt her.

Was he serious? He's joked like this before but this time was different.

There's really no doubt about that. His eyes, so much like Lyv's, left no room for questioning when they bore into mine. I know that if the day ever comes that I somehow screw this up with Lyv, Max will be there to personally deliver my sentence himself.

"What's on your mind?" Lyv breaks me from my thoughts as the wind flows her hair around her face. She tries and fails to keep the curled mess out of her eyes. "Is it Max? What did he say to you, anyway?"

I almost tell her as we pull onto the main road, out of her neighborhood, but when I see her humored grin stretch on her lips I stop myself. I don't want to ruin this day before it even gets started.

"Nothing major," I lie. "He was just being a protective brother."

She laughs lightly.

"It seems he's been really stepping up to that role as of late."

And then the silence returns, only this time it's more comfortable. She stares contentedly out the window. Her hand soars through the breeze the same way it did the day of mini golf.

She looks so peaceful with her eyes closed that I hate to interrupt the moment.

"So where are we headed?"

"It's a surprise."

Her teasing half-smile prompts an automatic one from me. It's an involuntary reaction on my part; my body responding to her without me telling it to.

"Well, since I'm the driver I think I should be privy to that information, don't you think?"

She shakes her head with a laugh.

"Nope."

"How do I get us there if I don't know where *there* is?"

My face hurts from the grin that's been permanently etched into place.

"I'll tell you when to turn," she pats my arm resting on the gearshift and my skin ignites.

For the hundredth time in the past four or five months I ask myself how I could've been so blind, so oblivious, to the wonderful creature sitting next to me. To think a person like this was breathing in my world all this time without me noticing leaves me puzzled.

"Turn right at the next light."

I do as she says.

For the next twenty minutes I continue following her directions, making every turn she tells me to make. Each course she tells me to take leads us farther away from Carter Springs until finally, we reach the entrance of an old, deserted parking lot.

Grass has grown up in the cracks of the pavement and rust covers the partly standing parking lot lights.

"We're here," she chimes.

Here being an abandoned amusement park on the outskirts of town. It's nowhere close to as big as one like King's Island or Six

Flags, but it's big enough for me to wonder how it's existed without me knowing until after its shutdown.

More and more I'm seeing that I'm oblivious to my surroundings.

"Where are we, exactly," I put the vehicle in park and glance around us. "And how do you know about this place?"

She opens the passenger door and hops out gleefully, pulling her camera bag behind her. I follow her quickly to match her fast pace.

"This is Funfair Island. It was abandoned in 1996 when the owners went bankrupt and couldn't pay for it anymore. No buyers were really invested, so it was just left behind to rot."

Her excitement about this old, run down park is contagious. My adrenaline starts pumping as I follow her to the side of the entrance, away from the front of the building.

"I read about it in a Facebook post on Colorado's most forgotten treasures, or something like that," she waves her hand as I stretch my stride out to keep up with her quick, short ones. "It's been on my photography bucket list ever since."

I nod even though she can't see it from where I walk behind her. She leads us through brush and over grown weeds until we reach a human-size hole in the outer perimeter fence of the park.

"This seems to be a trend with us," I mumble.

Her shoulders shake in a small giggle.

"At least this one is big enough to just walk through," she calls out behind her as she disappears behind the fence.

I follow close behind her, just as I've done since the beginning of the summer.

To be honest, I was surprised she'd asked me to go with her today in the first place. We've talked just about every night over the past couple of weeks since that amazing, soul shaking kiss on the pier and, up until that point, I could see a guard blocked around her.

Even after the night of the pier, I wasn't expecting her to be the one to ask me to go on an adventure. I had full intentions on asking her on a first, official date, but she beat me to it.

Not that I'm complaining. I'll take whatever she wants to give.

"So what else is on this photography bucket list of yours, besides old, creepy amusement   parks?"

369

We stop just inside the fence.

My jaw drops at the sight in front of me. It's no wonder she found this place so interesting. Rides and booths sit in place, half of them in the process of completely decaying and rusting to dust. It's like a ghost town. Everything is exactly like you'd imagine an amusement park to be, except it looks as if everyone just packed everything up and left it completely forgotten.

Stuffed animals hang from booths with stuffing falling out and graffiti covers the walls of buildings in colorful words.

"Loads of things," she whispers, "but this is all my mind can handle right now."

She pulls her camera out of her bag, puts it to her eye, and takes her first shot at the desolate grounds around us.

"It's so much more than I expected."

Lyv talks mostly to herself, but I still latch onto her every word.

That basically sums up this entire summer in one sentence. Coming home, having a new summer job, whatever this is between us; it is much more than I expected. Two months ago I was wandering aimlessly around campus, slightly mended from the ache

I had for her at the beginning of that first semester she was on campus. Two months ago I thought my brief infatuation with her was out of my system once she found her new boyfriend.

Yet, here I am, months later and wrapped around her finger.

And, as I think about everything that's happened this summer, I wouldn't want to be anywhere else than here beside her sidestepping old trash and weeds to get to the next stop on her photography venture.

The sun has just started setting behind the entrance of the park. Purples and pinks blend with yellows and oranges in the sky, spilling a perfect color scheme down on us. I follow in silence from one spot to the next, watching Lyv work diligently on getting photo after photo.

I've never seen her so intense and passionate before; so focused. I'm beginning to think she's forgotten I'm even there with her at all.

We eventually come across an old Ferris wheel and stop just at the bottom of it. It leans slightly and seats look like they would fall at the slightest bump of the structure. Lyv raises the camera to snap a shot of it with the setting   sun in the background.

"I think this is my favorite way of seeing you," I think.

Lyv pulls the camera down and looks at me slowly.

I realize all too late that I've said the words out loud. My cheeks burn and I scratch at my neck uncomfortably.

"I just meant, you seem so happy like this. Taking pictures seems like your happy place is all," I ramble on and a smile creeps onto her face. "It's just nice to see you dive into something so deep."

She bites her full bottom lip and hesitantly steps closer to me, eyes still glued down toward the ground.

Word vomit has taken over and I keep talking.

"I like that you have these spots that you feel comfortable in. I can tell being back home isn't fun for you, so when I see you like this," I wave my arm around us, "it makes me happy."

Finally, she looks up at me through long lashes.

"What makes you think home isn't fun for me?"

Now I hesitate.

I can't really put my finger on it exactly, but it's obvious she's not comfortable here. I can tell by the way she's constantly looking over her shoulder or avoiding certain people or places, like the day a couple weeks ago when she refused to go to the old amphitheater when Tilly suggested it.

"I don't know how to explain it. You just seem happier when you're away from Carter Springs."

She steps closer again, this time so that she's close enough to reach out and hold her if she asked me to.

"You make me happy," she whispers so low I'm sure I didn't hear her correctly. "You just—you make me feel so much. Too much."

The frown that takes over her stunning face squeezes at my heart.

"Is that such a bad thing?"

Piece by piece, wall by wall, I see her blooming right before my eyes. She looks at me boldly, more boldly than she ever has, and a smile teases at the corners of her mouth.

"I'm starting to think no, it isn't so bad."

And for the second time this summer, Lyv leans up on her tiptoes, brushes her lips across mine, and pulls the breath straight from my lungs.

Chapter Twenty Seven-Lyv

Sunday night shifts at The Cinema might be the slowest and most dreadful of them all. I wasn't originally scheduled for any Sunday shifts, but when a frantic Reggie called to say we were understaffed, I really had no choice but to help.

Apparently I have a problem with saying "no" when I need to most.

That's how I find myself here, scrubbing sticky counters on a slow Sunday night. We've had a grand total of two people buy tickets in the past hour, both of which were together as a couple.

A headache set in about fifteen minutes ago and no amount of temple massaging seems to help. Only the thought of Asher and our kiss—*second kiss*—keeps the headache at bay enough for me to at least function.

"I can't thank you enough for stepping in on such short notice, Lyv."

Reggie materializes at my elbow just as I begin feeling the phantom of Asher's lips moving against mine. I drop my fingers from my mouth where I'd been absentmindedly brushing my fingertips across my lips, as if that movement alone could conjure up the exact feeling from being with him yesterday.

Reggie smiles that gap-toothed grin and grabs a stray piece of popcorn off the counter. Before I can stop him he pops the buttery piece in his mouth followed by an "mmm" sound.

I hide my disgust behind a fake cough and Reggie shrugs with that same goofy grin.

"It's no problem, really," I go back to wiping down a particularly tough syrup spot by the drink fountain. "It's not like I had anything else to do tonight."

Nothing besides eating never-ending bowls of chocolate chip cookie ice cream in front of every New Girl episode on our DVR. Maybe a text here or there with Asher.

An epic night, in my opinion.

Reggie pats my shoulder.

"That's the spirit," he points to the door. "More customers!"

My temple thumps violently as I shift my gaze toward the oncoming moviegoers—and my stomach drops through the floor.

"Um, Reggie, can you take this one? I really need to use the restroom."

The customers stare down at their tickets, completely oblivious to me frantically running the wet towel between my hands.

Reggie knits his eyebrows together. Just as he's about to step in and save the day, the office phone rings.

"Shoot," he snaps his fingers together. "I've got to answer that."

Just like that, he leaves me alone to face the oncoming trio.

"Lyv?" Asher tilts his head a little like one of those cute, curious puppies.

The smirk playing on his lips turns my insides to Jell-O. He saunters up to the counter and the smile grows with each step he takes, the smile only a reminder of my bravery last night in making the first move on Asher.

"How are you?"

The pressure in my head has morphed into quick, jerking pulses. It's not that I'm unhappy to see him, but Asher has this uncanny ability of making me feel a lot of things all at once.

Last night was proof   enough of that.

I don't always have the energy to feel so much.

"I'm good, thanks. And you? I thought Tilly said you didn't work on weekends."

Mental note: Stop giving Tilly my work schedule.

"Typically I don't," he leans against the freshly cleaned counter with sparkling eyes and all I can picture is that kiss.

My words come out now in a hurried jumble.

"They were short staffed though, so I picked up a shift when they called this morning," I finish with a nod and heated face.

This reaction is a perfect example of why I wanted to avoid this interaction completely. I've never met someone who pulls and tugs at my heartstrings this much just by asking a simple question.

He stands there with his chin now propped on his hand, small smile never leaving his full lips. He looks at me straight in the eye as if he doesn't notice my ridiculous uniform or dorky uniform visor.

Like he's seeing straight through me.

Just when I'm close to pouring into a puddle on the floor there's a coughing sound behind Asher. I'd almost forgotten he wasn't alone.

Behind him are two girls, probably my brother's age or close to it. His sisters, I assume. While one has his exact dark eyes and hair, the other is blue-eyed and fair-haired.

All three are impeccably beautiful, though.

"Right," Asher moves aside. "These are my sisters, Mia and Cali."

The dark haired one, Cali, gives a wave and a smile. Her and Asher's similarities are never ending.

Mia with the blue eyes steps forward with a slow creeping smile and that's when the three siblings all sort of morph together. I've seen that same smile so many times on Asher, usually when he finds humor in something he shouldn't.

It's the mouth, I realize, that ties the three together.

"So you're *the* Lyv then, huh?" Mia elbows Asher out of the way and her smile grows wider.

I want to feel uneasy under her scrutiny, but Asher's rosy cheeks show enough embarrassment for the both of us. His tan face grows pinker and he scratches at the back of his neck.

I stifle my own amusement.

"I'm Lyv, but I don't   know about *the* Lyv."

Cali steps up next to Mia, blocking Asher out of the conversation entirely. It'd almost feel like an interrogation if not for their playful persona. Cali puts her chin in her propped hand much like Asher had just a few minutes ago.

"Oh, you are practically a legend in the Brooks household." Mia nods beside her sister. "Let me just tell you, Ash never stops tal—."

"Alright, that's enough out of you two."

Asher squeezes between them.

"Why don't you go find us seats and I'll get the stuff here?"

He poses it as a question with his back to me, but something in his voice pushes the girls to do as he says.

Meanwhile, my mind races with Cali's unfinished sentence. A rush jolts through me when I think of Asher at home talking to his family about me.

"So nice to finally meet you Lyv," Cali calls just before heading toward the theater hallway.

Mia wraps her arm through Cali's but turns slightly to say, "You're way prettier than he described, by the way."

The two giggle and disappear around the corner, leaving me stunned and laughing in their absence.

Asher groans behind his hands covering his blushing face.

"I'm going to kill them," he mutters. He doesn't even try to hide his humiliation. When he sneaks a peak at me between his fingers like a little kid, I know I'm a goner.

I'm a goner for this handsome, interesting man who still takes his little sisters to the movies and isn't afraid of being teased or picked at in front of people. I'm a goner for the way he gives his undivided attention to whoever is in the room with him so that they know he believes what they're saying is important.

I'm a goner, despite all my previous efforts of being the exact opposite of that.

"Hey, they're not doing their jobs if they aren't embarrassing you, remember?"

Just when I thought he couldn't get any more adorable he drops his hands to show a dimpled grin.

"They're obviously great at their jobs," but even now his cheeks have returned to their normal coloring and he's back to the confident guy I've seen all summer.

"I don't know. Those were some pretty stealth sibling moves. I think they deserve an extra popcorn for that."

I fight the smile as long as I can, but it slips out anyway.

Reggie chooses this moment to remind me he's here.

It's like I get tunnel vision whenever Asher is around so that all I see is him. Everything else blurs in comparison.

"Hi there," Reggie stands next to me and taps the counter cheerfully. "What can we get you?"

He sets off for the large popcorn Asher ordered while I get the drinks ready.

"I hope Lyv here isn't giving you too hard a time" Reggie jokes over his shoulder.

He laughs a boisterous laugh and I want to crawl under the counter. He talks like I'm a 12-year-old and he's my very over-bearing dad.

"She is, but I don't mind it too much."

I never used to see the allure of a wink before, but that was before I saw an Asher Brooks wink.

Reggie doesn't see it, but I do—I feel its power all the way to my toes.

I slide the drink carrier across the counter to Asher's receiving hands just as Reggie brings his popcorn over. The two exchange money and change before Reggie bids Asher a goodbye and heads back into the office.

"Well, I'd better get in there to the little rascals. I'll see you tomorrow. "

He plucks a piece of popcorn off the top of the bag that's tucked securely in the crook of his arm. The piece catches between his perfect teeth before disappearing behind his closed mouth. I'm so busy admiring the way he makes popcorn-eating an art form that I almost miss his comment.

Tomorrow?

My heart drops.

Fourth of July.

The worst day in the entire year.

I have my struggles with this day for reasons I try to forget, but with Asher mentioning it—and the inevitable bon fire at The Beach—I have no choice but to think about that stupid day.

The headache I'd forgotten about finds its way back to me and tears prick the corners of   my eyes.

One day.

Can't I just have one day where I don't think about that night or be reminded of just how bad one day can turn into?

Can't I just have one day where I forget?

My feet drag toward the office in the break we have between movies. Reggie's humming gets louder the closer I get. I'm surprised I can hear it at all over the loud, heavy *da-dum* of my heart beating.

"Hey Reggie, can I ask you something?"

I knock lightly on the doorframe as he sifts through papers on his desk. I cleaned it a week into the summer, just like I'd planned, but of course it's already a train wreck again.

"Hmm?" his head pops up and he smiles gently.

I want to tell him. Anyone. Talk about what's going on in my head so maybe he can help me fix it. He's not much older than me in reality, but Reggie's soul is years beyond its time, so I usually take comfort in his advice.

But instead of spilling my guts I focus on something I know Reggie can actually speak to instead.

"This is going to be a random and sort of personal question, so if you don't want to answer you don't have to," I inhale deeply when he doesn't stop me. "You told me before that you've made your peace about your wife's miscarriage. But how?"

It's a crude question, but I have to know how he carries on after something like that.

He doesn't look angry or sad or even shocked by my question.

He leans back in his chair and folds his hands against his stomach. Then he glances at the ceiling as if it has all the answers written there.

I follow his gaze, just in case.

"I mean," I continue frantically in his silence, "that's a huge bit of grief in someone's life. How do you get rid of that dark spot?"

Please, give me the answers, I silently beg. *How do I get rid of the dark spot in me?*

"To be honest, you don't really get rid of it per se."

My hope vanishes in a cloud.

"You just learn to live with it."

Frustration bubbles up inside; boiling water erupting over the edges.

"But how? How do you go through that and learn to live with it without going crazy? To remember it and not feel sad or angry or, or—*dead* inside because of what you've been through?"

He looks at me then, really looks at me, as if he's seeing me and hearing me for the first time. Curiously, he tilts his head.

Surely he hears my gulp and I'm afraid I've said too much. Given away too many details or emotions, because he removes his glasses and leans his elbows on the desk between us.

He studies my face like I'm an intricate painting at an art gallery.

I'm stone faced, but he stares me down, enunciating every word so it burrows deep in my brain.

"I think of the good parts. It's dark, yes. The miscarriage was bleak, yes. But in that dark, bleak moment in our lives I saw my wife stronger than I've ever seen her. We grew together and had to learn to depend on each other. That's the strongest we've ever been, after that miscarriage I mean. It was tough, but I had her with me."

And there it is, the great secret to how he survives with a smile.

He has someone to share in the darkness.

386

Someone to lay the burden on.

The one thing I struggle to do most.

"I could blame God or the universe or whatever source I thought the pain came from, but at the end of the day the blame game only made me more miserable. It felt better to just lean on my wife and find peace in the situation than to blame someone for the issue."

I nod like I get what he's saying, but I don't.

I wish I could just let it all go, kill the monster once and for all.

I wish, I wish, I wish.

"What's troubling you, Lyv?"

The worry in his voice threatens to bring on tears I didn't feel coming.

"Nothing," I say too quickly. "I was just curious, is all."

When I walk back to the counter he doesn't follow.

No matter.

I'm not so sure I'd have peace of mind either way.

Chapter Twenty Eight-Asher

It's always a hit or a miss with Fourth of July weather in Colorado.

This one, however, is a particularly hot one. In other places I guess 92 degrees isn't too hot, but in Carter Springs that qualifies as an all day pool day or all day air conditioning day.

Of course, I'm on duty on this miserably hot Fourth, but not for much longer.

Today, 5 pm is my favorite time of the day.

Because 5 pm is when I'm relieved from this shift.

And when I'm relieved from this shift, I get to go to The Beach and see Lyv.

The Beach isn't actually a beach like ones by the ocean, but more of a massive manmade sand pit at the edge of Emerald Lake.

The unexpected run in with Lyv yesterday was a pleasant surprise after our night at the abandoned amusement park and so I've been counting down the minutes to when I get to see her again. Just as I'm counting down again my boss comes over to the guard stand with a bright smile.

She's an interesting person-kind, but always a little too nosey for my taste. Maybe she does it to stay relevant with her employees, or maybe she really is just a curious person, but either way she tends to over share and expects people to return the favor.

"It's a hot one today, isn't it?"

She removes her sunglasses to wipe the sweat off the bridge of her nose.

"You can say that again."

I blow the whistle at two kids pushing in the high-dive line. One sticks his tongue out at me but he reminds me too much of Mia when she was younger, so I laugh it off.

"Rotten things," Jane shakes her head. "Anyway, I can't remember the last time it was this hot on the Fourth."

I brace myself for one of her painfully long stories. I'm not mean enough just yet to stop her once she gets going. Not like Tilly and some of the other veteran workers do, anyway.

Fifteen minutes, I tell myself. *Just last another fifteen minutes.*

"It must've been summer of senior year at CSU. Some of us had a couple of summer courses on the Fourth, of course-."

Jane goes on but this time I can't focus on anything she's saying.

This time I'm already miles away, recalling the image of Lyv in that terrible visor with The Cinema's logo wrapped across it. But on her it all fits. That's the thing about Lyv. She doesn't have to try to be pretty or funny or smart or kind.

She just is.

And tonight is the night I finally let her know.

No people standing between us this time. No punk guy getting to her first.

It's long overdue, considering the way we've been seeing each other more and more lately, but knowing something should've already happened doesn't really make it any easier to follow through with.

"-and I swear, the only way we didn't melt is by basically staying in the water the whole time."

Jane carries on and I nod in all the right places.

"Wow, that sounds awful," I chime.

"Oh, it was-and it wasn't, you know? Like, it was miserable in the physical sense of being hot, but perfect as far as memories go."

It's clear I've listened to way too many of her stories, because that part actually makes sense to me.

"Oh, look. There's Natalie."

I follow Jane's gaze to the side of the pool where Natalie marches towards us.

My heart leaps. My feet move quicker than my mind does and I jump down from the stand. Natalie barely catches the rescue tube before it smacks her in the face.

"I take it you're ready to get out of here," she chuckles.

She raises her brows almost to her white-blonde hairline but I shrug.

"I've got places to be."

It sounds rude even to my own ears, but Natalie's made it clear she's into me despite me making it clear I'm not into her. There's only room for Lyv in this head of mine.

Still, Natalie pushes at every chance she gets.

"Lucky you," she pouts her lip-gloss covered lips. "I wish I was off at some party with you, soaking up the sun and fireworks. Have a drink for me, will you?'

She winks but I turn toward Jane, pretending like I don't see it.

"Have a good evening. I'll see you next week."

The thought of being off work for a full week adds girth to the hop in my step.

"Bye Asher," Jane waves. "I hope you have a good evening too."

Natalie may have said something too, or maybe not, I'm already walking away toward my keys and clothes in the locker room.

Once I've changed clothes I practically run to my jeep.

The whole time hoping the night will give me a story worth telling. One of those long, boring, and memorable stories I'll still be telling years from now, just like Jane.

Chapter Twenty Nine-Tilly

"Pass me the tanning oil, would you?"

I reach across my towel and toss the brown bottle of oil at Emily without opening my eyes.

The sun fires down on us but I don't complain, though someone should tell Emily that sunscreen would probably be best for her pale skin. But me, I feel my best when I'm baking under a sunshiny sky, sweat pooling at the base of my neck before sliding down my back.

It's exactly why I suggested we spend this Fourth at The Beach instead of someone's pool like usual. Sure, The Beach isn't literally a beach on the ocean, but it's a nice switch of scenery.

"So where's Lyv, anyway?" I barely peek around my shades with a hand hovering over the unprotected eye. Emily sits next to me in the sand with her beach towel only a few centimeters away from my own.

She rubs tanning oil onto her already burning skin and I wish desperately for the friend in question to show up and save me.

"She'll be here soon," I reply as I drop my sunglasses back onto my nose. My face points back toward the sky. I love the way the heat warms my skin. It reminds me I'm alive and capable of feeling the beauty of the sunshine and summer around me.

"She's just waiting on Max and El to get back from her family's cookout."

Emily scoffs loudly and flops back onto her towel.

"Does she have to bring them everywhere now? Can she not go anywhere without her brother and his play thing?"

Her bitterness only makes me happier.

"Careful, now. Envy is an ugly color on anyone, even you."

I peak out of the side of my sunglasses to see her gaping mouth just seconds before a monsoon drops down on my stomach.

Now I'm the one gaping as Emily squeals next to me over the few drops that landed on her from my aftermath. What I assume to be a Mason prank turns out to be Max prank instead.

Befriending Lyv all those moons ago meant taking on her little brother baggage with it. Right now I'm cursing that first day in kindergarten when she helped me get my glued-together fingers apart.

"In Max's defense, babe," Mason, now standing beside Max, gets out between laughing breaths, "you do look pretty hot down there."

I stand and prepare to pounce with legs shaking from lying so long in the heat. Just as I'm about to show them what they can do with their apologies, Lyv walks up with Ellie at her side.

"I told them it was a bad idea but they didn't listen," El calls out and shakes her head, rustling the long, blonde locks of hair in the process.

Emily, at the sight of her competition, gets up, brushes the sand of her back, and stalks toward the water. But I don't care about the bucket of water or Emily's ridiculous jealousy, or even on getting revenge on Max and Mason.

My focus goes quickly back to Lyv, with the dark circles encasing her eyes and mouth drawn in a firm line. She hugs herself tightly.

I've seen that posture before.

It's the same posture she always gets when she tries to disappear into the crowd. As if she could vanish from sight if she just makes herself as small as   possible.

395

There's a distance already in her eyes as far-cast and wide as the water she stares out at.

My focus is only Lyv. It has been since the day I ran into Connor. That conversation brought life into more questions than I could keep track of.

But tonight—tonight I will get answers to put all my questions to rest once and for all.

Chapter Thirty-Lyv

Most mornings I'm up relatively early.

But on this particular morning I stay in bed hours after my usual wake time.

Even when my mom poked her head in just after 9 am to check in—even then, I "slept", pushing my breathing deeper in and out to give the illusion of sleep.

It worked, and I've been lying in bed ever since.

The beauty of taking the shift yesterday means Reggie had someone take mine today to balance everyone's hours.

It's perfect, really, because today is a day I don't really want to see or talk or even be around people at all. But unfortunately I'm obliged to show up at my best friend's Fourth of July party in a few hours.

I tossed and turned all night with little more than a few hours of actual sleep, so the party is the last place on earth I want to be today.

The past few years I've found ways of avoiding our "Friends Fourth", but this summer I'm actually home and I can feel the tension brewing like a storm inside me.

I find a little humor in how different life can go in such a short about of time. Just a few years ago I was exactly the kind of person who wanted to go to parties and meet new people and talk to all the cute guys.

A few years ago I was a different person.

Back then I didn't know what it meant to be bruised and battered. I'd lived a sheltered life without a worry in the world of what "danger" or "threat" meant.

But I quickly learned.

My rattling doorknob pulls me back to my bedroom and away from the murky memory lane I'd started down.

"Oh good, you're finally awake," my dad chimes in this time instead of mom.

His head pops around the door like a floating head and he bares one of his full-toothed grins.

"I am now," I mumble.

When I toss my blankets over my head he takes that as an invitation to come in. The weight of his body tilts me toward the side of the bed he now sits on.

"What's got you so under the weather this morning?"

He pats my covered hip and I want to tell him the truth.

To scream it out loud.

To him this day represents independence, but for me it represents a night I was forced to give up my freedom to walk away when I really wanted to. It was a night I was forced to grow up and stop looking at the world through a lens of innocence, even when I wasn't ready for it.

I want to spill it all because I'm so sick of hiding.

"Just tired from work," I pull the covers away from my face and smile, but it gets stuck somewhere between my mouth and my eyes.

"Well, don't waste the day away, lazy bones," he stands, already gliding back the way he came. Each step he takes away from me pulls my courage to confess away with him.

"What time is it?"

I glance at the broken alarm clock on my nightstand out of habit, then the window behind it. Judging by the light coming through I'd guess 10:30ish.

"Almost noon," he replies.

"Noon?" I shoot up into a seated position.

"I told you it was late," he stops in the doorway with his hand lingering on the knob. His other hand rests on his side. He looks back at me with creases lining his forehead.

"Are you sure you're OK?"

He sucks the inside of his jaw the way Max does all the time.

Just tell him, my heart pleads.

"I'm fine," I swallow the lie like a bitter pill. "I promise."

He pauses like he might add more but only nods in the end. The creases remain, making him seem much older than just 43 years old.

"If you say so," he begins shutting the door but holds it open enough for the floating head to reappear. "Oh, and I'm supposed to let you know your brother and Ellie will be here around 4 to leave for tonight."

"And don't forget sunscreen this time," he scolds. "You know how bad you burned the last time we all went to The Beach and your mom would kill me if I let you leave without it this time."

Just like that, he's gone, floating head and all.

My bed jostles as I crash back into my pillows.

Tears involuntarily brim my eyes and a sigh rises in my throat.

"It won't matter," I murmur after him.

Sunscreen doesn't protect anyone from the monsters that go bump in the night.

***

For whatever reason, this year everyone decided to have our "Friends Fourth" at The Beach instead of at Mason's or Tilly's pool.

Regardless of location, my energy for the night is quickly fading and we just got here.

"It's not a good idea. Lyv, could you please talk some sense into your brother?" Ellie scoffs next to me.

When I take too long to answer she turns around to look at me. Her smile fades slightly.

"Are you OK?"

The million-dollar question.

It catches Max's attention and he now frowns in my direction.

"I'm fine," I lie. "But trust me when I say that there's no amount of talking that can put sense into Max's head."

Ellie smiles at my attempt to seem engaged in the conversation but Max isn't as easily convinced. His eyes stay on me longer than I like. He searches my face like it's a puzzle. For a second there my heart skips a beat.

He knows.

But that's impossible. He can't know. Only two people in the entire world do, and Max isn't one of those people.

We stand on the splintered, wooden stairs that lead down to the sandy ground below. Our friends gather to the right of the staircase closest to the water and I spot Tilly lying among the sunbathers.

"Well," I start with a nod toward my oblivious best friend. "Are you going to do it or are you all talk?"

I raise my eyebrows in a challenge, waiting for Max to take the bait. Praying he takes the bait—and he does.

With just a slight hesitation he runs off to destroy Tilly's bliss, with Mason right on his haunches. My heart rate slows back to normal the farther away he gets from me.

"What a mess," Ellie chimes. I'm startled until I see she's smiling fondly after Max.

Breathe, I coach myself.

By the time we get to the group Tilly is already soaked in water. Meanwhile, Ellie apologizes for my brother's antics.

"No worries," Tilly waves them all off. "I was just about to head into the water anyway. Lyv, join me?"

Warning bells go off in my mind. Her face furrows a lot like Max's had on the stairs. I squirm like a bug under a microscope. My paranoia is getting the best of me; is clawing its way from my chest and into my throat until I struggle to breathe.

But Tilly stands waiting, feet pointed toward the water and head locked on me, so there's really no backing out.

"Sure," I mutter as I strip down to my high-waist bathing suit. Emily sulks at the edge of the water but stomps away when she sees us step into the calm waves.

"I'm glad you came out   this year," Tilly announces.

The water inches further and further up my body until we're chest high.

My arms stretch out and I smooth the water around me, ironing it under my hands as I move them forward and backward, forward and backward.

Tilly continues, "I know this isn't really your favorite event. You know, I never really understood why that is."

She gazes out at the water ahead of us. My eyes stay strained on the tree line just visible enough to see on the other side of the massive man-made beach we float in.

"It's just noisy, that's all. The big crowds and fireworks can get kind of loud and overwhelming, you know?"

It's only partly a lie, but a lousy one still, and Tilly knows it.

She pushes her sunglasses onto the top of her head and squints at me.

"Are we best friends?"

Her question catches me off guard.

"Yes," I assure her.

"And do you trust me?"

"I do."

She nods as if this clarifies some question she's asked herself. When I see the gulp at the base of her throat my nerves go on edge.

The anxious storm keeps rolling in.

"What happened with Connor? No bullshit answers this time. I know you guys struggled with getting serious or intimate with each other, and that it was mostly on your end. Why?"

Whatever I thought she was going to say, this wasn't it. This stream of questions makes me think she knows more than she's letting on.

My chest burns as she rambles on.

"What do you mean, you *know*?"

My voice barely travels over the sound of the water surrounding us. This time it's Tilly who hesitates.

"I saw him the other day," she mutters. "When we went to pick up Mona's dress I ran into him."

Red fogs my vision but it has nothing to do with the hot sun above us. My skin tingles and I've stopped smoothing the water around me.

"And what, you guys decided to have a little chat about me when I wasn't there?" I spit the words with so much anger I'm sure they'll burn if they reach Tilly completely.

I'm just so sick of being betrayed by people I trust.

"It wasn't like that. We're worried about you, Lyv," her almond eyes round and her pout only infuriates me more.

"Who is 'we'?"

She bites the pout away.

"Me, for starters," her bottom lip trembles, "and Connor. Max too. You're different, and it scares me."

For years I've wanted this exact conversation, wanted someone—anyone—to notice the change in me. To step in and pick up the pieces. But here I have it, and it feels all wrong.

This isn't by my choice.

This is an interrogation and the water flowing around me traps me. Once again, I'm backed into a corner and searching for some kind of quick escape from the danger in front of me.

"*You're* scared," I laugh in disbelief. "*You're* worried."

My chest rises and falls in a hurry.

"I don't need your worry, Tilly. Or Max's or Connor's or anyone else's. I don't *need* anyone.

Shut up! I scream at myself but keep rambling on anyway.

"You can't change what's happened to me. You can't take it all back for me, no matter how hard you or Max or even I try. Period."

I've said too much and Tilly bites down on the sob threatening to spill out. My eyes burn hot but the tears don't fall.

I ignore Tilly as I trudge through the water back to shore. She calls my name but I stop listening and start walking away from my friends and down the shoreline. The bathing suit cover I'd picked up from the sand falls swiftly around me, even as the wind threatens to blow it away.

I walk away from the laughter and the crackling fire that's already been lit. I keep walking until I'm alone with nothing but my own thoughts and memories.

It feels like hours that I stand there on my own.

Being by the water's edge I almost forget tonight. I almost forget *that* night. I almost forget, with the roar of the water crashing around me, the sound of his hushed "shh" from all those years ago.

With my toes sinking in the sand, I can almost forget the feel of fingertips sinking into my skin, or of his hot breath against my face.

Almost.

"Hey there."

A voice rings behind me and I jolt involuntarily.

When I turn Asher throws his hands up in surrender, ebony eyes wide.

"Sorry, I didn't mean to scare you. I thought you heard me coming."

"No, I'm sorry. My mind is a little distracted at the moment."

A piece of hair blows in the light breeze and I tuck it in place behind my ear.

"Anything I can help with?"

I almost say yes. I want so badly to let Asher in completely. I want to let him help take my mind off this burden.

But it's *my* burden and no one else's.

"Just girl drama," I smile up at him.

It seems lying has become a talent, because Asher doesn't call me out on it. His nose is a bit pinker today than the last time I saw him from the sun and he must've gotten a haircut at some point today. He looks too striking to be here on such an ugly night.

"Well, maybe I can distract you from your distraction," he scratches at the back of his neck in that nervous tick of his I've grown to adore.

Just as he opens his mouth to speak my brother interrupts him.

Max glides toward us and I wonder if he had anything to do with Tilly's probing earlier.

"Are you guys going to stay out here alone all night or come back and join the party?"

Asher sighs and whatever he was about to say fades with the breeze.

"You up for it?"

His grin beckons me forward.

Reels me in with him when only moments ago I wanted to sink further into myself.

To vanish entirely.

409

My hesitation comes like second nature. Asher holds his hand out for me but I struggle to take it right away. I look at his outstretched hand first and see the way his veins pop under the small dice tattoo they rest under. But when I look at his face, into his eyes, there's nothing but kindness.

I decide it's time to stop comparing him to the man of my nightmares. It's time to take a step toward letting that night—that monster—fade away.

Or at least try.

"Sure," I say, taking his hand and tugging my feet out of their sunken spot in the sand.

What could go wrong?

"I don't think I'm following. What did she mean by changing what happened to her?"

My whole body chills, despite the fading sun above.

"I don't know, Max. That's just what she said."

It was plain to see things didn't go so well between Lyv and Tilly when Lyv trudged out of the water about an hour ago, leaving Tilly completely behind.

Lyv had stormed off down the beach and has been gone ever since. It's taken me this long to make my way over to Tilly through the crowd of partygoers to get all the details.

"I think it's worse than we thought, Max."

Tears brim Tilly's eyes. I don't bother adding salt to the wound. I don't explain how I've already imagined the worst; already pictured what she's been hinting at over and over again.

The fact is I've just ignored all the warning signs up to this point.

But now they're bright and glaring as the bonfire crackling next to us.

There's no ignoring or running or hiding from them anymore.

Someone hurt Lyv and it's severely damaged her.

And now she's out of sight, which makes me sick to my stomach. Tilly has moved on to talk with Mason, or more so argue with him. She's yelling at him for inviting someone to the party, but I don't stop to ask who it is she doesn't want there.

Instead I walk away, looking for Lyv.

I run through the past few years in my head. That summer when Lyv turned in on herself replays like a broken movie reel. The distancing, the quietness, and the broken relationships—the root of the problem comes up in the back of my mind but I can't let it come to light.

If I let that idea come to light in my mind, what's stopping it from becoming a reality?

Not Lyv, I think. Beg. Pray.

But even as I deny it, I see it all so clear. Picture the vile act in my head until I can't see straight.

By some miracle, I find her and convince her to come back to the party. I'm not all that surprised to find Asher there too, since they've gotten so close this summer.

We walk back together, them following closely behind me. A few new people have joined our bonfire. Some I know from school and some are strangers. But one stranger catches my eye.

One stranger stands out among the rest.

He's vaguely familiar, but not enough to put a name to the face.

Tilly hops from side to side anxiously next to him.

"Hey Max, come here a sec. I have someone I want you to meet," Mason waves me toward him.

Tilly frowns and shakes her head slightly, but I can't decipher the look she's giving me. I manage to squeeze my way through to stand next to Mason. He claps one hand on my shoulder and the other on the stranger's shoulder.

My pulse quickens with some silent alarm going off in my head, warning me that disaster feels like it's on the brink of exploding around me.

"This is my cousin, Jackson. Jackson, this is Max. He was just a kid the last time you were in but..."

Jackson...

It can't be a coincidence, can it? Are things ever really a coincidence?

Mason rambles on but Jackson's eyes drift where I'd just come from. He smiles slowly.

The cat that ate the canary.

I follow his line of vision back to my sister.

Deep down I think I already knew it was Lyv he stared at before looking myself.

"Lyv?"

She stops.

Asher's hand rips out of hers and he stumbles after her. She's pale, much paler than she'd been seconds ago.

Slowly, she turns toward Jackson.

"Long time no see. How have you been?"

He sneers, like there's some secret between them that no one else knows.

She freezes in place.

And I know.

I know what's changed. I know *why* she's changed. I know my worst fear, that worse-case scenario I'd avoided all this time, has come to life after all no matter how much I tried to deny its existence.

My only thought now is to eliminate the problem. Eliminate Lyv's pain.

So, I lunge toward the problem with my closed fist cracking against his solid nose.

Chapter Thirty Two-Lyv

With my hand in Asher's I walk back to the bonfire with a small bit of hope still intact. I focus on the way his thumb rubs circles along the outside of my hand; let the way the sand jumps out in front of us with every step we take together keep me distracted.

Once we're back to the rest of the group Max trails off toward Mason, but I keep my eyes on Asher.

He pulls me with him around the fire like the tide. I follow willingly.

But I should know by now that good things just don't last.

"Lyv?"

It's one word. One syllable.

But that voice sends me back. It's the same voice that I hear on my worst days and when Asher's hand falls away from me it takes all my hope with it.

My body creaks toward the sound of my name and there he is.

That face that haunts my nightmares.

That smile I once thought was so perfect grows wide as he catches sight of me. I freeze, stuck in place with no voice to cry out with.

The warning bells drown out whatever he's saying next. Clanging and chiming loudly, they urge me to run as far and as fast as I can.

But I can't move.

I can't speak.

I can't even register how close the monster is to my baby brother—can't register the danger Max is in just standing that close to him.

My knees shake but before I can fall there's a blur in front of him. Jackson drops with a loud crack of what can only be a broken bone. My brave, loyal Max lands on top of him.

Chaos follows.

Some people run to watch the fight play out. Others run to try and break it up. I don't look to see who runs to do what. Asher has already headed toward the madness.

I quiver in his absence.

Slowly and quietly I back away from the crowd. I slip into the darkness and once I'm there I run.

I run until my bare feet blister and lungs burn. I run until the sounds of yelling and shouting fade to nothing around me.

And then I run more until I find the one place in the world I can disappear.

When you hear people say, "It all happened so fast," you never really grasp the concept fully.

Not until you're actually in the thick of it.

But here and now, when *I'm* the one in the thick of it, I can honestly say it all just happened so fast.

One minute I was yelling at a confused Mason for inviting his cousin, then the next moment bodies flew and blood flowed.

But just before all that there was this one second—this one terrible, painful second I'll remember until the day I die.

It was Lyv with a look of pure terror. I'll always remember how white her tanned face was, or how her mouth dropped open like some fish out of water, gasping for air. I'll never forget the way she looked at that man—no, that predator—as if all the breath had been pulled form her lungs.

I'd missed it.

In all this time, how had I missed it?

Was I really so caught up in myself that I hadn't once put all these pieces together to see what was really causing Lyv's agony?

They're all blinding now.

I see how she fell away from us. I understand why she couldn't get close to anyone. Even now, as Asher pulls Max to one side of the fire and Mason pulls Jackson to the other, I burn with anger at myself for not noticing Lyv's pain sooner.

Mason holds his cousin in a bear hug from behind, not that it matters. The amount of damage Max has done to him leaves Jackson powerless. Max, on the other hand, is barely scathed with just a busted lip and split eyebrow.

Jackson slouches slightly in Mason's arms with blood smeared allover his face and shirt.

He's barely recognizable under all the red.

I march toward that bloody face and stop just short of him. The snake glances up at me warily and I hate myself again for once thinking those vivid eyes were anything at all like Mason's kind ones.

Just as he opens his mouth to speak I bring my knee up with every bit of strength I can get.

Jackson drops to his knees in the sand as I connect with his groin. He lets out a pained groan and holds himself.

"Please stop," he begs.

Angry tears prick at the corners of my eyes but I refuse to let him see them.

"What about Lyv?" I hiss just inches from his face. "You didn't stop with her, did you?"

He has no time to answer before I grab a handful of his blonde hair, pulling his head up so he has no choice but to look at me.

"You don't deserve to breathe," I spit.

Another hand catches my fist before it can crash down on Jackson's already mauled face. When I turn with a huff I'm surprised to find Max is the one who stops me.

"Let go," I fight against him but he holds firmly.

"Tilly, wait," he rushes. "Lyv's gone."

I drop Jackson's head so quickly he falls forward from the sudden motion.

"Where did she go?"

I search the crowd frantically, looking from face to face and waiting on someone—anyone—to answer.

In the end it's Asher who steps forward.

"I think I know where she went."

***

When Asher first said to go to the old water tower I thought he'd finally lost it.

"She couldn't get that far on foot," I argued. "Or alone at night."

But he insisted, and as I pull into the gravel road at the base of the tower I'm glad I listened. Lyv's tiny form gets larger as I climb closer and closer to her.

In different circumstances I might voice my fear of getting tetanus on this rusty ladder, but I save that for another day.

Lyv doesn't look at me when I sit beside her.

She stares blankly ahead.

Tears fall warmly down my cheeks before I get the first word out.

"I'm so sorry," I mutter. My voice threatens to fade beneath the wave of new tears.

"For what?"

Still, she looks out at the vast darkness in front of us.

"You know what. It's me, Lyv," I reply, voice filled with grit. "You can tell me anything."

I enunciate that last word more than the rest, willing her to speak out.

To say the words aloud, maybe for the first time ever.

Because it has to be on her terms. She has to say it in her own words with her own gumption. I can't force the truth out of her or I'm no better than the person who made her this way in the first place.

But I can let her know I'm here if she wants to let it out.

I'm here, I silently cry. *I'm right here.*

She looks at me then. It's almost worse than when she wouldn't look at me at all. While tears continue to stream down my face, Lyv's eyes have none to give. That hazel gaze matches mine in volume, but hers has nothing left in its heaviness. It occurs to me that this is what real emptiness looks like.

That look there, of a girl who's spent years fighting invisible forces she's never let show.

Of bearing burdens she never should've had to bear on her own.

There's no emotion.

No inclination that there's any pain inside thanks to lots of practice at hiding it.

It's as if she's kept everything sealed up inside a Ziploc bag, so much to the point that she believes nothing's wrong anymore. Her eyes are bleak, but when she speaks she shows a thousand cracks.

Emotion slips through each crevice and with a shaking voice she utters, "He wasn't who I thought he was."

Chapter Thirty Four-Lyv

The summer before my junior year of high school had lots of firsts for me.

My first car, my first job, my first credit card.

It's strictly for building your credit, no splurging, my mother had told me the day she handed it to me.

It was also the summer where, for the first time in my life, a handsome boy noticed me. It sounds cliché to say that it was the summer where I actually felt worthy of attention for once.

But up to that point boys never really paid much attention to me. Sure, I had guy friends, but they saw me as just that—a friend. Nothing more. Nothing worth a second glance.

But that summer was different.

That summer a dreamy, beautiful boy came into town and spoke dreamy, beautiful words to me, and I had his undivided attention.

Undivided attention is a double-edged sword, a fickle thing. The beauty of it is feeling like

you matter, like you belong to someone and something important.
But the ugly side of it is there's always a drop once the high from it
fades. You rise and rise under the microscope of someone's affection
and then comes the hard tumble of that same someone losing
interest.

Because eventually they all lose interest, don't they?

For the first time in my life I had someone's undivided
attention.

Mason and Tilly started dating that summer, so that meant
where we usually were, Mason was there too. When he came to the
pool one day to see Tilly, I happened to be there, as well as his
cousin from Montana who was in for the summer.

Meeting Jackson was intoxicating.

He filled my head with pretty pictures of summer love and
romantic days together. He looked at me like I was the only one in
the room.

I'll remember his face until the day I die.

For better or worse.

Years from now when I'm old and wrinkly or losing all memory thanks to some brain-eating disease—I may forget his name, but I'll see his face.

And I'll remember.

I'll remember how his bold, blue eyes, so like Connor's when I first saw him at college, followed me wherever I went. I'll remember how his sneer looked more endearing back then than predatory to the clueless, teenage Lyv. I'll remember how my heart leaped when I heard his name.

It was beautiful.

He was beautiful, and he wanted *me*.

That summer was a dry summer, but *that* night it rained.

And when it rains...

Midnight rolled around and I put on my favorite champagne skater dress my mom bought me the prior Christmas. I brushed my fingers through my hair one last time then snuck down the rose trellis outside my bedroom window like I'd done so many times before to meet Tilly.

But that night was different.

That night I was meeting   Jackson.

No one knew about us meeting. No one even really knew just how serious we were that summer.

Or how serious I *thought* we were.

He waited under the old, rundown amphitheater awning like we'd planned. It was after midnight, so it was empty save for the two of us.

He looked marvelous in his jeans and dark blue t-shirt.

"You came," he'd said it plainly, not in the excited way I'd hoped. Like he knew I'd be there and it was just another known fact of life.

He grabbed my hips and pulled me to him with nothing else to say. His lips came down on mine heavy, like a smothering force to be reckoned with. One hand travelled to my hair and he gave a slight tug.

My head felt fuzzy from the way he held me and a stirring in the back of my mind slammed on the breaks of my speeding heartstrings.

Begging me to slow down.

Take a breath.

I broke away long enough to look into those vivid blue eyes I'd grown to trust so much over the couple of months of knowing him. Distance stared back at me and my palms clammed up.

"I can't believe you actually want me," I breathed, hoping to bring back any piece of him I was familiar with.

Hesitation flashed across his face and I pretended like I didn't see it.

He's just nervous I lied to myself.

"How could I resist these curls?" Another tug on my hair.

"Or these lips?" Another suffocating kiss.

"Or these curves?" Another wandering hand.

All at once I lost control of the situation. I was no longer in a position where I could get away easily. I was at his mercy with his hands holding tight enough to bruise and his body surrounding me like a cage.

When his hands slipped under the hem of my dress I pulled away as best as I could.

"Wait—we should—we should wait," I tried boldly, but my voice faltered.

It's like my throat turned against me and closed around all the words I wanted to say.

This wasn't the night I'd envisioned. This wasn't the guy I'd painted in my head. I didn't really know what I even expected or wanted to happen that night, but I knew it wasn't this.

"C'mon, you've been teasing me all summer. Don't back out on me now."

That snicker sent the alarms ringing.

Get out, Lyv. Get out now.

But I couldn't move. I couldn't speak.

Just like with my words, my body betrayed me and locked up long enough for him to move closer.

I'd finally been forced into a flight or fight situation, but instead of doing one of those I did the third option—the option people rarely talk about.

I froze.

When he grabbed my arms and pulled me behind the back wall of the amphitheater, I snapped out of my haze. But by then my attempts at kicking and shoving him away did nothing more than fuel the fire in his eyes.

Panic rose.

No one could see me struggle back here. No one could hear me yelp when he dug his fingers into my skin.

We were out of sight, out of mind to the world around us.

I couldn't make my limbs move anymore, though my heart beat out of my chest. He shoved me to the ground.

The cold concrete chilled the sweat trickling down my spine.

"Shhh, don't scream," he snarled. "Stay quiet and it'll all be over soon."

He hovered over me and my tears fell in sync with the rain finally dropping around the awning above. Still, I couldn't make the words come out.

No! Stop! I shouted from the deepest place in me but nothing came out of my mouth.

It wasn't some otherworldly experience Hollywood portrays. I didn't separate from my body and watch the horror while looking down at myself. I wasn't numb from the cold beneath me or closed off from what was happening.

I felt it all, every piece of him in me.

I felt the weight of him   on top of me.

431

I felt the splintering in my nails as I scratched them against the concrete beneath me as I tried distracting myself from his hot, erratic breathes against my face.

I felt it all.

He was quick, just like he'd promised, but in my heart I knew this was far from over—that it may never end, this feeling bubbling up inside.

He put it there, but the shame felt like my own fault. The dirtiness felt like a stamp I'd marked on my forehead myself.

IDIOT, the mark would read.

WEAK. NAIIVE. PATHETIC. TEASE.

When he finished he climbed off of me with a satisfied grin. He was full from his devouring of me and he'd left me empty in the process.

If I thought myself immobile before, now I was like a root grounded to the concrete below me. I didn't get up. I didn't back away. I didn't do anything. I just stared lifeless at the ceiling of that old, mildewed amphitheater like an empty shell.

He began buttoning his pants and I robotically pulled my dress back down.

"Let's keep this to ourselves, what do you say?"

Nothing.

"Hey! I'm talking to you."

The guy standing above me was unrecognizable. The hatefulness in his voice was a tone I'd never heard on him before, only adding to my self-blaming for not noticing his falsity sooner.

Finally I pulled myself off the ground. Legs shaking. Stomach full of vomit. I'd be sure to spill it all out the moment Jackson was gone.

"Keep your mouth shut, alright?" He moved toward me and I backed away like a roach scattering from the light.

I backed into the rain, hoping this once beautiful, dreamy boy would not follow me.

He didn't.

Instead he laughed, shook his head, and brushed me off with a wave of his hand. He pushed his perfect hair back but I avoided his eyes. Couldn't look into those treacherous, crystal eyes that tricked me so easily.

"See ya around, Lyv."

I prayed to God he   wouldn't.

The second he walked back out into the darkness my knees gave out and I crashed to the ground. Hugging my legs to my chest caused physical pain, but it was nothing compared to what hurt on the inside.

Sobs racked my chest and the vomit I'd been holding down came up without ceasing.

How could I have been so wrong about him? Were the signs there all along and I just hadn't paid attention? Was I really so high off the idea that someone would possibly like me that I didn't see how monstrous he was from the very beginning?

How could I have let this happen?

When I finally crawled back out of the rain I sat against the amphitheater wall, rocking myself into a trance.

Somewhere in the back of my mind I blamed Mason for it, holding onto that grudge for many years to follow. It wasn't his fault his cousin liked to take advantage of people, but if Mason hadn't have brought him here this wouldn't have happened.

But he did bring Jackson here.

And this did happen.

And nothing I said or did or wished for could ever change that.

The walk home was a blur. I don't remember passing houses or cars or anything, really. It's as if my mind blocked out the world around me like a safety shield.

What I can remember is the rain; the sloshing of my waterlogged shoes squishing in the mud.

When I got to the bathroom at home, miraculously getting through the back door without getting noticed, I avoided the mirror altogether. I couldn't stand to see the mascara inevitably running down my face or see the mop my hair had turned into on the walk home.

If it were possible to scrub skin off with nothing but soap and water I would've succeeded that night. The scalding hot water of the shower rained down on me, washing away the mud and blood.

But it didn't wash away what had happened.

Even after rubbing my skin raw, the bruises forming on my arms stayed as a reminder of him all over me.

I turned off the eventually cold water and dried off. After putting on my most worn in sleep shirt and a fresh pair of underwear I climbed into bed.

Only then did I let myself cry again. Though I muffled the noise against my childhood teddy bear with the lousy, torn button, the tears poured like a broken dam. The agony settled deep inside and I put a piece of me away, swearing to never speak a word of this as long as I lived.

No one would believe me anyway. After all, I was the one who met a boy late at night. What did I expect to happen, right?

I'd heard it all before, so there was no use telling.

The wound in my soul gaped open and I wanted to seal it shut in the only way I knew how.

I'd get away from this place and the home that was supposed to protect me from the monsters lurking outside my front door. I'd run from this town where I'd be reminded every day of the nightmare that had become my reality. I'd keep my head down and never let myself trust someone so deeply again.

That had worked until Connor, but even then I found a way to let my past catch up and ruin it.

But I promised myself that night that I'd bide my time until I could get away from this town and all that had happened here.

And I ignored the little voice inside saying I'd never be able to really get away from it all.

"I'm not going to push her, Hank. If she doesn't want to press charges we can't make her."

The aftermath of the Fourth can be best described as mass disarray.

Confusion. Anger. Guilt.

I can't decide which feeling to stick with the most as I listen to my parents argue downstairs. They don't know I'm listening, of course, but my spot on the top stair has kept me hidden for a while now.

"This is unacceptable, Ginny," my dad roars. "We can't let that, that—criminal get away with this! We just can't."

It's been the same argument since I took my seat here an hour ago. I used to sit in this same spot when I was a kid, eavesdropping on the conversations below. It's where I discovered Santa Claus wasn't real and where I heard about my great gran's heart attack.

But now, what I'm eavesdropping on in this moment is worse than all of the others.

"We just found out our daughter was *raped years ago,* and we knew nothing about it. I'm fully aware of how unacceptable this is, thank you."

I'd thought of that word a dozen times in my head. Hearing it out loud feels like a punch to the gut. But it's the new reality of this family and hearing it out loud is something I need to get used to.

Still, I struggle to swallow past the lump in my throat.

Lyv was raped, and shying away form that fact gives her no justice. Although, when she could've had justice by turning the ass hat in she didn't even take it. I don't pretend to understand her motives for not pressing charges. Like dad, I'm in the dark on why she'd just let the guy walk away free.

I want him to pay for what he did to my sister.

I want him to feel the pain and misery she felt from his hands.

But this isn't about what I want.

"It's her choice," my mom echoes my thoughts in a broken whisper. "It's either this, letting her come to her own peace about it, or it's dragging the whole mess out longer in a court room. She's chosen the former and we have to live with that. She's living with far worse."

Then mom goes quiet.

My dad doesn't offer a reply, most likely knowing mom's right.

I take that as my cue to go.

My feet carry me to Lyv's closed door instead of my own. I stand outside of it, listening with my ear pressed to the door like I had the night of the movie theater run-in with Ellie. But this time there's no channel surfing on the other side of the door, no Ellie pushing me to go in and talk to Lyv.

I press closer and hear nothing. Silence. Empty noise.

The night when all hell broke loose was easily the longest night of my life. By some miracle Tilly caught up to Lyv and that's when the truth came out. The morning after was when Lyv sat us down, my mom, dad, and I, to tell us everything.

She told us about her secret summer relationship with Jackson all those years ago. Then she told us how he was a phony, but she didn't realize it until the damage was done. He'd raped her that night when the rain came, when she rushed passed me soaked to the bone.

I was beginning to realize how important that moment was, but had I known exactly how important, things would've been different. I would've been more supportive. I would've tried to help her. I would've hunted that guy down and choked the life out of him with my bare hands.

The silence at Lyv's door now is more deafening than any sound she could be making.

A quiet *come in* answers my knock on her door. She lies on her side, facing the bedroom window with the covers pulled up to her chin.

Her red-rimmed eyes move from that window to land on me. I feel barer now than when we have to shower in the team showers after football practice. It's as if she's seeing right through me, looking right past the surface.

The past few days have given me loads of time to think about what I could say to try and make this all better. Up until this point I've been avoiding Lyv, telling myself I'm trying to give her space.

In reality, I think I've   been scared to face her.

And now, looking into her teary eyes, I know I was scared—and still am.

I'm scared of the possibility of this happening to her again. I'm scared she'll be stuck in this hollow state forever. But, more than anything, I'm scared that Lyv will blame me for not being there for her when she needed me the most.

I'd blame me if I were in her shoes.

The tears burn hot and come without warning. My chest heaves, up and down, up and down, and I blink furiously.

It's no use.

I tell myself to dry it up, that this isn't about me. It's about Lyv and being there for her right now.

But she scoots a little to the left and pats the now empty spot beside her with a sad drawl to her small smile.

They drop, those unexpected tears, like a torrential rain as I move to her side, crawling under the covers next to her.

It should be me comforting her, but in the end she's the one who wraps her arms around me. It's Lyv who rubs circles into my trembling back when I bury my head in her small shoulder. The painful sobs come in a hurry, never ending. My body shakes and I hiccup through the ache in my chest.

Still, Lyv holds on.

I'm sorry, I want to scream it but I have no voice to even whisper it out loud.

Chapter Thirty Six-Tilly

It's been almost three weeks since the Fourth.

A lot can happen in three weeks. In those three weeks we've sent Jackson away, threatening him with his life if he ever comes here or near Lyv again.

In those three weeks I also sat holding Lyv's hand at her kitchen table as she finally told her story, just as she had with me at the water tower. Only this time she tells it to her parents and Max.

In those three weeks Lyv decided not to press charges, which on some level I understand. Her mom also stopped me at their front door every day since then, telling me Lyv was sleeping or just needed alone time to process.

This is where my stomach knots.

The thing is, Lyv's had time to process-*years* to process what's happened. And she's done all of it on her own, carrying this terrible thing around with her.

Never letting it out.

Never freeing herself from it.

How had I been so stupid to miss it? There's no way she could've hid this assault that well, right? I had to have been oblivious, selfish and self-involved to the point that I never once dug deeper.

Not once did I stop and look at the obvious pain that was killing her daily.

"Whoa, Altoid, that's enough wiping off on this table," Mona pulls me back to the current task at hand, which is cleaning table clothes for the upcoming wedding. "You're going to rub a hole in the fabric."

The wedding is in two days and, sure, setting up for it has kept me somewhat distracted, but it can't take away what's happened in the past three weeks.

Or three years, if you're Lyv.

Mona's usually smooth forehead crinkles as she stares down at my defeated form. People bustle around us like bees in a hive, working in overdrive to get tables in their correct places and centerpieces put together.

But Mona drags a chair across from me and sits.

"What's going on in   there?"

445

She taps my forehead lightly but I shake my head in a firm *no*.

She shouldn't have to worry about me so close to her wedding day. We're just now getting back to some resemblance of mended sisterhood and I don't want to rock the boat. Instead of shrugging it away like I expected, she grabs both my hands in her freshly manicured ones, squeezing tightly.

The unusually kind gesture pulls the words out of me.

"She was raped," I mutter through my oncoming weeping. Mona's eyes widen but she doesn't interrupt. "Lyv was raped and I had no clue. It happened right under my nose and I didn't even know it for years."

One of her dainty hands pulls away to cover her gaping mouth as she shakes her head softly, rattling her perfectly laid hair.

"Oh Tilly, that's terrible," the softness of her voice eases some of the tension in my shoulders. But only a little. "No one should have to go through that."

She stares off into the distance for a moment then brings her onyx eyes back to meet my own.

"But you didn't know because Lyv wasn't ready for you to know, not because you're selfish or a lousy best friend," she takes a deep breath, squinting like she usually does when she's concentrating hard.

"Rape is something that takes a different kind of toll on each person it happens to. For my friend Allison that meant bouncing from one guy to the next, trying to find some sense of security afterwards. For Lyv, though, keeping it to herself may have been the only way she knew of protecting herself. It was her way of controlling the only part of all of this that she could."

All Lyv's changes-the distancing and the silence-that was her defense against having to relive it all. And how could I blame her for trying to salvage the rest of what was left?

"And now you know," Mona continues with a hopeful smile. She wipes tears from my cheeks. "So now you can be there for her like you couldn't before."

Chapter Thirty Seven-Lyv

I think I've stayed in bed longer these past few weeks than I did when Jackson first assaulted me. Back then, no one could know, and if no one could know, then I had to keep going on like normal.

Like nothing happened.

But the cat is out of the bag now. Everyone knows, or at least everyone who matters.

So now I can lie in bed and mourn in a way I couldn't before and no one will question it. But my decision to not press charges raised plenty of questions. Some people were more easily convinced in understanding that choice, like mom or Tilly. But it was harder to hear for Max and my dad.

For them, they couldn't grasp why I'd just let my rapist walk away so easily.

I haven't even entertained the thought of Asher and what he may think of all of this. That's just too painful to ponder.

Sometimes I hope someone's told him, but then I panic at him knowing Jackson has touched me in that way. I don't want him knowing something so dark and personal, so I quickly push the idea from my mind.

He's called a few times and texted a dozen, but I can't find the courage to even look at any messages or listen to the voicemails he leaves.

In terms of taking Jackson to the police, the choice was simple.

Pressing charges means exposure to the public and to strangers digging through the terrible experience, dissecting every dirty detail to decide if they believe me or not. Bringing Jackson to scrutiny in a courtroom also means bringing myself to that same scrutiny.

I know what happened, so I don't need a courtroom of strangers telling me if I was raped or not; telling me if I somehow brought it on myself or not.

I didn't.

No one does.

What happened to me is not on me, and the people I care about most know that. For me, that's all that matters.

In the beginning I blamed myself for what happened. If I wouldn't have done this, or if I wouldn't have done that, things may have played out differently.

But in the words of my wise baby brother, it doesn't matter what you're wearing or what time of day it happens—silence doesn't mean "yes" and rape is rape. Period.

But I won't lie and say it's easy.

Knowing I could someday run into him again hurts. Seeing my parents tiptoe around me like I'm a ticking time bomb hurts. Holding my strong, brave, sobbing brother to try and relieve his unnecessary guilt hurts.

And so, for the second or third week in a row (I've lost exact count) I wrap myself in a comforter cocoon on my bed. I lie in silence, tears randomly coming and going as they please. The birds I've stared at for days now outside my window flitter around, chirping songs of freedom I pray one day I can sing too.

When a light tapping sounds at my door I expect to see Max again. He's been coming in from time to time, keeping me up to date on the outside world.

Mona's wedding is in a couple of days and the buildup for that has been years in the making. I'm not so sure I can face everyone there, though.

"Sweetie, can we come in?"

I'm surprised to hear my mom's voice at the door.

When I sit up, pulling the covers up to my chest, she comes in with my dad following behind her.

They've been doing this sort of dance around me. One day they'll hover, serving me hand and foot. Then the next day they hardly come around me, giving me a wide berth of space to be by myself.

Today's dance is hovering.

"Come in," I croak.

It's been days since I've spoken above a whisper.

Someone, I'm assuming my mom, filled Reggie in enough that he's given me a pass from work for the time being.

My parents creep in, each taking a tentative seat on my bed.

"So," my dad starts hesitantly, "Mona's wedding is coming up. Any plans on going?"

I can see the question rip him up inside. The grimace on his face tells me he hates asking just as much as I hate hearing him ask. It's only more proof that I've completely secluded myself from everyone around me.

Again.

"I don't think so," I whisper.

The pity in both my parents' eyes twists the knife in my chest.

My mom clears her throat to my left.

"We love you, Lyv," she cups my face gently, smiling like I'm her shining star, "and if you want to stay in this bedroom for the rest of your life, we won't stop you. We're going to love you through this."

The last time I saw my mom cry was when I was eight and a five-year-old Max fell from the top of our new swing set, breaking his arm when he fell to the ground. My mom had cried more than Max did, and I haven't seen her do it since.

But now she stops, short of words to say next. Her crystal blue eyes well up and she bites hard on her trembling lip to hold the

452

tears at bay. Meanwhile my dad holds nothing back and lets his flow freely.

In a broken whisper she says, "I know you're scared. You have every right to be. But fear is a liar. It steals your hope and your joy, but is powerless if you choose it to be. And don't you think he's stolen enough from you already?"

Like my mother just seconds before, I'm at a loss for words.

I think of what I've sacrificed the past three years for a monster of a man I owe nothing to. I picture all those sleepless nights and fractured relationships I've suffered through because of his recklessness.

The loud, snot-filled sob wracks my body. My mom pulls me close and I cling to her like a lifeline.

"Don't let that bastard take anymore of your happiness, my sweet girl," my dad adds as he rubs gentle circles in my back. "He doesn't deserve anything you have to offer the world."

It's a new and sudden feeling, a welcome one; the feeling of finally deciding enough is enough.

It'll take some time to really get there, I'm sure, but I choose to really start trying here and   now.

My life is my own and no one else's.

What happened to me is just that—something that happened. It's not *who* I am. It doesn't define me. It's merely something I went through.

No more letting it dictate my every breath.

No more letting him control my mood and my life and my happiness.

My happiness is my own, and no one can take that away from me.

I've dealt with a lot of heartbreak in my young 21 years. I've lost family and friends. I've been dumped severely by people I gave my all to. I've lost my dad to cancer. But out of all of that, even my dad's death, nothing pierces my heart as much as knowing that Lyv was so brutally abused.

To know someone took advantage of her, violated her against her will, cut her down so viciously, breaks me apart more than anything else I've ever felt.

I almost didn't believe it when Tilly sat me down to tell me. I didn't want to believe it. But I couldn't deny the way her voice broke and sobs shook her violently so that she struggled to even get the words out.

I knew then why Max attacked Mason's asshole cousin. I understood why Tilly had kept on going, even after the scum was beaten down. I only wish now I'd known sooner so that it was me breaking him down to a pulp instead of Max or Tilly.

I've spent days trying to text and call Lyv, but nothing goes through.

I hope her phone is off or dead, that she's not just ignoring me altogether. I've gone to her house a couple of times, but her mom blocks me the moment I get to the doorstep.

I don't blame her, though.

Lyv's mom is a strong woman. She's protecting Lyv the only way she knows how, which is to keep everyone away from her.

It's naïve of me to think she'd be here at Mona's wedding.

I know that, but there's always this small part of me that hopes in the impossible in life. To believe light always squashes out the dark, eventually.

But the ceremony comes and goes and I see no sign of Lyv where I sit in the middle of the fold-up chairs.

The glamour of the wedding is overboard, but I barely notice. It's hard to focus on the chairs and tables decorating the outside lawn, or on the way the bride's train drapes halfway down the isle.

It's hard to focus on anything at all when I know Lyv is out there somewhere in any kind of pain. Mason nudges my shoulder and I quickly stand with the rest of the wedding crowd, clapping along with the whoops and cheers for the happy, new couple.

My hearts sinks as we file out of our rows toward the reception area, still no Lyv.

The wedding reception is also outside but is set up a few yards away from where the ceremony itself happened. White tents cover another large lawn but when I find my way to one of the less crowded tents none of it matters anymore.

Not the wedding or the bride or the fancy tents we stand under.

It all dulls in comparison to her, standing in a yellow sundress at the edge of the tent.

She stands alone with camera in hand, scanning the crowd over the top of her glass of lemonade. Her skin is slightly paler since I last saw her and the yellow in her long, flowing dress contrasts against her unruly, brown curls.

Finally, the moment comes for her eyes to fall on me.

It's one of my favorite things about her, her ever-changing eyes. One day they're tinted brown and the next they're as green as the sea. Today they're a mix of the two I can see even from this distance.

My heart hammers against my chest as she slowly walks toward me.

I meet her halfway.

"Hi," Lyv utters.

She stares up at me with her full lips parted slightly. Her breath comes out shaky, but she never breaks eye contact. I feel bad for Tilly's sister, for the fact that even on her wedding day she's not the one who stands out among the crowd.

Not with Lyv here.

It's impossible.

I thought it'd be uncomfortable, seeing her for the first time after knowing what I know now. But being here with her now, all I see is the strength and bravery it took to get her here. It radiates off her like sunrays.

"Hi," I manage to get out.

She gulps and I watch as her throat heaves up and down.

"I'm assuming you've heard?"

Her cheeks flush and I hate Jackson with every fiber in me now that I'm face to face with the aftermath of what he's done.

I nod.

She looks away then, nodding to herself as she focuses on something outside of the tent.

"I'm so proud of you," I speak evenly, enunciating each word slowly so she hears me plainly. "It's taken so much courage to come here, to carry on like you have all this time. You're not tainted in my eyes, if that's what you think. You're sweet and passionate and everything good. It's a sin you've not heard that over and over and over again."

A smile tugs at the corner of her mouth.

Slowly but surely, she looks back up at me.

"You really have a way with words, Asher Brooks," she finally declares.

There's a piece of the Lyv I've grown to care so much about that slips out in that one sentence. Now I'm the one fighting back the smile until it inevitably breaks.

"I'm more than words. I hope you let me stick around long enough to show you that."

She nods again, eyeing me cautiously.

I want to wipe the worry away. I want to clear her mind of the turmoil she's no doubt been handling for so long and distract her from the baggage she's been carrying.

"I'm also pretty good on the dance floor," I hold my hand out tentatively. "Care to test me on it?"

She hesitates, like she's battling some kind of war in her head.

She comes to some decision within herself and takes my hand. It fits perfectly into my own, as if the two were made to mold together.

The song is slow, but we step up onto the wooden dance floor and I want nothing more than to pull her close and never let her go.

We dance, then again when a second slow song comes on right after the first one.

It's not until Tilly shows up at my elbow that we stop.

There's a moment where Tilly and Lyv move off to the side, leaving Mason and I alone as they talk by themselves. Then they're done and a fast-paced song comes on.

At some point Max and Ellie join us and we jump and flail our bodies around in some form of "dancing" until my legs burn.

Either way, it's an end to summer that we all need.

And a beginning, I think, when I see the laughter flow so effortlessly from Lyv, with her arms raised high and the smile stretching wider than I've ever seen it.

Epilogue

"Could you stop fidgeting, please? You're going to—oh, there she is!"

I laugh as my mom swats at Max's hand that's tugging at the tie around his neck. My dad waves enthusiastically as my parents walk towards me, Max and Ellie following right behind them.

I can't imagine how much my brother probably complained about having to wear that tie the whole way here.

Here being my Photo Showcase for the photography program. My entry project was a major hit and I have to admit, I'm pretty proud of myself for all the hard work I put into it.

On top of it and the assault support group I've started on campus, I've been pretty busy this first semester back to CU Denver. It was Tilly's idea, starting up a support group on campus, but when I reached out and saw just how many people had been through a situation like mine, it was a no brainer.

There were voices muted all around me, and I felt an obligation to help them be heard. Those people needed to be listened to, to hear the words "you are more than what's happened to you" and really believe it.

Since coming back to campus it's been my mission to reach out to people, relaying the message that the goal shouldn't be "here's how to avoid sexual assault". Instead it should be "don't sexually assault someone. Period."

Today, though, my sole focus has been on the big reveal of my photo project. I finally came up with a topic and from there the inspiration came freely.

My mom and dad reach me first and each plant a kiss on my cheek before moving on to look at the gallery around us.

After a few pleasantries, I entwine my fingers through Asher's who stands at my side with a smile plastered on. He's been a steady force in the storm of the past few months and I thank God he's as genuine and pure of heart he's always claimed to be. He grins at me now with a proud twinkle in his dark eyes while I lead us toward Max and Ellie on the other side of the room.

"You've found my project, I see," I step up to the familiar faces in the series Max and Ellie stand in front of.

"These are amazing,   Lyv," Ellie boasts.

463

"Thank you."

"Eh, they're not half bad I guess."

Max shrugs and I shove him playfully before he wraps an arm around my shoulder. We all stand in front of my project titled "The Hopeful."

The idea came randomly toward the end of summer. Tilly had come over and we were talking about everything that had happened that summer; everything from my assault revelation to her and Mona's reconnection and everything in between. She talked about how we'd all made it to the other side of the storm, saying, "we sure are a hopeful group, aren't we?"

I'd jumped up from my chair so quickly I gave myself a head rush, declaring that the basis for my photo project.

In front of us now is Asher in one picture, smiling fondly at his sisters slouching in an old, raggedy armchair that belonged to his dad. The caption for that one is a simple *Dad's Chair*. The next one is Tilly's mom walking her sister down the isle at Mona's wedding. I'd taken the picture from the back of the isle while Tilly stood glassy eyed and grinning in the background by the other bridesmaids.

Then there's Mase hugging Tilly in his lap, who's been caught in the middle of a full laugh. This one I labeled *The Future.* Another one show's Reggie painting what will become a nursery with his very pregnant wife looking up at him happily.

The last one, though, is the one that draws me in no matter how many times I look at it.

It's the summer gang standing in a small huddle with me planted right in the middle. I didn't take the picture, obviously, but still used it in the gallery.

I still remember the day it was taken clearly.

It was the last day of summer break, right before everyone had to go back to school. Max and Ellie had already been back in their junior year of high school for a week, but that night they joined the rest of us since it was the last night before we all headed back to college.

Everyone is doing something goofy, like sticking out a tongue or flipping off the camera set to a timer to snap the picture, but I stand in the center of the posed group laughing. My smile is bright and Tilly hugs tightly to my left with Max close on my right. I've purposefully blurred everyone in the picture except for me.

The woman in this is far from the one who dreaded going home at the beginning of the summer. That girl was broken and weary of the fight she'd been struggling with for so many years.

But the woman smiling back at me now in that picture is bolder and happier.

Freer.

And when I step closer to the caption I gave this one it reads one simple, solid statement that I feel all the way to my core. It's a phrase that symbolizes just how much I've come through, and just how strong I've become because of it all; one that says my journey is far from over.

The woman in that photo is hopeful of all that's to come.

Her Leaves Remain.

ACKNOWLEDGMENTS

Thank you, God, for giving me mercy, grace, and love beyond what I can comprehend.

Thank you also to: Alicia, my incredibly supportive sister who stands in my corner every day of my life. Your enthusiasm through this process kept me going on days when I needed motivation the most (and to Daniel, for being one of my cheerleaders alongside her). You told me I had the power all along, and my life is changed because of it. Katelynn, who believed in me from day one when I'd force you to read every teeny, tiny piece of writing I could muster. You saw something in me in the beginning that I couldn't and pushed me to believe in myself. Your confidence in me helped me bloom and I'm so grateful. Thank you to Hannah because if it weren't for those childhood stories of yours that I'd sneak and read growing up, I'm not sure I would've known the joy of storytelling or felt comfortable enough to tell you about my own stories all these years later.

To my lovely friends, Bella and Paige, who read every terrible draft I sent. You were my first editors, my first critics, and you did so out of love and confidence in me. I love you both for listening to my ideas and reading my words with belief that I was capable of bringing this story to life. Your insight and suggestions were the guidance I needed along the way.

To my wonderful parents, my mighty Momma and Papa Bear, thank you for showing me unconditional love and teaching me that hard work pays off if you put the time and effort into it. You also taught me it was OK to dream big about writing and I love you so much for that.

Last but not least, to the Lyvs out there in the real world: I hear you, and I thank you for having the courage to keep living even after the trauma. You inspire me with your strength.

There are so many more people I could name specifically, and I wish I had the space to do so. But just know that I am so grateful and thankful for the army I've been blessed with. Your support is what pushes me to write, even on the bad days.

ABOUT THE AUTHOR

 Ashley Owens is a Language Arts teacher in the beautiful state of Kentucky and loves the randomness of teaching middle school students every day. She isn't a fancy, *New York Times* bestseller, but she's a dreamer of "some day", and for now that's enough. For more specifics, feel free to follow her on social media— though she can't promise it's all that exciting! :)

Instagram: ashley_owens

Facebook: Ashley Marie Owens

Made in the USA
Monee, IL
18 January 2020